The Christmas Deal

Also by Keira Andrews

The Christmas Deal

BY KEIRA ANDREWS

The Christmas Deal
Written and published by Keira Andrews
Cover by Dar Albert
Formatting by BB eBooks

Copyright © 2019 by Keira Andrews
Print Edition

ISBN: 978-1-988260-49-5

Acknowledgements

Many thanks to Anara, DJ, Mary, Leta, and Rai for their friendship and assistance with Logan and Seth's story. Ho, ho, ho! <3

Chapter One

WHEN THE PHONE rang again, Logan allowed himself a flicker of hope before snuffing it out. No, it wasn't the warehouse manager calling back to say he had the job after all. No Christmas miracle was coming.

He stared at the screen, dread sinking through him. It was Rencliffe Academy, which meant his balls were about to be busted because the kid had fucked up.

Again.

Logan shivered on the side of the bed in his skivvies, the battered parquet floor freezing under his bare feet since he'd put the heat down as low as possible in hopes of paying the bill. Fuck, he was tempted to huddle under the blankets and go back to sleep, dealing with whatever crap this was later.

But Veronica's disappointed face filled his mind. As foolish as the choice had been, he'd married her, and her son was his responsibility now. He swiped the screen and answered.

"Mr. Derwood? It's Assistant Headmaster Patel calling." She spoke calmly and smoothly in a British-type fancy accent. Logan braced himself. She said, "I'm afraid there's been another incident. Can you join us this morning for a get-together?"

He wasn't sure why Rencliffe insisted on making it sound as if they were inviting him over for finger foods and Chardonnay or some shit. "Yeah. I'll be there in—" He groaned to himself, remembering his Ford was broken in the shop. Because of course it was.

After a pause, she prompted, "Mr. Derwood? This is really quite urgent. Connor's behavioral issues—"

"Yeah, I know. I'll be there as soon as I can. Thanks." He hung up, bile rising in his throat. The only silver lining to apparently being unemployable was that he didn't have to take time off work for yet another school visit. Too bad his disability benefits had run out. That sure made being jobless a real son of a bitch.

Merry fucking Christmas.

There was nothing else to do but text Jenna:

Can I drive u 2 work and take the car? Will pick u up at 3.

His sister was working short days Monday to Thursday after having her second kid, and hopefully he'd caught her in time. The typing bubbles appeared on the screen, and she replied:

No prob. Just leaving day care. Everything okay?

He barked out a laugh in his empty bedroom. He couldn't even remember what *okay* felt like. Forget *good* or *great.* Those feelings were distant memories. He typed back:

Just have to run errand. Thx. They had to order a new part for the pickup.

A new part he couldn't afford, but he left that out. He also didn't mention Connor because it would only make Jenna worry, and she had enough on her plate. Shit, her plate had been overflowing since she was fourteen.

When the cancer finally got their mom, Jenna was the one who'd taken care of their father and the house while Logan had been in Iraq. He was seven years older than his baby sister, but she was the one who kept them all afloat.

She worked her ass off to include Connor in family stuff, and at least he tolerated her. For a moment, Logan considered whether he should ask Jenna to come with him to the school, but no. She had work, and she had to save her emergency time off for her own kids. Connor was his responsibility. Logan was thirty-eight years old, and he should be able to unfuck his own life.

He stood, wincing at the stiff ache in his muscles and the phantom twinges in his formerly broken bones. After being in traction, he'd never take moving his body for granted again, but goddamn, everything felt tighter than it used to. Of course, he hadn't done his stretches, so what did he expect?

There was no time to shower and shave, but he splashed his scruffy face, ran a comb through his cropped dark hair, and scrubbed a wet towel under his arms. He sniffed five shirts before finding a fresh-enough gray Henley and pulling it on over his jeans and combat boots. Maybe he should have dressed up a bit, but the folks at Rencliffe knew who he was. Putting lipstick on a pig wouldn't change anything.

After Jenna picked him up, he listened to her good-natured complaints about her kids and husband and Christmas shopping. She chattered nonstop until they reached the six-story, glass-fronted office building in a corporate park on the outskirts of Albany.

There was a puke stain on her shoulder, but Logan didn't tell her. She'd call it "spit-up," but from what he could tell, it was puke. But it was already dry and too late for her to change anyway.

Putting the SUV in park by the front of the building, she gave him a gleaming smile, dimples appearing in her cheeks. Logan and Jenna shared the same greenish-hazel eyes, but she'd been the only one to inherit their mother's sunny smile and optimism. "I haven't let you get a word in edgewise. Sorry." Her smile faded. "You sure everything's okay?"

"Yep. Have a good day at work."

But Jenna stayed put behind the wheel. "Look, I know it's still too soon to think about dating again—"

"Yet you're bringing it up anyway."

She sighed. "I just hate seeing you so miserable—and don't

bother telling me you aren't. I know you don't like me worrying, but newsflash: I worry anyway. And maybe dating would help."

"It wouldn't." The thought of meeting a woman and trying to impress her, getting to know her, inviting her into the shit show of his life—it was exhausting.

Hell, Logan hadn't even had the energy to hook up with guys beyond a half-hearted hand job in a bathroom stall at the mall a few weeks ago. It had been quick and rough, the way Logan liked it with men. No kissing, no hugging, no need to be tender and concerned about feelings.

That's how he knew he was straight. He only wanted that other stuff with women. Men were for getting off and nothing more.

Jenna sighed again. "You're right. I don't know why I said that."

He gave her a small smile. "Because you're desperate to fix things for me." Because Jenna was good and kind. He didn't deserve her. "Don't worry about me, all right? You'd better get inside or you'll be late."

"Oh, did you hear about the warehouse job?"

He shrugged. "Not yet." He'd put in a bunch of applications other places, so maybe one of them would call. For now, there was no point in worrying Jenna more by telling her he'd failed yet again.

"I'm knocking on wood." She rapped her knuckles on her head, then leaned over the console and pressed a kiss to his cheek. "Have a good day."

He walked around the vehicle, waving to her before she disappeared inside. Logan had a good foot on his baby sister, and as he adjusted the driver's seat and mirrors, his phone rang again. He pulled it from the pocket of his leather jacket, his stomach dropping. The landlord. He let it go to voicemail. He didn't need to hear Mrs. Politano tell him again that the rent was overdue.

He hadn't been able to afford the rent on Veronica's house after her death, and he'd moved into a tiny bungalow in a rundown neighborhood. Even if he'd had the money, the thought of sleeping every night in the room where Veronica died had been unbearable.

"Fuck," he muttered as he drove out toward Rencliffe. It was about forty-five minutes away, and Logan wished he could just be there already to get this over with.

He jabbed at the presets on the radio, and every one played commercials or Christmas songs with sleigh bells and peace on earth by a warm fireplace. He left it on a station blaring an ad for extended Black Friday deals. From what he could tell, Black Friday went for about six weeks at this point.

If that warehouse job had come through, maybe he'd have a hope of a decent Christmas. He could've at least bought Connor some presents. But the job hadn't come through, because no one would hire him once they found out he'd been fired from the railway and blamed for the accident.

No matter that he'd served his country for four years in the Marine Corps after 9/11 and earned a commendation medal. *Thank you for your service, but you're a useless sack of shit now.*

He struggled to take a deep breath, the low ache in his sternum that had never fully gone away flaring hot. Logan tugged at his seatbelt. His broken bones had healed, but sometimes he just couldn't fucking breathe. Usually it was only when he exerted himself, and he knew right now it was probably all in his fucked-up head, but it still hurt.

The sign marking Rencliffe's curving driveway was freshly painted in gold and navy, proclaiming:

Rencliffe Academy
The Brightest Minds Since 1909

Logan followed the driveway through the towering trees, only a few red, gold, and shit-brown leaves left hanging as winter quickly approached. Visitor parking was empty but for a silver Audi. Birds chirped almost desperately as he walked up the path to the main gray-brick building, which was decorated in massive red-ribboned holiday wreaths and lights that were currently off.

The school was a sprawl of five or six buildings, including the dorms. A newer addition had been constructed in the same style with big arches and turret-type things on the top like a castle. Veronica had called it Gothic, which apparently didn't actually mean scary, although Logan found it all pretty creepy. Rencliffe was definitely the type of place where a crazed murderer would strike in the movies.

He walked into the vaulted foyer of main building, his boots thudding. He stopped in front of a massive Christmas tree decorated in white lights and old-fashioned wooden ornaments shaped like birds, pinecones, and angels. Probably all made by the students.

The hush hanging over the polished wood and marble foyer made him think of church. They'd been Easter-and-Christmas Catholics when he was growing up, but he hadn't even done that much in years. Though Rencliffe wasn't a religious school, he still half-expected a priest or nun to appear to greet him. Instead it was an older woman, who led him down the eerily quiet hallways to Mira Patel's book-lined office.

She was surprisingly young—probably thirty. According to the framed diplomas behind her desk, she'd attended the University of Delhi and Oxford, so clearly she was pretty freaking smart. Her black hair was tied back in a twisty bun, and she had big eyes behind her gold-framed glasses.

If they were in a porno, she'd be about to let down her hair, take off her glasses, and rip open her cream blouse to reveal big tits. She'd hike up her skirt and—

"Thank you for coming, Mr. Derwood. It's good to meet

you." She sat in the padded leather chair behind her desk as Logan took one of the guest chairs and shoved away the stupid porno thoughts. "The headmaster's absent on personal business, so I'm handling Connor's case for the moment."

"Right. I'm sorry if the kid's been acting up again."

"Mmm." She leaned forward in her chair, folding her hands on the shiny wood desk, her nails gleaming with pale polish. "I hope you don't mind if I go back over the particulars with you?"

"Um, the particulars?" Jesus, he felt like he was back in high school about to fail an exam he hadn't studied for.

"Connor's background. How we've gotten to where we are now. I understand you were a recent addition to his life before his mother passed away?"

Dull pain throbbed in his chest, and he forced a breath. "Uh-huh. Veronica and I met about a year and a half ago. I was in an accident at work and had to be in the hospital for a few months. Veronica was my nurse."

A memory flashed—*the wedding march playing on someone's phone at the hospital chapel, Logan dragging an IV and Veronica still in her purple scrubs, her fellow nurses throwing confetti made of paper from the shredding bin.*

Clearing his throat, he added, "My life was shit, and she was the one good thing." He shifted on the hard-backed chair. "Um, excuse my language."

Ms. Patel smiled. "Shit happens. You're recovered now?"

"Mostly. If I push too hard, I get out of breath. But it's fine."

She nodded. "So you and Connor's mother married quite quickly?"

"Yeah. Within a couple months. Dumb, I know. But I loved her and was so sure we'd be together forever." He snorted. "Then, you know. Reality smacked us upside the head. She brought me home from the hospital, and in a few weeks we were driving each other crazy. Living with someone's not all roses and unicorns."

"No, it certainly isn't." Ms. Patel smiled wryly. "Compromise isn't easy."

He shifted, hot trickles of shame in his gut. "We tried, though. We did. We really cared about each other, even if we didn't fit."

"Of course."

"And I've tried with Connor. I really have." He cringed internally at his defensiveness.

She eyed him sympathetically. "I know you have. It's a challenging situation. Thirteen can be a tough age already, and Connor's faced a traumatic loss and major life changes. Plus, you've suddenly found yourself a single father. It's an adjustment, to say the least."

A single father.

It was so weird to think of himself that way. He wasn't qualified to be anyone's dad, let alone a single one. Logan nodded. "Yeah."

"What was your relationship like before his mother's passing?"

Passing. As if she'd drifted off down a lazy river in the sunshine. Logan hated when people didn't just call it what it was. Veronica hadn't *passed* anywhere—she was rotting in a hole in the ground. He choked down the resentment. Ms. Patel was only being polite.

"We didn't really have a relationship. He was pissed when I married his mom, and I can't blame the kid for that. He hardly talked to me when he was home on vacations from school, and I didn't know what to say to him anyway. Things got very tense with me and Veronica. Then she died."

"It was an aneurysm? That must have been quite a shock."

He tugged at a loose thread on the cuff of his Henley. "Yeah. I'd spent the night on my sister's couch since Veronica and I had been going at each other all day. They said even if I'd been home, it wouldn't have mattered." *But maybe the docs were wrong. If I'd been there...*

"Then Connor discovered her in the morning since he was home for the summer."

Hearing Ms. Patel say it out loud was a steel toe to Logan's nuts, guilt surging through him. Jaw clenched, he nodded. A clock ticked on the wall, each second louder than the last. His mind filled with red flashing lights, the sympathetic—yet definitely suspicious—cops escorting him inside his own place, a sheet over Veronica on the bedroom floor, waiting for a body bag. The poor kid sitting in the kitchen with a female cop.

Connor hadn't been crying, and Logan hadn't seen him shed a tear since. The kid was empty, although when Logan had clumsily tried to squeeze his shoulder, Connor had exploded with rage. It was apparently all he had left.

Ms. Patel quietly stated the fucking obvious. "It was extremely traumatic for him. We've endeavored to give Connor the support he needs, but he's simply not cooperating. His biological father isn't in the picture at all?"

Logan huffed. "Waste of space. Took off down to Florida years ago. Every once in a while he shows up with expensive presents and a bunch of bullshit stories. For a smart kid, you'd think Connor could see through him. The guy has zero interest in being a father."

"When was the last time you were in touch with Mr. Lisowski?"

"Dunno. After Veronica died. I don't know if Connor's talked to him."

"A few texts, apparently. You don't feel he can be any help in this situation?"

"Fucked if I know." He winced. "Excuse my language again."

She waved off his apology. "I'd need your permission to speak to Mr. Lisowski about Connor since you're the legal guardian. I understand Connor's mother had been a foster child? No family?"

"Right. If you think he can help, call him, but he probably

won't answer. Mike couldn't care less about the kid if he tried."

She picked up a gold and silver pen and wrote in a leather-bound notebook. Logan watched her pen making loops and swoops before she capped it and looked back at him. "I understand you're currently out of work?"

Anger flared, a hot burst in his veins. What she meant was: *I understand you're a useless sack of shit?* He barked, "Look, are we going to talk about whatever Connor did, or what?"

"Yes, of course." She folded her hands again, calm as anything. "You know that Connor's full scholarship is incumbent upon him keeping his grades at a minimum of a B average. And even more importantly, it requires him to behave in an orderly, respectable manner. To not put himself or any of his classmates in harm's way."

Fuck. "What did he do?"

"Connor dropped his backpack down the gap in the stairwell from an upper floor."

"Oh." That didn't seem so bad? "Did he break something?"

"The bag hit another student in the lower leg and caused significant pain and bruising. If it had hit him in the head, it very well could have killed him. This is no laughing matter or a 'boys will be boys' situation. Perhaps that recklessness would fly in a public school, but this is Rencliffe, Mr. Derwood."

All he could do was nod like he was back in the principal's office. "I understand. It was a stupid thing to do. It won't happen again."

She sighed, sitting back with a squeak of leather. "I sincerely hope not. We've attempted to engage him repeatedly, but he's sullen and uncooperative. Connor has a brilliant mind. He used to be one of our best students. We've been cutting him a lot of slack, but he needs to curb this destructive and harmful behavior. Not only toward his classmates, but himself."

Logan went very still. "What do you mean? Is he, like, cutting himself or something?"

"Not that we know of. But he's skipping classes, showing up late, and not completing assignments. Getting into fights, as you know from your discussion with Mr. Howard a few weeks ago. Connor's going to fail his courses, and we know it's not because of his intelligence. The term exams are next week, concluding on Friday, December twenty-first, followed by the holiday break."

"Right." The colorful ceramic tree in the corner of Ms. Patel's office seemed to mock him with its cheery lights and glossy snow. The holidays were supposed to be a magical time for kids, and what would Logan be able to give Connor? A roof over their heads if Logan was lucky.

"If Connor performs at a B level on his exams—which should be infinitely doable for him even without studying a word—and if he stays in line, he's welcome back in January to turn things around."

"And if he doesn't?" Logan gripped the arms of the chair.

"Then I'm afraid Connor's tenure here at Rencliffe will end. You should investigate the public school options in your neighborhood, although I sincerely hope it won't be necessary."

My neighborhood.

Where was that, exactly? The rented house he was about to be evicted from? He rubbed a hand over his face, a week of scruff scratching his palm. "Okay."

"Mr. Derwood, I assure you we want Connor to succeed. It would truly be a shame if he squanders his limitless potential. He's had a full scholarship here for two years because we believe in him. But he has to meet us halfway. It's been months of acting out, and while we're very sympathetic, we have to think of the other students. Connor has been too disruptive for too long."

"Yeah. I get it." He pushed to his feet. "You've been fair. Thank you." He stuck out his hand, and she shook it firmly.

"Connor's waiting in the atrium. I can take you there."

"I know the way. Thanks."

When he reached the high-ceilinged greenhouse down the hall—all glass and flowering plants and even a tinkling fountain, Logan found Connor tossing stones from a rock garden into the pool of water. Two stone fish were twisted together in the middle, water spouting out of their open mouths.

Connor didn't turn, instead plonking a rock right at one of the fish heads. His navy uniform jacket was stretched tightly across his narrow shoulders, gray pants a bit too short.

If he gets kicked out, I guess I don't have to pony up for new uniforms.

That wasn't much of a silver lining. "Hey," Logan said, jamming his fists in his pockets. Shit, he never knew what to say to this kid.

Connor ignored him, bending to scoop up more rocks. Logan stood there and let him finish that handful before he said, "Are you going to knock off the crap you've been pulling? You're smarter than this."

Another rock dinged off the stone fish's head. "You don't know anything about me. You're not my father."

"I know. But I'm…" Logan didn't know. In the eyes of Ms. Patel, he was a single dad, and he felt like such a fake. But he was all the kid had left.

"You're just the asshole loser my mom married because she hated being alone."

It shouldn't have hurt, yet Logan's chest tightened the way it did when he exerted himself too much, his breath coming short. Right now it was completely in his head, and he reminded himself of that as he forced in a gulp of air. He was sorely tempted to leave Connor to his sulking misery, but he had to be the grown-up.

"You took forever to show up." Connor turned, narrowing his dark gaze. The kid was maybe five-two, a full foot shorter than Logan and probably a hundred pounds soaking wet. Still, he internally cringed as Connor sized him up. "Bet you were hungover."

Logan breathed out evenly, ignoring the tug in his chest. *I'm the adult here. He doesn't really know me at all.* "I wasn't hungover. I had to borrow Jenna's car. Mine's in the shop."

"Sure. Bet you were out late screwing sluts, just like you were before my mom died."

"Hey!" Logan clenched his jaw, imagining they were being watched through all the glass windows, the heat of hidden eyes crawling on his skin. He gritted out, "First off, don't use that word. Second, I never cheated on your mother. Never."

Connor muttered, "Yeah, right."

"I didn't." Christ, he'd barely jerked off since she died. Didn't even wake up to morning wood anymore—even his dick knew how useless he was. "Listen to me—"

"Why?" Connor's sandy hair was a shaggy mess over his ears, which was probably a dress code violation or something. Was Logan supposed to take him to get his hair cut?

Connor's lip curled as Logan stayed silent. "You're such an idiot. No wonder you barely graduated high school."

Logan didn't argue for his own intelligence since the kid had a point. Look at the mess Logan had made of his life. But he was all Connor had, so he stood there and took it.

Veronica had loudly questioned his faithfulness a few months before she died. Logan didn't really blame her—he'd stayed out later and later to avoid their fights about everything from doing the dishes to which way to put the damn toilet paper. She'd assumed the worst about his absences, although he wasn't a cheater.

In the small house, of course Connor heard all their shouting matches. Logan wanted to comfort Connor in his grief—*their* grief—but everything was poisoned between them. He had no clue how to fix it.

Summoning patience, Logan unclenched his hands. He spoke calmly but firmly—the way the parenting vids he'd watched on YouTube advised. "Listen to me. They're going to expel you."

Connor rolled his eyes. "They won't go through with it. No way."

"They will. You're here on their good graces, and they've had enough of your shit. Ask Ms. Patel. You could have put that kid in the hospital with your prank. Why would you drop your bag like that?"

With a jerk of a shrug, Connor said, "Dunno. To see what would happen." He added defensively, "No one was down there when I let go! Then stupid Tim walked out."

"You know it wasn't his fault. But listen—Ms. Patel told me you're out if you don't get a B on your exams and stop acting up. This is serious. They're going to expel you. She told me to look into other schools."

Connor's perma-scowl evaporated as his brown eyes went wide. In a heartbeat, he looked so fucking young, his voice breaking. "Really? She said that?"

The poor kid was angry and hurt and surging with confusing new testosterone on top of it all. Logan tried to soften his voice. "Yeah. And if you get kicked out of here, you're stuck with me full time. So hit the books and cut the shit, okay?"

The bluster returned in an instant, and Connor raised his chin. "I'll go live with my dad in Florida. I'm sick of the cold anyway."

No, you won't, because your dad doesn't give a goddamn about you.

Forcing an even tone, Logan said, "Your mom always talked about what a genius you are. That she knew it from the time you could barely talk."

Connor's brows drew together, and he fidgeted with his fingers, shifting from foot to foot. "She… She did?"

"Yep. She was so proud of you, getting a full ride to Rencliffe out of elementary school. She used to smile so big when she talked about you. You know, how her eyes got squinty and her nose would crinkle?"

Connor nodded, biting his lip. Even with the pimples and attitude, he looked like a baby sometimes. Logan wanted to tell him everything would be okay and give him a hug the way kids deserved to be hugged, but the few times he'd awkwardly tried anything like that, it had resulted in Connor shoving him away.

Logan sighed. "I know you hate me. I don't blame you." He laughed hollowly. "There's plenty to hate. But you've got a good thing here. They want to help you. So let them. Okay? You can get a B on your exams in your sleep. Stop skipping class and screwing around. Make your mom proud."

After a few moments, Connor nodded, his jaw tight. He toyed with a plaid scarf hanging around his neck, and Logan eyed it. "Is that the one Jenna gave you at Thanksgiving?" They'd always done one gift for everyone at Thanksgiving in Logan's family for some reason. He didn't even know how the tradition had started.

Connor scoffed. "Dunno. I guess." He whipped it off and stuffed it in his uniform jacket pocket. "I was cold."

"She says hi, by the way."

"Whatever. Tell her hi back." He shrugged. "I don't care."

"Okay. I'll see you at the end of next week when school gets out." *Assuming you don't get expelled in the meantime.* Logan could only pray he'd somehow land a job so he could afford rent and food and maybe a few presents for the kid. If there was ever a time for a Christmas miracle, it was now.

Connor rolled his eyes. "Can't wait."

Ms. Patel appeared before Logan had to think of anything else to say. She smiled warmly. "Connor, are you up for a talk before you go back to class?"

Thank Christ the kid nodded and followed her out. Logan

gave her a tight smile and made his way back through the main building and out to the parking lot. The birds still chirped, the sun peeking out from steel clouds. His phone buzzed, and this time there was a text message from Mrs. Politano:

Without rent I can't eat. Time's up. Changing the locks in two days, so get your stuff out.

Logan tasted bile. That was a definite no-go on the holiday miracle. He climbed behind the wheel of his baby sister's shiny SUV and tried not to cry like the pathetic, useless sack of shit he was.

Chapter Two

WHEN THE STAFF email hit his inbox, Seth rolled his eyes at the all-caps "*URGENT!*" in the subject line and went back to his spreadsheet. To the receptionist/office manager, everything was *URGENT!*, including—but not limited to—running out of mochaccino coffee pods in the break room too quickly, overusing staples, and the minimum length of shorts on casual Fridays in summer (eleven-and-a-half-inch inseam).

At her desk a few feet away in their pod, Jenna gasped. "She's here! Oh my God."

"Hmm?" Seth glanced over as Jenna whirled around on her chair, her hand catching a garland and sending a bright pink ornament rolling across her desk.

Jenna's side of the pod was an explosion of life and holiday cheer. After Thanksgiving, she'd strung colored fairy lights over the top of her monitor, and sparkly red garlands snaked between framed family photographs on both sides of her desk, ornaments nestled throughout.

Seth had no such photos since he had no family at all—at least not any who would actually talk to him. The jagged edges of that particular pain had dulled after twelve years, but as another lonely Christmas approached, he had to force away the memories more than usual.

Jenna hissed, "Angela Barker is here!"

His heart skipped. "Wait, what? Why?"

"Surprise visit." Jenna pressed a hand to her chest. "What if they're doing a re-org? But the CEO wouldn't be the one to come and fire people. Right?"

"They promised our positions were safe when BRK bought us out." His stomach dropped. He'd moved to Albany. He'd bought a house. He'd been dumped by his boyfriend—was his job next? "They promised," he repeated weakly. Of course, everyone knew what a corporate promise was worth these days.

I'm going to have nothing but a half-finished house to my name.

"Why did she have to come the day I have spit-up on my blouse?" Jenna rubbed despairingly at the mark on her shoulder, which she'd dabbed with Seth's Tide pen when she'd arrived.

There was no denying the green blouse was stained, but Seth said, "It's not noticeable at all. Can barely see it now."

"You're a liar, but a sweet one." Jenna opened her top drawer and pulled out a compact. She blotted at her nose and then tugged her blond curls loose from her customary ponytail and squinted at her reflection in the little mirror. "Nope," she muttered before tying her hair back up again. "Frizz city."

"It's fine," Seth said. "You look great." He glanced down at himself. He wore a standard work outfit—pressed gray slacks, button-down shirt in blue, and a navy tie. His black Oxfords were polished. He ran a hand over his short, thick, brown hair, which he kept neatly combed back. "Do I look okay?"

Jenna didn't even glance up as she examined the stain on her blouse with her compact mirror. "Of course. You look perfect as always. I should have done my hair this morning, but the baby was being so fussy, and Ian refused to wear long sleeves even though it's supposed to snow today."

As she grumbled about what a pain in the butt five-year-olds were, Seth adjusted the knot on his tie half an inch higher before smoothing a palm down the subtly patterned silk. He snorted mentally. *Perfect.* Jenna always insisted he was classically handsome (*"like Jimmy Stewart!"*), but if he was so perfect, why had Brandon left him?

Nope. Abort. Focus on the current crisis.

He stopped himself from tumbling down the rabbit hole of *why*, a question he knew he'd never really answer. Brandon was gone. The end. It had been more than a year for Pete's sake.

Because I wasn't enough. That's why.

"Focus," Seth muttered to himself as Matt's head appeared over the partition that separated Seth and Jenna's desks from the next pod.

Matt's ruddy face was flushed even more than usual beneath his pale, shaggy hair. "Guys. I've got the scoop." Jenna wheeled her chair over to Seth's with one push, bumping into him. The other two desks behind them in their pod were empty since the interns had finished for the semester.

Matt glanced around and whispered over the partition, "They're implementing a new structure. Allegedly no one's getting fired, but we'll see. Angela's picking five new directors herself. It's this thing she does. You know how she's all about the company being like family?"

Jenna said, "Uh-huh. 'Family values' to the point where people married with kids get ahead more."

"What?" Seth sputtered. "But that's not fair."

Jenna and Matt stared at him like he had three heads. Matt said, "How do you not know this already? I sent you the link to the subreddit on Angela and BRK Sync when they bought us out last month." He fiddled with the collar of his suit jacket, which he wore over a T-shirt. There were undoubtedly dark suede sneakers on his feet instead of dress shoes, but since he was the graphic designer in the communications department, everyone let it go. Young creative types and all that.

"That message board?" Seth asked. "I've been busy working."

Matt rolled his eyes. "Well, this has happened at every other company BRK has absorbed. Married with kids gets you ahead. Becky said Angela's going to be here all week, and she's taking us on some family Christmas retreat next weekend, so cancel your plans. Her way of welcoming us to the clan."

Matt was sleeping with Becky, the alarmist receptionist/office manager, so Seth had no doubt the intel was good. Seth muttered, "Is this a corporation or a cult?"

"Little bit from column A, little bit from column B," Matt said. "It's batshit, but she's the boss, so…" He leaned closer, his head all the way over the partition. He clearly hadn't shaved in a few days. "Director of systems training is one of the roles. Everyone knows that should be yours, dude."

Seth's whole body clenched. "They're finally creating that role?"

"About time," Jenna said. "You've been doing the job since you transferred here."

He had. He *had*, and that job was *his*. He'd done the job without the title and raise he'd deserved, hoping that he'd be rewarded eventually. He'd uprooted his whole life to come to Albany—after very careful consideration—with the promise that he'd move up in the company. Now that BRK had bought them out, this was his chance.

Too bad about his utter lack of spouse or family. He hardly even had friends after the breakup. There were some people back home in Georgia he saw on Facebook and never actually *talked* to anymore, and acquaintances at work. While Jenna had been on maternity leave, Seth had realized how friendless he was.

He'd thought about joining some kind of club—although definitely not the pretentious wine tasting group he and Brandon had attended before Brandon dumped him.

But *which* club? Seth had been researching it for, well, almost a year. There were variables and pros and cons to consider! He didn't want to choose the *wrong* club. What if he ran into

Brandon and Brandon's new boyfriend? The thought was horrific. In the end, every weekend he'd wound up staying home. Alone.

Bitterness swelled. "Guess I'm not getting the director position. Single and gay won't cut it." He wasn't sure who he resented more—Brandon for leaving or himself for being so pitifully alone and indecisive. If he didn't deserve happiness in love, maybe he didn't deserve it at work.

"She doesn't care about the gay part." Matt's face lit up. "In fact, she's all about LGBTQ inclusion. Thinks everyone should experience the joy of having kids and all that shit. And she's got a real lady boner for showing off how open-minded she is. So just, you know, get married to some guy, stat. Tell her you're going to adopt a starving orphan. She'll love it." He jerked his head around, then hissed, "Here she comes!" before ducking back to his desk on the other side of partition.

Angela Barker's Texas accent and nasal tone preceded her as she made her way through the maze of pods. Jenna shoved a stack of paper into a desk drawer, then pawed at the stain on her blouse, muttering, "Why today of all days?"

Pulse racing, Seth straightened his little area, scooping a few stray paper clips into the jar by his keyboard. His pen and pad of sticky notes sat in their usual place by his phone, and his notebook rested on the other side of his computer. He adjusted the thumb tack pinning the calendar over his desk to make sure the December snowy sunrise landscape was centered on the bulletin board.

Said board also held a corporate lunch-and-learn schedule and a coupon for twenty percent off at Bed, Bath & Beyond Jenna had passed along to encourage him to buy more furniture for his house. He should have put up something Christmassy. He bet Angela loved Christmas.

Compared to Jenna's desk, Seth's looked hardly lived in. His black and white mug stated: "I really love my ~~boyfriend~~ cat." Considering his ex had given it to him as a birthday gift weeks before leaving him, Seth probably should have tossed it instead of adding a splash of masochism to his daily cup of coffee.

Especially since his cranky old calico, Agatha, had died a few months after Brandon left. Jenna had asked him once why he kept using the mug, and he'd said it was because it was the last thing Brandon had given him.

She'd tilted her head, mouth pulled down in pity. *"He's not dead. He dumped you, and he's dating a gym bunny from Schenectady. Which is what you should be doing. Get out there and hook up! You're only thirty-seven. You're still young!"*

Too bad the thought of hooking up left him feeling even emptier than Brandon's absence. Seth wished he was one of those guys—apparently every other man who walked the earth—who could have casual sex and not feel guilty and bleak.

Heck, he still felt guilty when he masturbated—although it didn't stop him when the need was too much. He hadn't been to church in years, yet he couldn't seem to completely let go of the strict rules he'd grown up with.

He straightened the ridiculous mug.

"Well, it's good to meet you, Lin!" Angela was a few pods away. Getting closer.

Seth's pulse raced. He'd been the de facto leader of the systems training team for three years. He planned worldwide training sessions for clients who purchased Greenware's corporate telecommunications system.

Now they were Greenware Sync after the takeover from BRK Sync, but the equipment and systems hadn't changed. Jenna didn't technically report to him, and neither did the revolving door of interns who helped with the sessions, but they should have.

When Seth had transferred to Albany from Atlanta a year and a half ago, it had been with the promise of a promotion and manager title. A pay raise. Yet he'd received excuse after excuse.

And now he'd be out of consideration for the director role because he wasn't married with kids? It just wasn't fair.

He muttered to Jenna, "I'm going to get screwed, aren't I?"

"And not in the way you need to get screwed."

"Hiya, Matt!" Angela Barker was right in front of their pod. Seth glimpsed the top of her poufy bleached hair over the partition. As she talked to Matt and a few other people, Seth's mind spun. He wanted the promotion. He needed the promotion. Most of all, he *deserved* the promotion.

He rolled over to Jenna and whispered, "Too bad I don't have a magic wand to create an instant family." He pushed off the thin beige carpet and rolled back to his spot, clicking on his spreadsheet as he tried to look both busy and casual at the same time. It was what it was. There was nothing he could do to—

A framed picture suddenly appeared on the left side of his desk, Jenna diving back to her chair just before Angela popped into the wide entry to their pod.

Angela grinned. "Well, howdy!"

Before Seth could process the new addition to his desk, he had to stand and meet Angela's firm grip. Around fifty, she was petite and slim, her gray pantsuit neatly pressed, a fuchsia scarf knotted around her throat. Her earrings were delicate little silver Christmas trees decorated with what was probably Swarovski crystals or even diamonds.

He said, "I'm Seth Marston."

Jenna shook Angela's hand next. "Jenna Derwood-Kim."

"Hiya," Angela said. "Not sure how much you know about me, but a few years ago, I took over the family business. My daddy built BRK Sync from the ground up in the eighties, and as technology and the times have changed, so have we."

Seth wondered how many times she'd delivered the spiel. Probably millions. He said, "It's wonderful to meet you, Ms. Barker."

"Oh, I'm a proud missus, but you can call me Angela." Her gaze went to Jenna's colorful desk, and she neared it to peer at the photo frames. "And who do we have here, Jenna?"

"That's my husband, Jun-hwan—but he usually just goes by Jun—and our two boys. Ian's five and Noah's almost six months."

"Jun. Is that Korean?" Angela asked.

Jenna smiled. "It is! His parents moved here just before he was born."

"Wonderful. I hope you're transitioning back to work all right after the baby?"

"Yes, I came back part time a few weeks ago. It's been a much better transition with the extended maternity leave option you introduced. Thank you."

"Oh, my pleasure, sugar! I know how tough it can be as a working mom."

Jenna said, "Seth's been carrying so much of the workload. He's incredible. The training department would fall apart without him!"

He cringed internally as Jenna laid it on but kept a smile on his face as Angela turned her attention back to him and his desk—with the new addition from Jenna.

Angela leaned over the framed photo, which Seth realized was a new picture Jenna had put on her desk after Thanksgiving of her brother and his stepson. It was framed in cheery, multicolored wood squares, but Logan and the boy were barely smiling, their spines stiff as if they were lined up in front of a firing squad instead of posing for a family snap by the newly decorated Christmas tree.

Jenna's brother was handsome in that craggy, Daniel Craig kind of way. The kind of rough-and-tumble guy Seth's mother would have called a "bruiser" with a disapproving sniff. His wife had died suddenly in the summer, and Jenna worried a lot about him and the boy. It was all very sad from what Seth knew.

"And who's this?" Angela asked.

Before Seth could hope to formulate a response to explain the picture, Jenna said, "That's Logan, Seth's fiancé, and their son, Connor. Seth has such a lovely little family."

Angela clapped her hands together, appearing genuinely delighted. "Isn't that something? You know I've always said gay folks are just as the good lord made 'em."

My parents and their church would strenuously beg to differ. Seth kept smiling robotically. *Say something!* "Uh, yes. Thank you?"

"Families are at the heart of our biggest successes in this world. Too many people try to go it alone." Angela shook her head sadly.

Seth wanted to argue that single people could certainly be just as happy and successful—his own miserable single life notwithstanding—and that some people were thrown out of their families, but he just nodded and smiled.

Angela beamed. "When's the big day?"

"Oh, uh… We haven't set the date yet."

Jenna said, "They're thinking next summer."

"I look forward to seeing the wedding pictures." Angela eyed Seth speculatively. "Now, Seth—if I recall correctly, your name's come up for one of the director roles we're fixin' to fill."

"Has it?" he asked, trying not to look too excited. But maybe he didn't look excited enough? "I'd love to discuss it further with you." *And if I pretend to have a fiancé while you're around, what's the harm if it helps me get the promotion?*

"Seth's really been holding down the fort for systems training since he came here," Jenna said. "He'd be an excellent director."

"Good to hear it! Seth, we'll have to sit down soon and have a confab." Angela checked her gleaming Rolex. "I've got to get going now—duty and lunch call."

As if summoned from thin air, a short, slight young man with dark skin stepped into the pod. He wore a suit and glasses and spoke in a deep murmur. "I'll alert the driver that you're on your way down."

"Thank you, Dale." Angela motioned to him with a wide smile. "My right-hand man. Wouldn't know if I was comin' or goin' without him." Before Seth or Jenna could reply, she chuckled as she glanced around. "Now I told y'all I didn't need an escort while I toured the office, but darned if I'm not turned around."

Dale opened his mouth, but Seth quickly offered, "We'll walk you out!" Between beige partitions, he could feel the eyes of coworkers, the floor unnaturally hushed as he and Jenna guided Angela and Dale back toward reception.

"How did you and your fiancé meet?" Angela asked as they passed Becky's immaculate desk and approached the glass doors leading to the elevators. Becky sat almost comically straight, smiling with gleaming white teeth.

"We—Uh, we met through Jenna, actually." Seth debated whether to dart ahead and open the door for Angela. Was that anti-feminist? Or rude not to? Dale wasn't opening it for her. Should Seth—

In the time he was trying to decide, Angela had already pushed open the glass door. "Oh, here's your fiancé now!"

As Seth attempted to process the cheery, absolutely *horrifying* words ringing in his ears, he stared at Logan Derwood. Logan was all scruffy and—wow, *gorgeous*—in his black leather jacket, somehow standing there in the flesh. In real life.

Seth prayed the polished tile beneath his feet would open up and swallow him whole in one merciful gulp.

Chapter Three

AS THE ELEVATOR doors slid shut behind him, cutting off the damn cheery instrumental version of "Jingle Bells," Logan gripped Jenna's car key in his pocket, the metal digging into his palm. At least if he dropped off the key early and bussed it back, he wouldn't have to make conversation and pretend everything was fine and that he wasn't about to be homeless.

"Oh, here's your fiancé now!" a woman exclaimed. Small and aggressively blond, her teeth flashed in a blinding smile. Beside her was a tall, slim man with dark brown hair and blue eyes gone comically wide. The vaguely familiar man gaped at Logan as the woman stuck out her hand. "Logan, wasn't it?"

He automatically shook her hand. "Uh, yes. Logan." That part was right, although he sure as hell wasn't anyone's fiancé, least of all this stuffed shirt's. Clothes perfectly ironed and tucked in, not a hair out of place. Although at the moment, the man's face was bright red, and he looked as if he might puke all over the woman's fancy stilettos.

Jenna and another man trailed them, Jenna's frozen expression of horror making Logan tense. He hated seeing her upset. That's when it clicked into place—the tall guy was Jenna's co-worker. Her boss, maybe? Logan recognized him from the odd Facebook post.

Since Jenna and her boss didn't seem able to do anything but stare mutely, and the short man only came to stand beside the blond woman with a passive expression, Logan was forced to speak. "Um, good to meet you…"

"Angela Barker from Dallas, Texas. President and CEO of BRK Sync, which owns Greenware now. I'm getting out in the field and meeting the family, like your fiancé. Seth was telling me about your wedding plans."

"Was he?" Logan asked. Behind Angela, Jenna nodded frantically at him, making a rolling motion with her hand, gaze imploring. Logan tried to smile, glancing at this Seth, who appeared close to hyperventilating, his chest rising and falling rapidly.

What the fuck is all this?

Angela beamed. "I think it's so wonderful you two will be creating a family with your son. Family first, I always say. Gay or straight!"

My son? He wanted to scoff as he thought of Connor's hunched shoulders and hateful scowl. Shit, Logan just wanted to be alone, but Jenna pleaded with her eyes, and he couldn't deny her anything.

He bit down the knee-jerk denial that he was gay and kept what he hoped was a friendly expression on his face. Clearly he'd been roped into some kind of weird scheme, although for the life of him he couldn't guess what the hell it was about. Seth stood beside Angela with a rigid smile.

"And what do you do, Logan?" Angela asked.

There it was again, the shame somehow jaggedly icy yet burning as it ripped through him. *I don't do anything. I'm a useless waste of fucking space.* He cleared his throat and said, "Railway work." At least it had been true for more than ten years.

"Oh, how fascinating!" A gleam entered Angela's eye. "You know, I have been on the road so much lately, and I would kill for a home-cooked meal." She glanced at Seth. "What would you two say if I shamelessly invited myself over for dinner while I'm in town?"

Logan would say he had no fucking idea what was going on, but he only raised an eyebrow at Seth, who said, "Uh, th—that would be wonderful, Angela! It would be our pleasure."

To the short young man in the suit, who was probably her assistant, Angela said, "Talk to Seth and schedule something for next week before the retreat." She turned back to the rest of them. "I hope you're as excited about the retreat as I am! Going to be fun for the whole family. I know I'm springing it on y'all, but I hope you can make it."

The tinny notes of a pop song echoed from Angela's dark-pink purse, and she exclaimed, "I'm so sorry, but that's my daughter's ring tone. She loves that Shawn Mendes." She swiped to answer. "Hey, sugar! Hold on a sec." To Logan and Seth, she smiled widely. "So wonderful to meet you. I look forward to seeing you both again soon! Don't worry, I'm not a fussy eater!"

Logan took the opportunity to turn and press the elevator call button so he wouldn't have to say anything else. Thank fuck it had parked on the floor, and the doors opened immediately. He nodded and tried to smile as Angela stepped on with her assistant, chattering to her daughter about a dog named "Pom-pom" who was pissing on the furniture.

Jenna twisted a loose curl from her ponytail around her finger the way she did when she was stressed as hell. As soon as the elevator doors shut, she and Seth exhaled loudly. Seth rubbed his face, mumbling, "This was a terrible idea." Then he hissed to Jenna, "This was a terrible idea!"

Jenna glanced around the empty foyer, and Logan looked as well. To the right, through glass doors, a young redheaded woman at reception watched them with sharp-eyed interest.

Jenna whispered, "I was just trying to help!"

"Someone want to fill me in on what the hell's going on?" Logan asked.

Seth winced. "I'm so sorry. Thank you for playing along."

"Anything for my fiancé," Logan said dryly. "Seth, is it?"

"Seth Marston." He extended his hand. "I work with Jenna."

Logan shook Seth's sweaty palm. "Right. And how did we get engaged? Neat trick since we've never met and I'm not gay."

"Let's discuss this in a breakout room," Jenna said, leading the way into the carpeted main area past the redhead, who didn't try to hide her curiosity as they went by. Jenna chose the first of the rooms that ran down a long wall. After knocking and poking her head in, she ushered them in and closed the door.

Jenna stood by the oval table in the middle of the narrow, windowless room. "I thought you were coming to pick me up at three?"

"Got done early. I'll bus it back. Sorry to mess up your little plan, whatever the hell it is." Logan crossed his arms and glared at Seth. "You in the habit of telling people I'm your boyfriend?"

"No! I swear I'm not. I'm sorry. Jeez, this is messed up." He tugged at his tie as if he couldn't breathe.

Jenna sighed. "It was all me. Spur of the moment thing. We found out Angela was here, and she's going to be choosing new directors in the company. Seth *so* deserves a director role, but he's single, and Angela has this thing about families. Nine times out of ten she always promotes someone married with kids."

"That's fucking weird," Logan said.

"It is, but it's her company, and thanks to even more deregulation lately, she can hire, fire, and promote however she wants. Anyway, I framed that pic I took of you and Connor at Thanksgiving. You know, after we put up the tree?"

"Uh-huh." Logan remembered Connor's bony, rigid shoulder beneath his palm, Jenna trying to get them to smile, her cheeks rosy from a glass of wine. He'd been surprised Connor had even agreed to pose, but Jenna had that way with people.

"Well…" She grimaced. "I put the picture on Seth's desk at

the last second and told Angela you're Seth's fiancé. It was all me. Seth had no choice but to go along with it or it would have been awkward and bizarre."

Logan said flatly, "Good thing we avoided that."

"I didn't expect you to show up!" Jenna actually looked indignant.

"So it's *my* fault?"

"Let's not argue." Seth looked between them, holding up his hands. "It's definitely Jenna's fault."

Logan tensed, his protective instinct kicking in even though Seth was on his side. It was one thing for Logan to say his sister was wrong…

But Jenna huffed out a laugh and lightly slapped Seth's arm. "Okay, yes. It's my fault. Obviously I didn't have time to think through all the ramifications. I thought it could just be a little white lie to help Seth get the promotion."

"And I went along with it," Seth said. "I'm sorry. It was wrong to involve you and your son."

"Stepson." Connor's voice echoed in Logan's head. *"You're not my father! I hate you!"* That had been after Mike had said he didn't want custody, giving Connor a load of excuses and empty promises about how Mike would be in a better position "soon."

Jenna frowned. "Not that that matters. He's part of the family."

Logan snorted. "For now. He'd never see me again if he had his way." People might act like Logan was his dad now, but Connor sure wasn't fooled.

"He's thirteen." She shook her head. "Connor doesn't know what he wants. Don't be butt-hurt over a teenager acting out."

"I'm not." Fine, maybe he was. He wished like hell it didn't bother him. For so many years he'd avoided big emotional commitments, and this bullshit was why. He'd been better off alone. "Speaking of family, what's this retreat Angela mentioned?

It sounded like she expected me there?"

Jenna and Seth shared a glance, frowning. Jenna said, "We actually don't have the details yet. Let me just... I'll be right back." She jerked her thumb toward the door, leaving and closing it behind her.

Logan and Seth stared at each other. Seth dropped his eyes to his fingernails and leaned against the edge of a white board that had bullet points on it about meeting goals or some shit.

Aim high!
But be realistic
Ask for help when needed
Work as a team
Manage stress
We're all in this together!
What a load of crap.

Seth cleared his throat. "Are you back at work on the railway? Jenna never said. I remember when you were in that terrible accident. I'm glad you're better now."

His cheeks going hot with shame, Logan stared at the ugly beige carpet. "Nah. Never going back. I'm looking for something else, but it's a pain in the ass explaining it all to strangers."

"Ah. I understand. I'm sure you'll find something soon."

Logan only shrugged, still unable to meet Seth's gaze. Seconds ticked by in awkward silence, and thank Christ, Jenna returned quickly. She leaned back against the door and bit her lip.

"Well, the good news is that the company is paying for us to have a weekend in Lake Placid. Staying at a lodge, winter activities, etc." She grimaced, and Logan braced and waited for the rest. She said, "The bad news is that they want our spouses and kids to come."

Seth frowned. "When is it? Not this weekend but next? The weekend of the twenty-second?" When Jenna nodded, he half-laughed disbelievingly. "On such short notice? That's ridiculous. People have plans—especially at the holidays. They have lives."

Jenna gave Seth a wry smile. "Yes, some of us do."

"I have a life!" Seth insisted. "Regardless, I'll just say we can't make it. Surely not everyone is going to drop everything and attend because Angela Barker wants us to jump when she snaps her fingers. Obviously we're not going to ask Logan and his stepson to come on this retreat and play fake family for a weekend."

Logan said, "Good. Can I go? If you want to tell the boss lady I'm your boyfriend, feel free. Just leave me out of this. I have enough crap on my plate right now." He made a move toward the door, but Jenna blocked his path, her forehead creasing.

"Wait, what happened?"

He tried to laugh it off. "Nothing. Just stressed about the job situation. You know." He had to figure out a plan before he dumped the latest disasters from his garbage life on her.

But Jenna didn't budge. "I know that tone. Something's wrong."

There was a knock at the door, and she turned to open it, ushering in a shaggy-haired guy who whispered, "What's going on? Becky said you guys were talking to Angela by the elevators and now you're hiding in here." He nodded to Logan and stuck out his hand. "Hey, man. I'm Matt. You're Jenna's brother, right?"

Logan shook his hand. "Right. I was just leaving."

Matt gave him a quizzical look. "The weird thing is that Becky thought she heard that you and Seth are getting married?"

Seth groaned. "That means everyone will know in the next ten minutes."

"No, it's okay," Matt said. "Becky's holding it in for now. I figured I should buy you some time. So how exactly did you two end up engaged? I mean, *mazel tov*, but this is a surprise."

Jenna quickly filled him in, then added, "We can just make up an excuse about why Logan and Connor can't attend the family retreat."

Matt winced. "Word is that when Angela springs these retreats on people, you'd better go unless there's a life-or-death excuse. It's completely unreasonable, but basically it's a test. She's paying for everything, which is generous, but the catch is that we only get 10 days' notice, and we have to prove we're BRK team players whether we're single or married or whatever. And if you have kids, you should definitely bring them. I guess it's not such a big deal when it doesn't fall near the holidays. But it's happening, and if she thinks Logan and Seth are together..."

"Which we aren't," Logan said. "Can I go now?" He needed to find another place to live before the landlord locked him out, and definitely before the kid got off school for the holidays. Had to find some way to put down a deposit. Crashing at Jenna's would be the last resort.

Jenna groaned, ignoring him. To Matt, she said, "Angela also invited herself over to Seth and Logan's for dinner."

"Whoa. This is..." Matt grinned, which was bizarre. "This is *awesome*. It's, like, a *caper*. Who doesn't love a caper?"

Logan stared at him, wondering what planet Matt was from, as Seth said, "*Me*. And I can't have Angela over for dinner regardless. My kitchen's not finished. I don't have a dining table. There's so much to do. I don't even know where to start."

"But the demo's done and the drywall's up," Jenna said. "Don't you have all the cabinets and stuff sitting in the garage? It would only take a couple days to fix it up. You know, our dad was a contractor. If you can find the muscle, Pop could supervise. Would give him something to do other than watch TV all day—and get him moving at least a little. He still refuses to do his exercises."

Seth shook his head. "This is crazy, Jenna. Even if I could fix up the house in time, why would Logan want to pretend to be my fiancé?"

An idea popped into Logan's head, accompanied by a flash of unfamiliar emotion that left him a little breathless. Was it...*hope*? This whole situation was batshit, but maybe there was a way to temporarily solve his problem and Seth's.

What the fuck do I have to lose?

Jenna was saying, "Logan, I know it's so much to ask, but..."

He spoke before he could talk himself out of it, a twist of acid in his gut reminding him he and Connor were about to be homeless. "I could do the renovation stuff. Would need a hand to carry things and get it all in place, but I worked with Pop when I was a teenager. I can do it. The thing is..."

He hesitated. The itchy heat of Jenna, Seth, and Matt staring at him, waiting, made him sweat. Humiliation prickled the back of his neck, and he considered just shutting up and telling them to forget it.

Jenna stepped closer, concern softening her face. "What's going on?"

Logan spit it out, afraid he might puke at the same time. "I was evicted. Connor and I need a place to stay. Not for long—just over the holidays until he goes back to school. I'll find a job in January for sure." Had to. There was no other option.

"*What?*" Jenna grabbed hold of his arm, awful sympathy shining from her eyes. Logan was so sick of his baby sister feeling sorry for him. Being worried about him all the time since he was a mess. She said, "Why didn't you tell me?"

He scowled. "You have enough going on with the kids and Pop. You don't need me on the couch, and what about Connor? There isn't enough room. Besides, it just happened this morning. I have to be out by Friday, and I *did* hear from the factory. I didn't get the job." He shrugged, dislodging Jenna's hand and pretending he didn't care. "It's fine."

There were a few beats of awkward silence before Matt exclaimed, "Guys, this is perfect." He quickly added, "Not that you're getting evicted, man. That sucks. But Seth needs a fake boyfriend, and you need a place to stay. Two birds, one stone." He made a motion like he was dunking a basketball. "Nothing but net."

As Seth and Logan looked at each other dubiously, Jenna bounced on her toes. "Yes! You guys can finish the kitchen with Pop this weekend. Have Angela over for dinner, and then play happy family next weekend on the retreat. Seth's been alone out there in that house too long anyway."

Seth shot her a glare. "I have not."

Jenna gave him an impatient, disbelieving look Logan had seen many, many times. She said, "Seth, I know you'd prefer to make an extensive pro and con list and examine it for a week before committing, but there's no time. You deserve this promotion. What do you have to lose?"

"My job if she finds out this was all a lie?"

"Oh, right." Jenna made a face. "Valid point. But she won't. Think of how many employees Angela Barker has. BRK has offices around the world. We won't see her again for years."

"What about everyone else you work with?" Logan asked.

Jenna shrugged. "We'll just say I set up you and Seth, and it's been a whirlwind romance."

"Everyone will definitely believe Jenna played matchmaker," Matt said. "Less believable that you didn't tell every last person here about it, including the janitor."

Logan wanted to defend her, but, well… Jenna huffed. "I can keep a secret! I knew for months you and Becky were hooking up before you went public."

"Fair enough." To Seth and Logan, Matt said, "Well? You two ready to make a deal?" He grinned.

Seth fidgeted, cracking his knuckles. "It does seem like it would be a mutually beneficial arrangement?" He looked to Logan, his expression creasing. "But I know you're grieving, and if it feels inappropriate, I'd completely understand."

Logan shifted uncomfortably, aware of being watched by everyone in the room. "It's fine."

Yes, Logan did grieve Veronica's death, but he missed the awesome, caring nurse he'd known before it had all gone to crap. And that probably made him a complete shit-brick to not miss her as his wife, but he couldn't make himself feel something he didn't. Maybe he was just broken.

Seth said, "You'd be welcome to stay through the holidays and until you can figure out something in the new year."

"I'd earn my keep." The thought of taking any charity had Logan defensive.

"Of course!" Seth agreed. "Trust me, there's plenty of work for you." He laughed incredulously. "This is completely insane, but maybe it could work?"

"Caper, caper, caper!" Matt chanted, raising a fist in the air.

Jenna bit her lip. "Might take some convincing to get Connor on board."

Logan grunted. "We'll deal with that. Things aren't great at school. I'll fill you in later."

"And you know you're both always welcome at my house," Jenna insisted. "We'd make it work. It's not even a question."

Warm, familiar affection for her flowed through Logan. "I know. But if we could pull this off, maybe it's not the worst idea ever."

"Caper, caper, caper," Matt whispered, pumping his fist again.

Logan looked at Seth, and they shared a laugh. Logan hadn't imagined smiling on this crappy day, let alone laughing. That little flare of hope burned brighter. The plan was nuts, but it was all he had.

With a rueful smile, Seth asked, "It's a deal, then? Think you can pretend to be in love with me for a couple weeks?" He held out his hand.

Logan sure as hell didn't do *love* with men, but it had to be easy enough to fake. He grasped Seth's palm firmly. "Deal."

Chapter Four

THE NEXT DAY after work, Seth made the drive over to the suburb where Logan lived. Apparently neither of them had regained their right minds, and they were actually going to stick with the crazy deal they'd made. Granted, Logan was being evicted and didn't have much choice. Seth couldn't exactly back out and leave the guy out in the cold.

Light snow fell in the early darkness after five p.m., and he shivered, turning up the heater. He wasn't sure he'd ever get used to northern winters. Where he'd grown up in Georgia, if there was even a hint of a flurry everything ground to a halt. Of course, they didn't have snow tires down south, and now his SUV was fully equipped for the worst Mother Nature could—and would—throw at him.

So far there was just a dusting of snow over everything, and as Seth turned off the main road and into a residential area, colored Christmas lights gleamed on houses and wrapped around trees, the snow making everything magical. "I'll be Home for Christmas" played on the radio, and though Seth braced for the pang of longing, it still stole his breath when it hit.

Christmas had always been his favorite time of year, with the lights and music, the smell of fresh cookies baking, and presents under the tree. Friends and family gathered together to celebrate that holy holiday. He'd actually liked going to church around Christmas, singing carols joyfully until his voice was hoarse, no one minding that he couldn't carry a tune to save his life.

He snapped off the radio. It would definitely be only in his foolish dreams that he would ever be home for Christmas again. He didn't even own decorations. Brandon had never been keen on celebrating, and after the terrible holiday twelve years ago, it had all seemed poisoned to Seth. Christmas wasn't for him now.

Following his phone's directions, Seth turned down a few streets, the houses getting a little more rundown and ramshackle. Number eighty-two was a small bungalow and didn't have any holiday lights or decorations. He recognized Jenna's SUV outside and parked behind it, his headlights illuminating the boxes already packed high inside.

Snow crunched under Seth's boots as he got out and walked up the driveway, keeping his bare hands in his coat pockets. The wind was calm, fat snow drifting down peacefully. However, that peace was broken by the shouts exploding out of the house like the *rat-tat-tat* of gunfire even though the front door was closed. Seth stood on the stoop, debating whether to knock.

"That's my shit! Don't touch anything else!"

Logan's rough voice rumbled. "I'm only trying to help."

"You had no right to touch *anything* of mine!" a young voice screeched. That had to be Connor, the stepson.

"For fuck's sake, I only packed the clothes hanging in the closet. I could have just moved all your stuff without telling you, but I didn't want to invade your privacy. Now hurry up, because whatever you don't get into these boxes in the next half hour is staying behind. You've wasted enough time arguing."

"Fuck you! I'm not going anywhere."

Logan's voice rose. "Yes, you damn well are. We're moving our shit over to Seth's, and then I'm taking you back to school before curfew. So get a move on."

Listening to the foul language in shock, Seth decided he'd better knock instead of eavesdrop, so he rapped his knuckles against the door. He knew he was laughably repressed when it came to cursing, but Logan and Connor just sounded so horribly angry towards each other.

When the door opened, Connor was still complaining loudly, but Seth blocked it out and focused on Logan, who ushered him in with a grimace. He wore a black T-shirt and jeans, the cotton hugging the firm, broad muscles of his chest and back. And jeez, his arms were nothing to sneeze at either. Seth had always thought Logan looked handsome in Jenna's pictures, but in person he really was...*wow.*

"Hi. Sorry, it's a bit..." As Connor screamed more curses, Logan winced, rubbing a hand over the scruff on his face with an audible rasp. Seth wondered what that would feel like against his own face.

"Chaotic?" Seth offered. "Moving always is." He peered into the living room, which was still furnished with a plaid couch and a wooden coffee table. "You said the furniture isn't yours?"

"Right. Rented a furnished place." He glanced over his shoulder, dropping his voice. "When Veronica died, there were a lot of bills, and that was on top of what I still owed for my insurance copay on my hospital bills after the accident. Had to sell just about everything."

Seth nodded, shame that he'd been ogling Logan twisting in his gut. *The man's wife died barely six months ago. Have some decency.* "I understand. Well, I put the back seats down, so should be plenty of room for what's left."

"Thank you." Logan winced at a thump from the direction of what had to be Connor's room. "There's still time to back out."

A little voice did pipe up saying that Seth was biting off more than he could chew, but he couldn't exactly leave Logan high and dry, now could he? He tried for an easy smile. "Nah, we made a deal. You're helping me out just as much."

Logan snorted. "Not sure if that's true. But thanks." He

glanced down the hall. The cursing from Connor had faded. Logan still spoke softly. "I didn't want to go through his stuff, so I picked him up after school to tell him in person. Give him a chance to pack up his things so he wasn't completely blindsided."

"Sounds like it's been a barrel of laughs." This earned him a sardonic smile from Logan, and Seth tried to ignore the sexy little dimples that appeared in Logan's cheeks. Before Seth could say anything else, a gangly boy who needed a haircut appeared down the short hall. He wore uniform slacks and a white dress shirt, the sleeves rolled up to his bony elbows, his tie missing. He scowled at Seth.

"Oh, hello," Seth said with a smile. "You must be Connor. I work with your Aunt Jenna. It's nice to meet you."

"She's not really my aunt," Connor muttered, crossing his arms.

"*Connor*," Logan warned.

Seth smiled awkwardly. "Well… It's still nice to meet you."

"Whatever. I'm calling my dad, and he's going to fly me to Florida for Christmas, so I'm not staying with you."

Seth glanced at Logan, who only shrugged, his face impassive as he said, "Okay. Go ahead and call him."

Connor glared. "I did. I left a message. He'll call me back any minute. He's probably still at work. He actually *has* a job since he's not a loser like you."

Waiting for Logan to scold Connor for the rude insult, Seth bit his tongue. But Logan didn't rise to the bait, only saying, "In the meantime, keep packing." He picked up a box in the hallway. "Seth, there isn't too much to go into your SUV. It'll mostly be Connor's stuff."

"Right. Uh, okay." Seth fished out his keys and opened the front door for Logan, following him out into the snow. Flakes caught in Logan's dark hair, his wide shoulders rigid as he walked out. At the SUV, Seth opened the back and said, "Don't you want your coat?"

Logan's muscles flexed as he pushed the box into the back. He straightened and blew out a long breath, his exhalation clouding in the cold air. "I'll grab it in a sec. Just had to get out of there before we got in another fight."

"Understood. I didn't realize his father was still in the picture?"

Logan shook his head derisively. "He's not—selfish piece of shit is what he is. He probably won't even call back for days, and when he does, he'll be full of excuses. But I try not to say a bad word about him to Connor."

"Right," Seth repeated. "That's smart. Let him figure it out for himself."

Logan shivered, rubbing his bare arms. Jenna'd mentioned that Logan had worked hard to get back in shape after recovering from the accident, and Seth couldn't imagine how good he'd looked before it, although his brain stubbornly tried.

Logan said, "For a smart kid, it's sure as hell taking him a while to get the message."

Seth thought of his own parents—his mother's round face and big eighties-style curls, his father's balding head and wire-framed glasses—wondering what they would do if he actually called. "It can be hard to accept." He knew without a doubt his parents would hang up on him, yet he still thought, *Maybe...*

"Although the kid's right that his asswipe father does have a job, at least."

"Hey, it's not your fault you're out of work."

"That's not what the railway says. Worked there more than a decade, and I'm out with nothing. I wasn't speeding, and I know I braked in time. I *know* it."

He was obviously referring to the accident. "I'm sure you did."

"Doesn't matter anyway. Except for the fact that I can't seem to get another job without a reference since I worked there so long." He headed back to the house. "Anyway."

Seth followed him inside, standing in the doorway as Logan put on a black leather jacket and gloves. It was quiet from down the hall, and Seth hoped that meant Connor was packing. "In the new year, something will turn up."

"Let's hope so. For both our sakes." Logan grimaced. "But don't worry, I'll figure something out. The deal is just until January and we'll be out of your life. Thanks again."

"Hey, you really are doing me just as big a favor."

"What favor?" Connor asked. He must have been listening, and now he neared them in the foyer, his socked feet slapping on the parquet.

Seth's heart sank at the thought of explaining it, embarrassment prickling his skin. He glanced at Logan, who sighed and mumbled to Seth, "Hadn't got there yet." Logan faced Connor. "It's no big deal. Seth needs to pretend he's getting married so he gets a promotion at work that he really deserves. So I'm going to be his fake fiancé."

Connor's face creased with confusion and possibly disgust. "What the fuck?"

It was entirely strange for Seth to hear a kid swear the way Connor did without being reprimanded. Seth would have been belted if so much as a "damn" or "hell" slipped out. Even "darn" or "jeez" or "heck" had been forbidden since they were clear derivatives of curses. Logan seemed to swear regularly, but he was an adult, at least.

Seth cleared his throat. "I'm sure it sounds a little confusing to you." He tried to smile. "It's a little confusing to us as well. It started as a white lie and snowballed into this…*caper*, I suppose you could call it."

Connor stared at Seth, then Logan. To Logan, he hurled, "You're gay now?" as if it was a barbed accusation.

"No. I'll just be pretending for a little while. It's not a big deal."

Grunting, Connor shifted his focus to Seth, eyeing him up and down, his lip curling. "So you're a fag no one wants to date?"

Seth flinched, not sure whether the slur or the accurate assessment of his love life hurt more. "Uh…"

Logan stared at Connor in apparent disbelief before drawing himself up even taller and barking, "What the hell kind of word is that? Jesus Christ, you know better."

Connor opened his mouth as if to shout back, but then his pimply face flushed, his gaze dropping to his feet. He muttered, "Sorry."

"What would your mother say, hearing you talk like that?"

In a flash, the defiant rage returned, Connor's head snapping up and his eyes flashing. "She wouldn't say anything. She's dead. Because of you."

Seth blinked in surprise. From what he recalled, it had been natural causes—an aneurysm, perhaps? Heart attack? But guilt definitely flinched across Logan's face, his shoulders hunching as he muttered, "You know she'd hate to hear you talk like this anyway."

To Seth, Logan added, "Sorry. Look, if you want to back out, I don't blame you." His gaze flicked up to Seth's and then away miserably.

Resisting the urge to reach out and touch Logan's arm, to give some kind of comfort, Seth shook his head. "No. We had a deal. Trust me, I've heard worse."

Logan's nostrils flared. "Well, you shouldn't have to. And you *won't*, at least not from Connor." He raised an eyebrow at the boy. "Since when do you call gay people names? Isn't your buddy Jayden gay?"

Connor fidgeted, his expression miserable. "Yes." Then panic seemed to seize him, and he sucked in a breath and pleaded with Logan, eyes wide. "Don't tell him I said that word!"

"I won't," Logan assured him. "I think it would hurt his feelings a lot."

Exhaling, Connor nodded. To Seth, he added, "I didn't mean it. I'm really sorry. I don't know why I said it."

Because you're angry and confused and lashing out. Seth gave the kid a little smile. "Apology accepted. I'd really like to be friends. What do you say?" He extended his hand. Connor peered at it suspiciously before shaking it briefly, his small hand damp.

Fortunately, Connor was quiet after that, finishing packing his room and helping to carry the boxes without any more complaints. They piled up the back of Seth's SUV and drove back to Saratoga Springs, Logan and Connor following in Jenna's vehicle.

Turning into his hundred-foot driveway, Seth glanced at the retro metal mailbox by the curb, his stomach tightening at the flyers sticking out. He hadn't checked the mail for two weeks. He should just bite the bullet and face what was likely inside, but...

I'll look tomorrow.

After parking at the top of the drive, he followed the unshoveled brick path and climbed the two steps to the front door. The outdoor light had switched on automatically, and it illuminated the fluffy snow that was still drifting down. Logan and Connor approached, both gazing around.

Logan whistled softly. "Real beautiful home you have. Lots of land."

"Thanks." He pointed left and right. "You can see the lights of the neighbors through the trees. They're close, but not too close, which is perfect for me." He ushered them inside, all of them stamping their feet on the mat and taking off their snowy boots in the little foyer.

Seth pointed up the stairs, which extended back on the right-hand side of the house. "Two bedrooms and bathrooms up there." To the left, he led them through the little sitting room area, which currently only held an armchair. "Uh, you can tell I haven't finished furnishing the place yet." He laughed awkwardly and continued on into the kitchen on the left and empty dining space to the right.

Logan examined the kitchen. "Did you demo some walls and open this up when you moved in?"

"Yes." He winced, looking at the wide island and counters that were still covered in plywood, and the complete lack of cabinets. At least the medium hardwood flooring that ran through the whole main floor was done, although the walls where the blue-tinted subway tile back-splash would go were still bare.

"As you can see, it still needs some work. The pantry's finished in the corner, so I've been storing food and whatnot in there." He glanced to the bare room on the right. "Still need the dining table and chairs. When we moved up from Georgia we were going to buy most things new."

Connor, who had poked his nose into the long pantry, asked, "Who's 'we'?"

Logan looked like he was about to chastise him, but Seth spoke before he could, keeping his tone light. "Well, 'we' was me and Brandon. We met in Atlanta at my first job out of college. Both worked in HR back then. We were together a long time, and when I was transferred here about a year and a half ago, I bought this house and Brandon came with me." His throat got tight, and he cleared it. "But it didn't work out. We broke up last October."

"That sucks," Connor said, going back to the pantry. He seemed to be eyeing the little collection of Halloween treats Seth had bought at half price on November first and hadn't finished yet. He'd hidden up in his room on Halloween instead of shelling out, although he wasn't sure any kids would have come by anyway.

Seth asked, "Are you hungry? Help yourself to whatever you like."

Logan swore under his breath. "Forgot about dinner."

"I'll order a pizza." Seth pulled out his phone. "What do you guys like?"

"No, I'll order it. You already went out of your way to help us move our crap." Logan took out his own phone.

Seth shook his head. "I insist. You can get the next pizza." Of course he had no plans to let Logan pay for anything. For goodness' sake, the man was jobless and evicted. He joked, "Trust me, there will be plenty of opportunities. I don't cook as much as I should." When it was just him, it didn't seem worth the bother.

"Pepperoni and extra cheese," Connor said. "Um, please. Thanks." He held up a snack pack of Doritos. "Cool if I have these?"

"Absolutely," Seth said. "Logan, what's your pizza order?"

He shrugged. "Anything." He examined the kitchen. "You said you have the cabinets and the counters already?"

"Yep. It's all in the garage." Seth tapped in an order for one pepperoni pizza and one sausage and mushroom, both with extra cheese. "Think it's doable?"

"Definitely." Logan glanced at the dining space. "You're definitely going to need a table and chairs if the boss lady's coming for dinner. It's all painted, at least."

"Right. Yes." The white trim was done along with the pale gray walls. Seth groaned. "I shouldn't have put it off so long."

"We'll figure something out. Don't worry."

"Whoa!" Connor's exclamation echoed from beyond the short little space, barely a hall, that led to the great room at the back of the house.

Seth smiled as he and Logan joined him, taking the two steps down into the room. This was the space Seth could actually be proud of—a vaulted white ceiling with wood beams, tall and wide windows, a sleek gas fireplace stove in one corner and a massive TV in the other. A curved black leather sectional with chaises on both ends dominated the right side, facing the fireplace and the

TV. On the far side of the room there was a sliding glass door to the patio.

"This is dope," Connor said, gazing around in apparent awe.

Seth felt ridiculously pleased to have impressed him. "Thanks."

Logan seemed equally awed. "Wow." He walked across the thick area rug, which was a navy and gray diamond pattern, and cupped his hands around his eyes to peek out the sliding door. "Is that a built-in barbecue?"

"Yep. We had a gas line put in, so figured why not?" He'd barely used it, and shifted guiltily. "There's a fire pit back there too. The outdoor space was a big selling point. And this room, of course. Got them to vault the ceiling and put in new windows. It was small and dim before, and now it's, well, this. An improvement, I think."

Logan gave him a look. "You could say that. Anyway, we should bring in the boxes. Have to get Connor back to school by nine."

Mouth full of Doritos, Connor said, "Yeah, you'll be in shit if you don't."

It was still jarring to hear the way Connor and Logan cursed freely around each other, but it wasn't Seth's place to say anything. Logan didn't seem to think anything of it, but of course he'd been in the military. Seth imagined he'd become inured to obscenity.

They put their boots back on and went out, unloading the boxes and bags into the foyer. Between the three of them, it didn't take long. There were some boxes of kitchen and miscellaneous items that Seth left in the empty sitting room before they took Connor's things up to the spare room. It was a nondescript guest room—a double bed, dresser, closet, and generic art of a sailboat and a country road up on the pale gray walls.

Seth cleared his throat as Logan and Connor came in. "So, there's only the one extra room. I figured two bedrooms would be

enough since I don't have any family and Brandon's are real
homebodies who don't travel much. There was another small
room, but we sacrificed it for the great room ceiling."

Connor frowned. "Why don't you have any family?"

"Don't be nosy," Logan snapped, a little harshly in Seth's
opinion.

Before Connor could retaliate, Seth said calmly, "It's all right.
I don't mind talking about it." It wasn't pleasant, but he tried to
be matter of fact about it when it came up. "My family cut me out
of their lives after I told them I was gay. It was twelve years ago
now. They're very religious, and their church is quite homophobic. They believe I'm choosing a life of sin and all that kind of
stuff." He shrugged tightly. "I knew this could happen when I
came out, but I'd hoped for the best anyway."

Connor and Logan seemed to be taking it in. Logan shook his
head and said, "Sorry, man."

"It's okay." Seth forced a laugh. "I mean, it's not *okay*, but it is
what it is. I couldn't stay in the closet. I like to believe in a God
who made people the way they're supposed to be."

Connor was watching him silently. Then he said, "Your family
are dicks, huh?"

Seth had to laugh for real this time. "They are." Of course
guilt slammed him immediately, and his smile faded. "I shouldn't
say that. They're good people—they just have their beliefs."

"That gay people are going to hell?" Connor asked, eyebrows
shooting up. "That's bullshit. Good people shouldn't think that.
And good people shouldn't choose to never see their own kid
again because of the way they were born."

Logan said, "Hard to argue with that."

"My friend Jayden? His parents are awesome. They love him
the way he is. That's what parents are supposed to do."

Guilt still lingered, leaving sticky trails like gum on the bottom of Seth's shoe, stuck in the crevices. He simply said,

"Anyhow, we should get the sleeping arrangements sorted out."

"Right. I'll sleep on the couch if that's okay?" Logan asked. "Connor, this can be your room while we're staying with Seth."

"You could stay in here while Connor's at school." Seth knew the couch was comfy, but he felt like a bad host regardless.

Connor stared at the wood floor. Logan said, "No, I'll be good on the couch. Connor, why don't you unpack a bit? We'll bring the rest up before the pizza gets here."

"Yes, should be soon," Seth said. "The place I order from takes a while, but it's worth it." He gave Connor a smile and went back downstairs with Logan.

In the foyer, Logan glanced up behind him and whispered, "Hope it's okay if I stay on the couch? He already had to move after his mom, and now this. I think it'll help if he has his own space without me in it at all."

"Of course. That makes perfect sense. He's been through a lot of upheaval."

"Thanks for getting it. And we'll be out of your hair ASAP. I'm job searching every day, and either way we'll be out in January." He grimaced. "You're sure it's okay to be here over the holidays? You probably have plans."

That would require having a life. "No, actually. I'm not really big on Christmas."

"Oh." His brow furrowed.

"What?" Seth shifted uneasily, trying to smile.

"You just seem like you'd be into all that wholesome holiday stuff."

He probably finds me incredibly lame. Seth admitted, "I was, but…"

Understanding seemed to wash over Logan's stubbly, handsome face. "Right. The family thing."

"Yeah. Will you and Connor be with Jenna on Christmas? I know she loves it." Poor Connor. His first Christmas without his mother, and he didn't have a proper home.

"On Christmas Eve, I guess. She'll be with her husband's family on Christmas Day." He waved a hand. "But we'll do our best to stay out of your way. Thanks again for this." Logan clapped a calloused hand on Seth's shoulder, and Seth tried to ignore the tingle that spread through him at the strong, warm touch.

They went back to work, taking the rest of Connor's boxes upstairs. The pizza arrived, and they all sat on the couch in the great room, the pizza sitting on the iron and wood coffee table on top of tea towels Seth spread so the grease didn't seep through. He realized he was out of napkins, but they didn't seem fazed by using paper towels.

He and Logan let Connor pick something on the TV, and he went for *Mythbusters* on one of the streaming channels, complimenting Seth on the surround sound from the home theater speakers he'd had installed. Seth sipped a Sprite and put a coaster under Connor's cola.

He'd ordered a six-pack of soda since he realized he only had water, coffee, and tea on hand. He should make a list of what they liked and stock up, especially for Logan since Connor would still be at school before the family retreat.

Seth had to choke down his bite of pizza at the reminder of the retreat, the extra cheese almost lodging in his throat. Could he and Logan really fool everyone—and Angela in particular—into believing they were a *couple*? Was Connor going to behave? Would he even agree to go?

Maybe it was best if he didn't, but Angela was so keen on families that it would probably help if he did. Assuming he didn't blow their cover, of course. Seth wasn't above bribing him handsomely.

They ate and watched a segment about whether drifting a car around a corner was faster than just slowing down and reaccelerating. It turned out to be a myth that drifting was faster. Seth said, "Guess no one gave Vin Diesel the memo."

Logan chuckled, wiping his mouth with a paper towel. "To be fair, that's the only *Fast and the Furious* movie he's not in."

Connor huffed. "He is too. He has a scene at the end." He shook his head as if Logan was a complete idiot, and it set Seth's teeth on edge.

But Logan only shrugged. "Yeah, okay."

Seth supposed Logan had learned to pick his battles, but Connor's bursts of hostility just seemed so…unnecessary. Seth knew the boy was grieving and hurt, but it was a shame he was dedicated to regarding Logan as the enemy.

After they ate, they drove in tandem to drop Connor off at school, where he slouched away without a wave goodbye, and then to Jenna's to drop off her SUV. Seth had gotten a bit behind when he was caught at a yellow light, and he was surprised to see Logan waiting for him on the curb. Jenna's modest house was alight with golden Christmas lights and Santa decorations beyond him.

And if Seth's gut tightened with a spark of lust as the headlights caught Logan's tall, muscular frame, that was no big deal. So Logan was hot and looked like a classic bad boy in his leather jacket and combat boots. Nothing wrong with Seth enjoying the view. Yes, Logan was a widower, but looking was harmless.

I'm allowed to be attracted to other men even if I'm not in love with them!

Yet no matter how many times he told himself that, guilt lingered. With Brandon, Seth had assured himself it wasn't sinful because they'd loved each other. But now Brandon was long gone, and Seth should be able to admire another guy without feeling like he was doing something wrong. It was… Well, it was a work in progress.

Logan climbed into the passenger side. He opened his mouth, but then his rough face creased. "You okay?"

"What? Oh, yes! I'm fine." Seth's cheeks flamed hot, and he was glad it was relatively dark in the SUV. "Uh-huh."

"I gave the keys to Jun. Jenna's busy getting the kids down, and I don't feel like talking to her right now."

"Oh. Sure." Seth headed down the street. Truthfully, it was getting late, and he didn't much feel like talking to her either.

"Not that I don't love my sister. She's amazing. But sometimes she's…"

"A little exhausting?"

Logan smirked. "Damn right." He quickly added, "But she's the best."

"Absolutely! She's been so kind and supportive of me since I moved here." Seth stopped for a red light, glad the snow had tapered off. "I don't know what I would have done without her last year after Brandon… After we split."

"Right."

Silence fell, and Seth was about to flick on the radio when Logan asked, "It was only a few months after you moved here that you broke up?"

Seth's fingers tightened on the wheel before he fiddled with the wipers even though the windshield was clear. "Yes. Four months. The renovation had been dragging on, and it was stressful for both of us on top of moving across the country, but it was almost finished. Things hadn't been great, but I thought the light was at the end of the tunnel. We'd been together so many years."

He sprayed fluid on the windshield, the wipers thumping across before he turned them off and tried to laugh. "Turns out he'd blasted a hole through the side of the tunnel and made his escape with some guy he met at the gym who's not even thirty yet." Seth winced at how bitter he sounded.

"Fuck. That's brutal."

"Yeah." Seth did flip on the radio then, scanning past endless Christmas songs until he found someone talking about global warming. "This okay?"

"Whatever you want."

The planet's doom should have been more depressing than his failed relationship with Brandon, but Seth decided it was a tie. It was strange to be with Jenna's brother driving back to the house—which wasn't really *home* the way Seth had dreamed it would be when he'd planned the renovation.

He should have known back then that Brandon had one foot out the door. Brandon had let Seth make all the decisions, like he'd known deep down he wouldn't be around to live in the final product.

As the people on the radio talked about islands of plastic in the ocean, Seth turned onto the 87, careful of the slush that was accumulating. He peeked at Logan from the corner of his eye. Odd to think that Logan would be staying at the house.

Odder still to think that they'd be posing as loving partners. How were they going to pull it off? He supposed they should come up with a plan, but he stayed silent.

How much PDA do we need to make it look real?

Heat flowed through Seth, very much in a southerly direction. Logan was like his secret young fantasies about Dylan McKay come to life, but minus the nineties hair and sideburns.

Seth swallowed through the pang of hurt as he remembered huddling late at night with his big sister, Christine, the volume down low on their secretly recorded VHS episodes of *90210* after everyone had gone to bed.

Now she won't even acknowledge I'm alive.

He exhaled sharply, annoyed at himself for thinking about Logan and PDAs and teen fantasies in the first place. This was a deal he and Logan had made, and he had to stay...professional, for lack of a better word. Logan was going to be sleeping in his house. Seth had a responsibility to be a good host.

Does he sleep in underwear or pajamas? Or maybe in nothing at all... And what kind of underwear does he wear? Is he hairy?

No. It was wrong for Seth to be thinking about that, even if it was only in his screwed-up head. He shifted, blowing out a long breath. Yes, Logan was handsome—fine, incredibly gorgeous and sexy—

"You okay?" Logan asked.

"Huh?" Seth said too loudly. "Oh, yeah. Just frustrated about all this plastic in the environment. It's terrible."

"Oh. Yeah."

Seth turned up the volume and put all thoughts of Logan, leather jackets, and *especially* underwear firmly out of his mind.

BOXER BRIEFS.

Black and clinging to a spectacular rear and meaty thighs. Seth stood frozen atop the two steps down into the sunken great room, gripping the mug of coffee he was bringing Logan.

Logan was sprawled on his belly on the couch at the far end, his left arm stretched out on the chaise, the sheet twisted beneath him and duvet pushed down to his feet. He'd asked about putting on the gas fireplace, and Seth had told him to feel free. Now it was overly warm, condensation glistening on the windows.

"Need to set the maximum temperature so it shuts off and doesn't get too hot." Seth realized a second later that he'd said the words aloud. His heart raced as he tried to focus on anything but the lust sizzling through him at the sight of Logan's half-naked—more like three-quarters—and splayed body.

Jenna was right. Seth was ridiculously pent-up and needed to try dating before he humiliated himself and tented his slacks in front of his guest.

Grunting, Logan pushed himself up. "Huh? What?" He peered around in a daze, his sexy voice sleep-scratchy.

Yep. Hairy chest. Would it feel rough under Seth's fingers? He tore his gaze back up to Logan's bleary face. "Sorry! I'm so used to talking to myself I apparently don't even realize I'm doing it." He waved a hand around at the fogged windows. "It got too hot, huh? I can set the fireplace so it turns off after it hits a certain temp." His other hand was still gripping the mug, which he thrust forward. "Coffee? This is black, but I have milk and sugar if you want?"

"Black's great. Thanks."

Seth crossed to the couch, concentrating on breathing. He put the mug on the table, afraid he'd spill it on all that exposed skin if he tried to pass it to Logan directly.

Mmm, hair on his legs and arms too.

Standing upright, Seth backed away. What was the matter with him? He encountered attractive men all the time and kept his libido in check. Was it that he'd been alone and celibate so long now that he was cracking under the pressure? Or was it that there was something undeniably intimate about having Logan sleeping under his roof? In his boxer briefs?

As Matt would say: *Little bit from column A, little bit from column B.*

"I'd better get to work. Have a good day! Make yourself at home. Oh, let me get you some towels." He spun to escape before Logan could reply and tried not to think of Logan naked and wet in the shower.

He failed badly, but at least he tried.

Chapter Five

"I'LL PAY YOU back."

Expertly balancing the car seat with a sleeping Noah inside, Jenna opened her front door and called, "Hi, Pop!" To Logan, she said, "I know. I heard you the first three times."

Logan nodded and kicked the door shut behind him, his hands occupied with canvas grocery bags. He'd had to borrow the money from Jenna to pay for the repair on his truck. The garage had been impatient for him to pick it up right away, and if Logan was going to be staying out in Saratoga Springs, he needed wheels.

Friday was Jenna's temporary day off until she went back to work full time in the new year, so she'd picked him up at Seth's and taken him to the garage.

He took off his boots and leather jacket and followed her through into the kitchen. Noah was somehow still fast asleep in the car seat, which Jenna put on the kitchen table. Logan took things out of the bags and put them on the island for her.

"Seth's house is so beautiful," she said for the hundredth time, tightening her ponytail. She wore sweats with a dark stain of something that had dripped down her chest. Peering around her beige and pink kitchen with a miserable expression, she sighed. "God, this is so nineties. All this laminate. Ugh."

"It's nice."

Jenna narrowed her gaze. "Don't shit a shitter. I'm dying for a new kitchen, but these kids keep wanting to eat and stuff, so." Her face lit up again. "But wow, Seth's great room looks incredible now. I only saw it once, back before Brandon sleazed off and I'd shamelessly invited myself over. It's gorgeous now."

"Yeah. Slept like a baby on that couch." The wide leather had been soft, yet firm, and Seth had given him a pillow with cool foam in it. Logan had gotten more sleep than he had in weeks even though it had gotten too hot with the fireplace on.

He was a jobless loser who couldn't afford rent, but Seth had brought him a steaming mug of coffee and acted like he was a real guest, not just a freeloader. They'd made a deal, but Logan was sure as hell getting more out of it.

He'd found himself thinking about Seth a lot. Seth wasn't like most people he knew. He was…fancier. Not arrogant, though. But the way he didn't swear, and how he did everything so neat and orderly…

For some weird reason it reminded Logan of his grandma's sitting room, with fake flowers in vases and plastic on the couches. Which probably sounded like an insult even though he didn't mean it that way. He'd always wanted to rip the plastic off those couches and bounce on them.

Logan asked, "He's a good boss?"

"Oh yeah, the best. I mean, he's technically not my boss, but he should be. *Will* be after this caper." She grinned, waggling her eyebrows and adding fresh bananas to the fruit bowl by the toaster. "I still can't believe you're doing this."

He snorted. "Me either. Not a lot of options."

Her face softened. "I know. But Seth really is so great. Kind, generous, patient. He deserves this promotion so much. I'm really glad you're helping each other. I can't tell you how many times he covered for me when I was pregnant and puking. Picked up so much of my slack. I just wish he wasn't so tough on himself. I think it's because of his upbringing."

"Right. Crazy religious parents?"

Jenna grimaced. "Yup. I mean, we grew up with standard-issue Catholic guilt, but his family's evangelical church took it to a whole new level. Seth's always been a bit reserved, but when Brandon dumped him, it was a big shock. Really did a number on him."

"What happened there?" Logan had already decided this Brandon was a fucking idiot.

"Ugh." She opened the fridge and loaded up the crisper drawer. "I guess Brandon was already having doubts before they moved, but he thought the change of scenery would fix their problems or something. Like a fresh start would make him fall back in love with Seth. That's apparently what he told Seth when he was leaving. Obviously that never works, so when he met another guy at the gym, he bailed. That was over a year ago now, and Seth seems...stuck."

She opened a cupboard and pulled out a jar of natural peanut butter, taking a spoonful and saying through it, "I think this caper will do wonders for him. At least he'll finish his house." She held out the jar, the spoon inside.

Logan filled his mouth with the sticky peanut butter, pondering what Jenna had told him. When he swallowed, his tongue still coated with thick residue, he asked, "Seth's not seeing anyone else?"

"Not that I know of. Of course, I don't want to pry."

"Of course not," Logan said dryly.

She smirked. "Shut up. But as far as I can tell, he hasn't dated at all the past year. He's such a catch! Handsome and sweet. Don't you think?"

Shrugging, Logan said, "Sure." He didn't usually think of men's looks or personalities that way since that stuff didn't matter when it came to simply getting off.

But yeah, Seth was in good shape and had a nice smile and blue eyes. And a lot of people would have backed the hell out of the deal after Logan and Connor started going at it, but Seth had been patient with them.

"I'm sure he could get laid easy," Logan said.

Jenna sighed. "He could if he wanted to, but I think he's got some hang-ups about casual sex. When I suggested he try Grindr, he almost choked on his tongue."

Logan had to laugh. "Do you ever mind your own business?"

"Nope."

"You know, I was wondering about the house. Seth said *he* bought it, not *they* bought it."

"Yeah, apparently Brandon's never been good with money." She swirled the spoon around the peanut butter jar. "It's a blessing that Seth was smart enough not to put the house in both their names. Honestly makes me think he had his doubts too, even if he hadn't admitted it to himself."

"I guess." Logan thought of that voice that had told him marrying Veronica was nuts and that they barely even knew each other. But his life had been garbage, and there she was, beautiful and kind and taking care of him.

"Do you think Connor's going to agree to go on the retreat next weekend?" Jenna asked. "And, more importantly, that he'll behave?"

"Maybe. Guess he won't have much choice. And he'll be stuck with me all the time if he doesn't get in line at school." Logan hesitated. Might as well just spit it out. "He's getting kicked out if he doesn't."

The spoon clattered to the counter. "Shit."

"Yup."

"But he's a genius. I remember Veronica saying he practically had a photographic memory."

"Yeah, but he's been skipping class and blowing off assignments. Being an asshole to other kids. Acting reckless. He has to do good on his exams next week, or else."

"Maybe it would help to supervise him this weekend. Make sure he studies."

Logan unpacked a jumbo box of bran cereal. "Maybe."

"I think Seth can be a good influence on him. And you."

"Me? I ain't studying for jack shit." He slid some jars of baby food across the island. "Thank Christ. You know school wasn't my strong suit."

She rolled her eyes. "I mean just that you and Seth could, you know." She shrugged. "Become friends."

The back of his neck prickling, he shrugged. "I'm going to go say hi to Pop."

"No, no, no." She blocked his path and stared at him, hands on her hips. "You always blow me off when I bring this up. You used to hang out with your buddies from the railway all the time. But when was the last time you talked to them? Saw them? Liked one of their Facebook posts?"

He huffed. "You know I hate that shit."

"Yes, I'm well aware you and social media are not on the same wavelength. But you used to go out drinking and watching football games with those guys every week. Why don't you call them up?"

His lungs tightened, and he forced a jagged breath. "Just leave it alone."

"But those guys—"

"Those guys never came to see me in the hospital." He raised his voice, clenching his fists. "Okay?"

She blinked, jutting her chin forward. "What?"

"The bosses said the accident was my fault. Huey went along with it—said he couldn't remember anything. Everyone knew I was taking the fall for faulty equipment, and since it happened in the train yard and not out on the line, and no one got killed, there was no investigation. Maybe they paid off the feds, I dunno. But they said Huey got hurt because of me. I was poison after that. I haven't fucking seen my friends once since I woke up broken on a ventilator."

Jenna opened and closed her mouth. Then her eyes glistened with tears, and Logan felt like a piece of shit. He begged, "Don't cry. It's fine. Really."

"It's not fine! I should have known!" She hugged him fiercely, standing on her tiptoes. She smelled like Vaseline and spit-up, and Logan held her tightly. Voice tight, she whispered, "It makes so much more sense—why you moved so fast with Veronica."

No sense in denying it. "Yeah."

"I should have known." She stepped back and shook her head. "Why didn't I know?"

"Because I never told you?"

"I should have realized."

"You can't read my mind. You've spent your whole life taking care of other people. What do I ever do for you?"

She slapped his arm. "You do plenty. You're my big brother. Remember when you terrified that asshole Billy Morgan after he made fun of my training bra? Not that I condone the threat of violence, of course."

Laughing softly, he swiped at her tears with his thumb. "Haven't done much for you lately."

"True," she joked with a wink. "Think you can keep an eye on Noah for half an hour or so before I have to pick up Ian from his half day of preschool?"

Logan was more than happy to stop talking about all this emotional shit. "Sure." The kid was still fast asleep, so it would be simple enough.

"Awesome. I know eventually when Ian is Connor's age and wants nothing to do with me that I'll long for these days when he wants to be with me every second he can, but sometimes it's just so nice to go to the bathroom by myself. Maybe even have a shower all alone."

"Go nuts. Noah and I'll be fine." Then he frowned. "If you need help with the kids during the day, I can come over. It's not like I have a job." He should have offered ages ago and kicked himself silently. *Useless sack of shit. Can't even babysit.*

"No, no, we're fine. Jun helps before and after work. I shouldn't complain."

"Why not? Wanting to drop a deuce in peace isn't exactly asking for the moon."

She grimaced. "Must you use Pop's old classics? And I know, but the kids already spend time away from me at preschool and daycare. In January, I have to work full days. I'm lucky I've been able to ease back part time."

"If boss lady's got such a hard-on for families, she should pay for more maternity leave."

Jenna smirked. "Indeed. But she gives a lot, comparatively. I was damn lucky to get almost six months off because BRK took over—it was barely a month with Ian. Okay, if he gets fussy, just shout." Smiling down at Noah, she ghosted a kiss over his forehead before straightening. "And just... I'm sorry I pressed. I only want you to be happy again."

"I know. Now go read Facebook and take your dump." He kissed her cheek and waved her off before easing out a chair at the round kitchen table. Sunlight beamed in over the sink, which was full of dirty dishes. Logan wondered if he could wash them quietly enough.

The TV murmured distantly from the den, Pop watching some morning game show by the sounds of it. Noah was still fast asleep, making little whimpers from time to time, opening and closing his round little mouth. His dark hair was spiky the way Ian's had been.

It was strange to imagine Ian and Noah at Connor's age, and just as hard to imagine Connor ever being so small and peaceful. Of course he had been—Logan had seen the pictures. Veronica had said Connor was a happy, easy baby, and a good toddler until his father had abandoned them.

As Noah fidgeted, kicking out his little boot-covered foot and grasping the air with tiny fingers, Logan wondered if Connor would ever be happy again. God, he hoped so. He wanted to help, but he was so unqualified to be a father figure. And had Mike bothered to return Connor's messages? Sometimes it took weeks.

He gave Noah his finger to grasp, the baby gripping on with surprising strength and blinking blearily. Logan tried to imagine actually abandoning your own kid and couldn't. There was a special place in hell for cowardly fucks like Mike.

When Noah started kicking harder and whining, Logan carefully unbuckled him and lifted him out, taking off his coat and boots and holding him. The kid seemed to settle a bit when Logan walked around with him, patting his back and making soothing noises the way Jenna and Jun did.

Logan headed into the den as Noah gurgled against him wetly. The blinds were shut, probably to avoid glare on the TV. The Christmas tree was lit with gold in the corner, strands of silver decoration stuff all over the carpet. There weren't any presents under it yet.

"Hey, Pop," Logan said, walking closer to the tree with Noah still in his arms.

On his ancient stuffed armchair, slippered feet up on the matching orange footstool, Pop grunted. He'd never been much of a talker, but after the stroke, he talked even less. He *could* after a lot of speech therapy Jenna paid for, but chose not to most of the time, especially when watching TV. On the screen, a contestant played Plinko.

"Anyone guess an exact price today?" Logan asked, peering at the tree's glass balls and icicle ornaments along with the old decorations he remembered from his childhood. He smirked at the butt-ugly beagle he'd made in Boy Scouts, its tongue too long and ears too short. He didn't know why Jenna had hung on to all that stuff, but he had to admit it wasn't bad to see it every December.

"Pop?"

"Nah. These guys are guessing for shit." Pop took a sip from his mug of coffee, which was probably stone cold by now. He folded his hands over his gut, the TV reflecting in his glasses.

He was only sixty, but after the stroke five years before, he'd stopped dyeing his thinning hair, and it had gone completely gray now. His glasses slid down to the end of his nose, and he was constantly pushing them up.

Shifting Noah to his other arm, Logan reached up to the treetop to brush his fingers along the fringed bottom of the old angel's dress. His mom had loved that angel with her gold-flecked halo that got bent one year in storage. It was still bent, but the angel beamed like everything in the world was perfect.

"Getting big already," Pop said.

Logan rocked Noah gently. "He is."

"How's Connor?"

"Fine," Logan lied, lowering himself and Noah to the worn couch carefully.

Pop grunted, watching the TV again. They sat in peaceful enough silence until the next commercial break. "Jenny says you need help finishing a kitchen."

"Yeah. The bones are all in place. Just needs the finishing touches." Truthfully, Logan probably could have done the work himself as long as there were enough extra hands to carry the heavy pieces. But it would be good to get Pop out of his chair. "Could really use your help."

He grunted again. "If it'll make you and Jenny happy." Pop was the only person allowed to call Jenna anything but her proper name.

"Thanks. Maybe we can go over and take a look. See what equipment or materials we need."

The grunt was accompanied by a shrug this time. "After the Showcase Showdown."

"Sounds good."

"It's Jenny's boss's kitchen? She said you're staying over there."

"Yeah. Just temporarily." They'd decided there was no need to tell Pop about the deal Seth and Logan had made. It would probably just confuse him. Mostly Logan didn't want to go there. His father had never seemed to have an issue with gay people, but... Yeah. Just didn't want to go there.

"That warehouse job fell through?"

Shame simmered in his gut, and he braced for Pop's judgment. Yet Pop only grunted when Logan nodded. After a few moments, Logan added, "I'll get a job soon." Noah gurgled and squirmed, and he rocked him. "I'm trying."

Pop actually looked away from the TV, bushy eyebrows drawn tight. "'Course you are. Those bums at the railway fucked you over. Sons of bitches. You always tried hard. Skinned your knees raw, but you rode a bike before any of the other kids."

Logan blinked. He couldn't remember the last time Pop had talked about something from the past. After the stroke, just getting him to talk about *The Price is Right* had been a massive win. He tried to think of something to say, a swell of emotion sticking in his throat.

Pop turned back to the TV and farted. Smiling to himself, Logan settled back on the couch. Maybe he wasn't good or great, but he hadn't felt so *okay* in a long time. He still didn't have a job, and his stepson still hated him, but at least thanks to this deal with Seth, he wasn't homeless.

He watched the Showcase Showdown with his Pop, yelling at the contestants for their stupid bets, and let Noah suck on his finger until the kid started screaming for the real thing.

Chapter Six

"LEFT!" BILL DERWOOD barked, leaning on his cane.

Straining, Seth, Logan, and Jun shifted, trying to line up the quartz counter just right on the island. When Bill gave them the okay, they lowered it, and Seth exhaled and rolled his wrists when he could let go.

From where he was playing with a toy dump truck in the would-be sitting room, Ian clapped. Strapped in his car seat, Noah kicked and gurgled. Jun raised his palms, and Seth and Logan high fived him.

Jenna's husband was on the shorter side, wore round glasses, and had a build Seth's mother would have called "husky," with the implication that "fat" might not be far behind if he wasn't careful.

Why he still cataloged people's appearance through the prism of his mother's judgment, Seth wished he knew. Maybe because when he looked in the mirror, deep down he was still imagining how she might judge him.

She'd always favored short, trimmed hair, clean-shaven faces, shirts tucked in, and slacks creased down the middle. Brandon used to tease Seth about how he ironed his pajamas.

Seth squirmed with embarrassment now as he looked at how he was dressed—polo shirt tucked into his khakis and Oxfords since Bill had insisted everyone wear sturdy shoes while the work was being done. Bill, Logan, and Jun were all in jeans and old tees, Bill with a ratty cardigan over top, and work boots.

Seth tried not to stare as Logan bent over, denim stretching tight over his firm butt as he examined something near the base of the island.

Now if I could find a rear end like that on Grindr, maybe I'd swipe right. Or left, or whatever you're supposed to do.

Scoffing to himself, Seth turned away and ran his palm over the new counter around the rectangular apron sink. The hard, cold truth was that he was too terrified to try any of the gay hookup apps. Partly because of his hang-ups about casual sex, and partly because he hadn't been with anyone but Brandon and it was…daunting. The whole reason he was lusting after Logan was because it would never happen in a million years.

"Hi!" Jenna's voice rang out. "Wow, you guys have been busy!" Leaning in the front door beyond the little sitting room, she kicked snow off her boots on the edge of the top step. "Hi, baby!" she exclaimed as Ian hurtled toward her, grabbing her around the legs as if it had been days since he'd seen her instead of a few hours.

She shuffled inside with difficulty, and Connor appeared behind her at the top of the makeshift ramp they'd constructed to wheel the cabinets and quartz inside.

"Connor!" Seth smiled, saying a little prayer that there wouldn't be any screaming arguments. "So glad to see you."

Shoulders practically up to his ears, Connor regarded Seth dubiously. Jenna had apparently taken him for a haircut, since it was clipped neatly. "Hey." His gaze skittered over to Logan. "She said you needed my help."

Logan glanced at Jenna, seemingly at a loss for words, so Seth jumped in. "We do! All hands on deck. We'll be putting Noah to work any minute." Fortunately, Jun laughed at the lame joke as he plucked Noah out of the car seat.

Jenna gave Connor's shoulders a big squeeze, Ian still attached to her legs. "We always need you around."

Connor rolled his eyes, but Seth noticed he couldn't hide a tiny smile, and he wasn't trying to get out of her grasp. He mumbled, "Sure," glancing at Logan.

Unfortunately, Logan said, "Are you sure you shouldn't be studying for your exams?"

Now Connor did squirm away from Jenna. "I've studied more in the past couple days than you probably have in your whole life." He reminded Seth of a stray dog who wanted so desperately to be loved but would bark and bite out of fear.

"Good," Logan bit back, his jaw clenching.

Jun had Noah in his arms, and he beckoned Ian over with the lure of cookies. Bill had plonked down into a folding chair Seth had brought out from the garage and seemed to be staring off into nothing.

Jenna kept her tone low and even as she said, "Logan, I know you're just concerned about Connor's future. Right?" She glanced at Connor, who scowled, his hands jammed in the front pockets of his jeans.

"Right," Logan said. "Of course."

She smiled, her voice soothing. "You both want the same thing—for Connor to ace his exams and go back to Rencliffe in January. Connor and I talked about how important it is for him to do his best." She glanced at her father, her voice still low. "We also talked about how important the family retreat is next weekend. He understands, don't you?"

"Yeah," Connor muttered. "I won't screw it up."

"Thank you," Seth said. "I really appreciate your help." He looked to Logan, who was watching the exchange warily, as if ready for Connor to act out. When Logan didn't say anything, Seth added, "We both appreciate it very much."

"Yeah." Logan nodded.

"Am I getting lunch soon?" Bill asked loudly.

"Yes!" Seth was happy for an excuse to do something to break the awkward moment. They'd moved the fridge over into the sitting room, and he hurried to take out the sandwich fixings.

They had lunch in the great room, Jenna managing to keep the conversation flowing and noncombative. They all laughed as she told a story about an explosive diaper incident with Noah. It might not have been the best topic while they ate, but if there was one thing that could unite most people, it was embarrassing poop stories.

As they howled with laughter, Jenna standing now to animate her story, Seth realized it had been so long since he'd heard true laughter in the house. Not just the odd chuckle when he was watching *The Good Place*, but full-throated, belly-busting *laughter*. It echoed off the high ceiling, filling him with cozy warmth.

He knew that come January, once their caper was done and Logan moved on, that he'd be alone again, but at least Seth could enjoy having a family around him for the moment. Even if they weren't *his* family, there was something profound and beautiful about three generations together, sharing food and jokes.

After lunch, Seth and Logan left the others relaxing in the great room for the time being, Jun reading Ian a story before he had his nap, Jenna nursing Noah with her feet up on the chaise and a blanket draped across her, Bill dozing on the other side of the couch.

Seth and Logan put on their boots and coats, and Seth impulsively asked Connor to come along. He shrugged but followed without complaint.

In the garage, which ideally would soon hold Seth's SUV instead of the unfinished renovation materials, they had to take the cabinets out of their crates and load them onto a dolly. Logan said to Connor, "Hold the dolly still once we get the cabinets out."

Connor rolled his eyes. "I can do more than that."

"Oh, for fuck's sake," Logan snapped. "Can you just do as

70

you're told for once?"

"Screw you! I knew you didn't really want me here." With a dramatic huff, Connor spun on his heel and marched off down the driveway, snow crunching under his boots.

Seth stared after him in shock, boggled at how quickly that had gone south. Everything had been fine, and then *bam*. Logan and Connor couldn't seem to communicate at all without anger and resentment exploding between them. Over nothing—although Seth knew it wasn't really about the dolly.

He cleared his throat. "Should I go after him?"

Logan's face was flushed, his nostrils flaring. "No. Just let him sulk." He muttered something under his breath and got to work, taking a crowbar to the crates with gusto.

Seth tried to help but mostly stayed out of the way since Logan was apparently working off his frustration, prying open the crates, removing the cabinets, and loading them on the dolly. But when a grunt morphed into a gasp, Seth reached for him.

"Okay?" Seth asked. Logan's face was an alarming red, and his arms shook where he held a cabinet. Seth tugged it free and thunked it down onto the garage floor, his heart skipping. "Logan?"

Panting now, Logan pressed a palm to his chest as if he couldn't breathe. Seth's own breath caught as Logan dropped to his knees on the concrete, his shoulders heaving. Squatting, Seth checked to make sure Logan wasn't wearing a medical alert bracelet or necklace he hadn't noticed.

"Is it asthma? Do you have chest pain?" Seth asked. Logan shook his head, but his eyes were wild and he still couldn't seem to breathe. "I'm calling 911. I'll be right back!" Seth jumped up, but Logan caught his wrist in an iron grip.

Logan shook his head. He gasped out, "Will...pass."

He still had hold of Seth's wrist, his strong, callused hand freezing. Seth sank back down, letting Logan hold on, angling himself so he could tentatively reach out with his other hand and stroke Logan's back. Not thumping—that didn't work for choking, let alone whatever this was. A panic attack? Seth prayed it wasn't actually a heart attack and that Logan wasn't just being a stereotypical tough guy by insisting he was fine.

"What's wrong with him?"

Seth looked over his shoulder to see Connor with one foot in the garage, his eyes wide as he stared at Logan. Logan released Seth's wrist, sucking in a breath and wheezing out, "It's nothing." He pushed to his feet, still breathing hard, sweat glistening on his brow despite the frosty air, his exhalations clouding.

Seth added, "Everything's okay. It was just a little…" He had no idea what, and grasped for a word, landing on the one his gram would have used. "Just a little turn."

Connor stared at them, his gaze jumping back and forth between Logan and Seth. To Seth, he said, "He's supposed to be better now." He bit it out like an accusation, but Seth could sense the terror beneath it. The poor kid had lost his mother suddenly and been through so much upheaval. Seth managed a smile and approached him.

He hoped he wasn't lying when he said, "He is." He squeezed Connor's shoulder, and he could feel little tremors despite Connor lifting his chin and putting on a careless tone.

"Fine. Whatever."

Seth ignored that. "I'm glad you came back. We really do need your help."

"I didn't have my phone," Connor replied flatly.

Heh. Should have known. "Right. Well, I'm still glad. How about you help me get these first few cabinets inside? I'll push and you pull." Seth motioned to the long dolly. He glanced at Logan, who nodded, gratitude clear in his brown eyes.

It gave Seth a satisfied little flush of warmth to help Logan. He grasped the cold metal handles, yelping. "Yikes! We need to get our gloves when we go in. Think we can tough it out?"

Connor nodded as Seth hoped he would, glancing at Logan as he took hold of the dolly's handles at the other end and pulled. *Wants to prove he's tough,* Seth thought. He bet Connor wanted Logan's approval far more than either of them realized.

Nodding encouragingly, Seth pushed, and they made their way out of the garage and along the front walk over the temporary plywood path. It wasn't too heavy, and they were able to get up the ramp without too much struggle on Seth's end, his thighs flexing as he dug in and shoved.

Inside, he asked Connor, "You want to help Jun unload these and warm up for a minute? I'll be back." Seth grabbed his gloves and hurried out. He exhaled in relief when he saw Logan standing in the garage, his color back to normal and seemingly breathing okay.

"You all right?" Seth asked as he neared. He rubbed Logan's arm, the leather of his jacket and Seth's gloves creaking. Wait, was he being too familiar? He dropped his hand.

Logan nodded and rasped, "Thanks."

"What happened?"

"It's fine." Logan shrugged. "No big deal. Let's get back to work."

Seth stayed put. "I thought you were having a heart attack. It was a pretty big deal."

Logan rubbed a hand over his face, making that scratchy sound that sent a thrill down Seth's spine. "I guess I pushed a little too hard. Docs have a fancy word for it: dyspnea. Just means shortness of breath. Because of the accident."

"Ah." Maybe he was being nosy, but Seth's curiosity got the better of him. "It was a derailment?"

"Yeah." Logan's jaw tightened, his gaze on the concrete. "I was driving the engine, just moving it to the other side of the yard. The conductor had released the other cars, thank fuck. It would have been much worse. They said I was going too fast, being a hotshot or something. I know I wasn't. The brakes failed. I wasn't speeding, and I braked in plenty of time, but it was just..." He shuddered. "Screeching metal like you've never heard before."

"My goodness," Seth whispered. He could only imagine the terror.

"Track curved, and we went over. Last thing I remember was my buddy Huey screaming, and this punch to my chest, like being stomped by an elephant."

Logan swallowed hard, raising his head and looking off somewhere beyond Seth, unfocused. "One of the monitors had come loose, and it hit me square in the chest. Massive pulmonary contusion. My lungs were so bruised, I needed to be on a ventilator to breathe. Woke up like that—tube down my throat."

Seth shuddered. "That must have been horrendous."

"Yeah." His gaze was still distant. "Dislocated my shoulder and broke my arm, and it had to be in traction. Cracked ribs. Everything was just...broken." He inhaled and seemed to give himself a shake, meeting Seth's eyes. "Anyway. Once in a while I get short of breath. I guess it's in my head sometimes, but today I just pushed too fast. Connor must think I'm pathetic." He looked away. "You too."

"What? No, not at all. I'm just relieved there's an explanation. I can't imagine how much work you had to do to recover the way you have. I'd never know you'd been so badly injured."

"The physio helped. Having a goal. And Veronica..." He shrugged. "She helped a lot."

"Connor's mother? I'm so sorry for your loss."

"'*My loss*,'" he muttered darkly. "I always feel like shit when people say that."

"Oh. I'm sorry." Seth tried to think of something better to say.

"No, it's not your fault." Logan lifted his hands out to his sides before dropping them. "It's just that we were done. It was over between us. So I feel like an asshole acting like she was still…mine. You know what I mean?"

"Yes, I understand that. I didn't realize."

"Not that I'm *not* sad she's dead. I did love her. She was a good woman, but we were a mess together. I wish I could change a lot about what happened." He shrugged tightly. "I guess that's life. She dropped dead at thirty-four, and I can't fix it. Connor got the shit end of the stick, that's for sure."

"The poor boy. It's heartbreaking." Seth frowned, going back to what Logan had said before. "But you know, I don't agree that Connor thinks you're pathetic, or that he truly dislikes you. He was scared to see you like that."

Logan scoffed. "He'd probably be thrilled if I dropped dead."

"You can't really believe that? As much as he may want his biological father to be in the picture, you're the one who's here. If you two could stop butting heads for five minutes…"

Logan was silent a few moments. "But he's never liked me from the day we met. I try not to lose my temper, but he just—" He made a stabbing motion with his index finger.

"Pushes your buttons. I noticed." Seth glanced out of the garage to make sure they were still alone. "I don't think you should take what Connor says to heart. I realize that's easy for me to say. But he's lashing out and angry at the world. You're a convenient target."

"Yeah." Logan gave Seth a rueful smile. "And since I'm not thirteen, I should try to be the adult, huh? Not fly off the handle."

"Right," Seth agreed gently. "Praise him. Try to build up his confidence."

"But he doesn't care what I think."

"I'd argue he cares very much what you think. Despite what he might say."

Logan seemed to ponder that. "I guess so. Shit, Jenna and Jun are so good at this stuff. I'm useless."

"Doesn't Jenna…talk to you about this kind of thing?" He tried to phrase it delicately. "She's usually eager to…help."

Barking out what sounded like a genuine laugh, Logan scratched his head. "That's a polite way to put it. She does help, but she's always given me more credit than I deserve. And she's got so much with the kids and Pop and working. When our mom died…"

"You were teenagers, right?"

"Jenna was. Fourteen. I was twenty-one and in the Marines. Pop only had the stroke five years ago, but when Mom died, he needed taking care of. Hell, I don't think he could even use the microwave. Jenna stepped up, like she always does. She barely had the chance to move out after college. Pop had the stroke, and he ended up moving in with her and Jun. He'll be there until he has to go in an old-folks home or they take him out feet first."

Logan took a deep breath and blew it out. "I was working long hours on the railway. On call, never knowing exactly when I'd have to go in, and for how long. Just depended on the shipments and where they had to go. I'd be away a couple days sometimes since we had to wait at least ten hours in the bunkhouse upstate before we could come back. Regulations and all. Pop needed stability."

Seth tried to assure him. "Of course. It's not your fault you couldn't be the primary caregiver. And with Connor, you're still learning. From what I gather, parenthood takes practice."

Logan scowled. "That's just it. It's not like I'm a *parent*. I'm totally fucking unqualified for that."

"But…you are. A parent, I mean. Whether you're ready or not, Connor needs you." Seth thought of his mother and father with a pang of longing, a bite of pain quick on its heels. "His mother's gone, and his father's MIA. He needs a dad he can depend on. Who will look out for him, no matter what. Being rejected by your parents, it's… I wouldn't wish it on anyone. Let alone a confused kid."

After a moment, Logan softly said, "Parenthood," as if he was trying out the word, weighing it on his tongue and in his heart. "The lady at the school called me a 'single father.' It's weird as hell to think of myself like this. Me actually being…a *parent*."

Footsteps approached, and they turned as Connor pulled the long dolly back into the garage, wearing gloves now. For a moment, no one said anything. Then Connor frowned and glanced at the dolly. "Did I do it wrong?"

"No, not at all," Seth quickly assured him.

Logan cleared his throat. "You did a great job. Thanks."

It was silly for Seth to be proud and pleased that Logan had taken his advice, but he was nonetheless.

Connor watched Logan warily. "Okay." Then he waved a hand toward him. "Are you…?"

"Oh yeah, I'm fine. It's nothing to worry about."

Connor glanced at Seth, as if looking for affirmation, so Seth nodded and smiled. "Let's get back to work! Team Caper needs to finish this kitchen, right?" He held up his palms for high fives, which was probably a nerdy thing to do, but he'd never pretended to be cool.

After a moment, Logan and Connor dutifully slapped his palms, and Seth grinned as they got to work.

ALONG THE MAIN street in town late on Sunday afternoon, fluffy flakes of snow drifted down, the sun already setting by four-thirty, the trees glowing in white Christmas lights. Red-ribboned wreaths hung from the old-fashioned streetlight poles, and other shoppers popped in and out of the antique stores and gift shops.

"I think that's the one," Seth said. "I can't imagine we're going to find another dining table in store without waiting for a custom build or warehouse delivery." Although it made him a bit nauseous to think of buying a major piece of furniture without looking in *all* the stores in the area. And online. And after making an exhaustive list of the pros and cons.

Logan said, "Looked good to me. A table's a table, right?"

Seth laughed. "You just want to finish shopping, don't you? Your eyes glazed over in the second store two hours ago."

"Guilty as charged." Logan gave him a sexy little smirk.

Stop thinking about how sexy he is.

The struggle was real. As much as Seth tried not to think about how hot Logan was, his sexiness was *right there.* And aside from the way he looked, it was very attractive that Logan had gone furniture shopping with him and not complained once, even though all the talk of wood grains and rustic vs. classic vs. modern had surely bored him to tears.

Seth might have pretended once or twice that Logan *was* his boyfriend, and when a few shopkeepers had made the assumption, he hadn't corrected them. He'd told himself it was only for practice purposes, but he was full of it. If he only cared about faking it, he wouldn't be imagining what it would be like to hold Logan's hand as they walked down the street.

Or what it would be like to steal a kiss under one of the boughs of mistletoe that hung outside the bookstore. Their lips cold and noses red in the frosty air... How they'd warm each other up, Logan's arms strong around him and pulling him close...

Seth cleared his throat. "Okay, let's look in one more store down here and—" Breath punching out of him, he staggered to a halt, almost tripping over his own feet.

Oh, merciful lord.

Or cruel and not merciful at *all* as the case may be, because there was Brandon. Seth blinked, willing the nightmare to end. But no, that was definitely, one hundred percent Brandon standing twenty feet away looking in a store window, snow catching in the bushy hipster beard he'd grown that year. Which Seth only knew about from stalking public Facebook posts.

He closed his eyes and opened them. Still Brandon.

Of course—because the horror had to be complete—Brandon was talking to Peter, who even at a distance in a parka was clearly still climbing ropes and lifting cars one-handed or whatever people did at CrossFit.

They were with Bethany and Jake—no, Joe—from the wine club, which shouldn't have bothered Seth at all—he hadn't even liked the pretentious wine club in the first place. Why should he care that Brandon had kept going with Peter? Why had he been Facebook stalking in the first place?

That Seth had been dumped and replaced, seemingly without missing a beat, *hurt*.

His feet felt locked in ice. "You've got to be kidding me," he muttered. With Logan stopped beside him, clearly confused, Seth had never wanted to make a run for it so badly in his life.

Chapter Seven

SQUINTING DOWN THE sidewalk, Logan tried to see what was making Seth look like he might puke, his face going red the way it had when Logan had shown up unexpectedly and met Angela Barker.

Seth's mouth was open as he stared at four people nearby peering in the window of a store that looked like it sold candles and oil and that kind of froufrou stuff Logan's long-ago ex Jacinta had loved. If Logan never smelled lavender and that sandalwood shit again it would be too soon.

Grabbing Logan's arm, his fingers digging in through the leather, Seth took a step back. Then he froze as one of the people glanced over and did a double-take. She was a blonde around thirty and had a nice rack under her tight jacket.

Her eyes went wide for a moment as she and Seth stared at each other, and then she slapped on a fake-looking smile and called, "Oh my God, is that you, Seth?"

Seth dropped Logan's arm like it was burning and laughed shakily, calling back, "Hi, Bethany. Joe." He paused as the other people looked over. "Brandon."

Oh fuck. Logan wasn't sure which of the three men was Brandon, but he assumed it was one of the guys who immediately linked hands and put on bullshit smiles. The two couples approached, Seth still frozen beside Logan, his breath clouding the frosty air in shallow bursts.

He looked scared shitless, and Logan wondered if he'd looked like that himself in the garage when he couldn't breathe. Fuck, he hated when he was like that—so helpless and…bare. Seth had been good to him, and seeing his fear now, Logan wanted to protect him.

Hell, they were supposed to be pretending to be engaged— that was the deal, wasn't it? Might as well get in some practice.

He slung his arm around Seth's shoulders, squeezing when he felt how Seth was trembling. This breakup had kicked Seth in the nuts, and Logan wasn't going to let any shit-brick ex make him feel worse. In a world full of assholes, Seth was good.

Putting on his own bullshit smile, Logan said, "Hey there!" He stuck out his free right hand to the closest guy. "Logan Derwood. Seth's boyfriend."

The man's eyebrows shot up so far they might never come back down. He looked between Logan and Seth, his smile faltering. "Oh! Wow! Uh, hi." He had to let go of his boyfriend's hand to shake Logan's. "Brandon Templeton."

Logan squeezed. Hard. "Great to meet you." He let his eyes drop down over Brandon—short, teeth too big for his mouth, and one of those bushy beards that must be making up for a small dick.

Then he looked away dismissively, moving on to shake the hand of Brandon's boyfriend, Peter—thick neck, probably took steroids but could kick Logan's ass—and the male/female couple whose names Logan forgot as soon as he heard them.

Brandon gave Seth an uneasy smile. "Babe, I didn't realize you were seeing anyone."

What an asshole. He had no right to call Seth any names like that—and right in front of Logan! The fucking nerve. Sure, they were fake boyfriends, but Brandon didn't know that. Seth was rigid against Logan's side, and Logan willed him to unclench.

"Uh-huh," Seth managed, his voice higher than Logan had heard it.

"That's great, babe." Brandon tilted his head and touched his hand to his chest. "I'm so happy for you."

Would Seth be mad if Logan punched the condescending prick? Logan wished he was a better actor. He couldn't think of anything to say that wasn't telling Brandon, his hipster beard, and tiny dick where they could go.

But it got easier when Seth exhaled and slipped his arm around Logan's waist. Maybe it should have felt weird, but it was reassuring. They were faking this together.

Seth said, "I'm happy for us too," his voice calmer.

Act like Seth's your boyfriend!

Logan tried to think of something cheesy and in-love sounding. He went with "Me, three," and leaned close and pressed a slow kiss to Seth's smooth cheek, just the hint of five o'clock shadow under his lips.

He made it a lingering kiss—a kiss promising more once they were alone. A tremor vibrated through Seth, and he turned his head to meet Logan's gaze.

His blue eyes were dark, and he licked his lips. Logan looked down at the movement and then back into Seth's eyes, a bolt of lust shooting to his balls and waking up his dick.

Whoa.

The woman laughed awkwardly. "Well, I guess we should leave you lovebirds to it!"

Tearing his eyes away from Seth's, Logan looked at her like she was incredibly boring, which she probably was. "I guess you should." He didn't even glance at the others as he strode forward with Seth at his side, forcing them to move out of the way or be stomped on by his combat boots.

He could feel them watching—the back of his neck practically sizzled with it—and he knew they were whispering even though he and Seth were too far away now to hear. It was in the air, swirling with the snow.

Seth matched his strides, arm snug around Logan's waist. "Wow."

"Oh, look, pookie—that kind of chair would be perfect for

our new table," Logan said, stopping in front of a furniture shop's window. He added under his breath, "Smile and play along, but don't look back, whatever you do."

"That *is* a great chair!" Seth exclaimed, pointing at it. He whispered, "You think they're still watching?"

"You bet your ass they're watching." He needed to do something else a boyfriend would do, so he brushed some fresh snow from Seth's dark hair. He leaned in and murmured, "Think I should grab your ass?"

Seth swallowed so hard Logan could hear it. "Okay."

Slowly, Logan ran a gloved hand down Seth's straight back, keeping their faces close as if they were nuzzling. Seth's jacket was one of those pea coats, and Logan stroked his nice, round ass and slipped up under the hem of his coat, gripping the firm flesh.

He whispered in Seth's ear, "Imagine I'm saying something really dirty."

Seth made a sharp little sound that had to be a laugh. He reached around Logan, grabbing his shoulders before stroking one hand over Logan's head. He teased the back of Logan's neck and ran his blunt fingernails over the short scrub of Logan's hair at the base of his skull, sending sparks through Logan and getting his dick interested again.

With guys it was always fast and rough—this was different. Logan figured it was definitely boyfriend-like. He had to hold up his end of the deal, so he'd do what it took.

Besides, he liked Seth, and that ex was a fucking idiot for dumping him for the thick-neck who probably also had a tiny dick thanks to steroids. Seth deserved a hell of a lot better from where Logan was standing, and it was satisfying showing Brandon that Seth didn't miss him one little bit.

Then he wondered if Seth *did* miss him. "Do you wish he hadn't left you?" he asked before he could tell himself to mind his own damn business.

Seth was toying with the ends of Logan's hair, sending nice little shivers through Logan. He stopped, resting his bare hand on the back of Logan's neck, warm and heavy.

"You know what? No." A smile lifted his mouth, his lips wide. He laughed like he couldn't believe it. "Seeing him now made me realize how much I *don't* miss him. Not that we didn't have good times over the years. We did—a lot of good times."

"I'll take your word for it."

Laughing, Seth said, "We did. But it seems so long ago. Seeing him now, it was the strangest thing. I've looked him up on Facebook and found pictures, but it's been over a year since I saw him in person. And he's so familiar to me—aside from that ridiculous beard. I knew him so well. So...intimately. I think I recognized his body before his face. But now he's someone different. I wouldn't want him back. I *don't*."

"Good. He's a shit-brick." Logan realized his hand was still resting on Seth's ass, but he didn't move it, just pressed firmly.

Seth was breathy as he asked, "Think they're still watching?"

"Maybe. Let's go a bit longer to make sure." If they were going to do a job, they should do it right. He massaged Seth's ass and nipped at his jaw, scraping with his teeth and grinning at Seth's gasp.

"Okay, I'm going to look," Seth murmured, his breath hot across Logan's mouth. A moment later, he sighed and eased away. Logan dropped his hand, and Seth did the same.

"All clear," Seth said. He squinted at the store window. "You know, that chair really is great. Let's see how many they have."

Logan shoved his hands in his pockets, suddenly not sure what to do with them. "Sure."

As Seth opened the door, a bell tingled. He glanced back at Logan. "Thanks for all that, by the way." He laughed, his cheeks going red. "You were very convincing."

"Sure," Logan repeated, feeling his own face go hot. "Anytime."

Chapter Eight

*"I*MAGINE *I'M SAYING something really dirty."*

Although Seth's imagination when it came to sex was admittedly lacking, that hot gust of a whisper echoed through his head endlessly the next day, accompanied by wisps of thrilling, forbidden words. Like *suck* and even *fuck*. Or *co—*

"I haven't seen Logan smile so much in a long time."

Seth jumped so violently at Jenna's words that his knees rattled the keyboard tray. She laughed and said, "Sorry. Didn't mean to interrupt your deep thoughts."

He spun in his chair. "My thoughts aren't deep!" He winced at how strange he was being. "I mean—yeah. Um, I was miles away." *Thinking dirty thoughts that are probably pathetically tame by most people's standards.* "What did you say?"

"Oh, that Logan was smiling for once on the weekend." She kept her voice low, rolling closer on her chair.

Seth's heart skipped, thinking of Logan's grin when he'd called Seth "pookie." "Oh, well… That's nice."

"I mean, obviously his problems aren't magically fixed, but he's been so beat down. It's a relief to know he'll have a few weeks with you. I think you'll be a good influence. You handle Connor really well."

"Has that relationship always been so…fraught?"

She crossed her legs, her foot swinging as she made a face, the low pump hanging off her foot. "Oh yeah. From day one, it was snippy comments and butting heads. Connor was deeply suspicious of Logan, and I can't say I blame him considering how quickly Logan and Veronica got married. I mean, Logan was still in the hospital. He hadn't even met Connor. I can imagine that was a shock for a kid."

"A heck of a shock."

Jenna smiled briefly. "A heck indeed. And when Veronica brought Logan home with her, it went to hell fast. They really seemed to love each other, and he needed her so much. I think she *needed* to be needed. If that makes any sense? But once he healed, that connection faded. It was like, the Florence Nightingale syndrome or something. Nurses and patients falling for each other." She laughed. "I don't think that's what it's called. I need to apply more coffee."

Seth smiled. "I understand what you're saying." He passed her his ridiculous cat mug, and she finished the last few gulps of dark roast with a grateful smile.

"Anyway. He just seemed a bit unclenched this weekend. He's been wound tight for a long time. And you're wound pretty freaking tight yourself, if we're being honest."

He could only laugh. "Which apparently we are. Yes, I'm wound tight. I can't deny it."

Jenna tilted her head. "You're both uptight in different ways, but maybe together you can loosen each other up." She laughed, slapping a hand to her forehead and whispering, "Oh my god, listen to me! I'm talking like you two are really a couple and this isn't a fake relationship."

Seth laughed, then blurted, "We ran into Brandon and Peter yesterday."

She sat up comically straight, eyes wide. "What? How? Where?"

"Saratoga Springs. We were shopping for a table and chairs."

Jenna's eyebrows sailed north. "Okay, I need a minute to

process the idea of my brother…*antiquing.*"

"He was a good sport. In more ways than one."

After a pause, Jenna poked Seth's arm. "What happened? Tell me already."

Seth gave her a quick version of events. "So he pretended to be my boyfriend, and we walked off like… Like Brandon and Peter and the others didn't matter at all."

"Yes!" She pumped her fist and whispered, "I love it."

He had to grin. "It felt pretty good." *So did your brother's hand on my butt.* Seth imagined he could still feel the pressure of Logan's palm and fingers, firm against the swell of his backside.

She asked, "Hey, did Dale set up the dinner?"

"Oh. Let me check." Seth typically checked his work email at home in evenings and over the weekends in case of anything urgent, but realized he hadn't.

His brain helpfully supplied a collage of images of what he'd been doing instead—seeing Brandon and Peter, Logan's hot breath and scruff against his face, his hand on Seth's rear…

"Imagine I'm saying something really dirty."

"You sure you're okay?"

"Yep!" Seth could feel Jenna's gaze on him, his skin prickling as he clicked the mouse too hard to open his email. There it was:

Sender: Gupta, Dale Subject: Dinner with Angela Barker

Seth double-clicked and read the short message. To Jenna, he quietly said, "Thursday night, seven p.m."

She scanned the email, leaning in close, smelling like apples and Tide. "Okay. This works."

He took a deep breath. "Dinner Thursday. Then we leave Friday after work for the retreat."

Jenna said, "It is blowing my mind to think of Logan…canoodling with you."

"Well, we are in a committed fake relationship," he murmured. "He did a great job. I admit I was surprised." He quickly added, "Not that I thought Logan was a homophobe or anything.

He just comes across very macho, I guess."

"Yeah, between the Marines and the railroad, he's not used to being in touch with his feelings or anything. Not that all gay men are in touch with their feelings." She eyed him speculatively. "Speaking of which, I'd expect you to be moping today, and probably pining after seeing Brandon. Ruminating at the very least."

Huh. She was right. "How do you know I'm not?"

"Not what?" Matt's shaggy head appeared over the partition between their pods. "What are you whispering about?" He mouthed, *"Caper?"*

Jenna nodded and waved him over impatiently. In his usual sneakers and dark jeans, Matt came around and wheeled over one of the desk chairs the interns had used, spinning it to sit backwards and lean his forearms on the top of the backrest. Under his suit jacket, his graphic T-shirt had the image of a guitar and the name of a band Seth had never heard of.

After Jenna filled him in, Matt grinned. "Oh, man. How much do I love that you got to rub your hot new boyfriend in that douchenozzle's face?"

"Fake boyfriend," Seth whispered. "Well, fake fiancé, actually-ly."

"Whatever. Douchenozzle doesn't have to know that." Matt's brow furrowed. "But yeah, I'm shocked you're not brooding about the whole thing."

"Again, how do you know I'm not?"

"No fidgeting," Jenna said. "It's your brooding-about-Brandon tell. You fidget endlessly, like you want to climb out of your skin."

Matt said, "I can hear your chair when you do it. *Squeak, creak, squeak.*"

"Oh." Seth was taken aback. He shifted then, recrossing his legs, feeling dangerously exposed. His chair *creak-squeeeeeaked.* He froze. "Uh. Guilty as charged, it seems."

"Oh, don't forget decorations for your house!" Jenna said. "Angela loves the holidays."

Ugh. "Oh. Right. I'll have to buy some stuff." It was silly to dread decorating. "It's not really my thing."

Matt's eyebrows rose. "Seriously? Huh. I thought you'd be all about hanging stockings by the chimney with care and visions of sugarplums."

I don't deserve Christmas.

The thought filled his mind, but fortunately was blocked before it could reach his tongue. The swirl of memories of Christmases past made him ache—his family's stockings hanging from the mantel cluttered with his mom's ugly Christmas figurines and nativity scene, the paint chipped on the three wise men.

Jenna said, "I'll arrange a tree and talk to Logan about what to get. Our cousin manages a tree lot, so he'll give us a great deal."

"Uh, okay." Seth's head was spinning. He was going to have a real Christmas tree. He'd only ever known his parents' artificial one, which had become rather threadbare the last time he saw it. Years ago, of course. Surely they had a replacement by now. There were probably lots of things different at home now.

Home.

"Ho-ho-ho!" Tara from accounting appeared at the entrance to the pod, her Santa hat slipping down over her forehead. She shoved it up, the bell on the end making a faint *ding.* "Have you contributed to the food bank collection? We want it to be the biggest donation ever this year! Angela will be in on Friday when the volunteers come to collect."

They all agreed to bring in more cans of tuna and jars of peanut butter, guilt tugging at Seth that he actually hadn't contributed at all yet. He'd been meaning to stop by the grocery store and stock up, but admittedly had wished he could just write a check or give cash instead.

Matt returned to his pod, and Jenna wheeled back to her desk. Seth tapped his keyboard and scanned a few new emails—this time checking to see what Becky had deemed *URGENT!* It was something about printer toner.

As Seth scanned another email, his gaze drifted to the framed photo of Logan and Connor on his desk. Logan really was handsome and…masculine. He remembered the sensation of Logan's hand on his butt, then imagined Logan in his boxer briefs, sprawled on the couch with the blankets shoved down…

Clicking his mouse, Seth cleared this throat. He realized Jenna was right—he really wasn't brooding over Brandon. Running into Brandon and Peter would have sent him into a tailspin in the past, yet he'd barely thought of them at all. Instead, his mind had been occupied with Logan, and that secret whisper in Seth's ear.

AS SETH PULLED into the driveway in the early darkness, his heart skipped to see Logan up on a ladder in front of the house. The jolt wasn't specifically because he was on a ladder, but just that he was there, period.

Seth eyed the already-familiar shape of his broad shoulders in the leather jacket, the way his jeans clung to his rear, on display as Logan reached up to attach a section of Christmas lights to the edge of the slanted roof.

There was no denying the flutter in Seth's belly or the excitement that spun through him. He grinned to himself as he parked on the driveway and turned off the engine. So maybe he had a little crush. It was a heck of a lot better than mooning over Brandon. Maybe a little crush was exactly what he needed to move on.

Seth left the bags of canned goods in the back of the SUV and juggled the other cloth bags while he locked the car with a *chirp*. On the walkway, he called up, "Looking great!" His face went hot even as his breath clouded in the frigid air. Should he clarify that he meant the lights? Although the lights weren't even on yet, it was just a dark string of bulbs. Why had he said that?

"Should be okay," Logan replied. He looked down and gave Seth a pleased little smile that softened his face, and despite his best efforts, Seth's heart foolishly swelled.

As Logan strung another few feet, stretching precariously to his right, Seth inhaled sharply. "Be careful up there!" He dropped the bags on the shoveled walk and held the ladder.

Grunting, Logan climbed back down before shifting the ladder over. "It's fine. One more section to go." He frowned down at the groceries. "Those are getting wet."

"Right! I'll just..." Seth grabbed the handles and carried the bags inside, stamping his feet and taking off his boots, the door still open.

A colorful wreath made of glittery ornaments now hung on the front door, a mix of traditional holiday colors as well as pinks and purples. He'd admired similar wreaths while driving through the neighborhood, and it gave him a pulse of pleasure to have his own.

But this is just for Angela. For show. It's not really mine.

Seth leaned outside. "The wreath is gorgeous."

"Yeah? Jenna said to get an ornament wreath, and that one looked good."

"It's perfect." *It's not really mine. This is all pretend. I don't get to have this.*

"Can you flip the switch?" Logan called down.

Seth turned on the switch by the front door and leaned out. Multicolored lights adorned the lines of the roof, fat snowflakes drifting down to make it even more perfect. "It really does look great!"

Logan climbed down the ladder and stood back on the edge of the snow-covered lawn, craning his neck. He nodded. "This works."

"You must be freezing! Come inside. I'll make dinner. Well, I'll nuke the rotisserie chicken and cheesy mashed potatoes I grabbed from the ready-made section."

Logan grinned. "I'll just put away the ladder and shit."

"Right. I love the wreath too, by the way. Thank you."

"Yeah? I wasn't sure if it had too many colors. But it looked pretty. Jenna gave me a list of indoor stuff to get too, but I only had time for outdoor today. Had to take Pop to a doctor's appointment."

"I hope everything's okay?"

He shrugged. "Same old shit. Pop won't listen about cutting out the junk. Not to mention red meat and scotch."

"Ah. I admit I enjoy a good scotch myself."

"Yeah? Although I don't think Pop drinks the good stuff." He grabbed the ladder and carried it back to the garage.

Seth hurried to unpack the groceries, trying to ignore persistent flutters of excitement. It was a crush! No one had to know. He and Logan didn't have a real relationship, but Seth could enjoy his company. He could enjoy not being so terribly alone.

As he opened the pantry, he stopped. This was the part when he typically would have thought of Brandon with a pang of loss that was at turns dull or deathly sharp. But tonight…

Nope. It wasn't there. He didn't miss Brandon. Maybe he hadn't actually missed Brandon for a long time.

"Need a hand?"

He jumped, whirling around and dropping a bag of macaroni, which rattled. "No. I'm good."

Logan eyed him warily. "Okay."

Seth needed to say something else, and he cast about for a topic as he bent to grab the pasta. "How's Connor doing?"

After a pause, Logan said, "Um, fine? I guess."

"You haven't spoken to him today?" Seth went back to unpacking.

Brows drawing together, Logan said, "No. We don't really... He doesn't want to talk to me."

"Right. I hear what you're saying."

"But?" Logan snorted. "Go ahead. I can take it."

"Well, I know you two tend to butt heads, but..." Seth tried to find a way to say it without offending. "The thing is, if you don't make the effort with him, he'll think you don't care. Even if you end up arguing, I think it still helps to reach out. He's angry and scared and difficult, but if you keep trying, he'll surely come around."

Logan frowned, seeming to ponder it. "I don't want to bug him. You know?"

"Right. I get that. It doesn't have to be a big thing. Maybe send him a text every day asking how he's doing. Or it could be something like talking about sports or sending him a link to a funny video. Just...contact. Show him you're thinking of him. That you care."

"That makes sense." Shaking his head, Logan rubbed a hand over his short hair, smiling ruefully. "Told you I'm useless at all this."

"You're not useless. It's new. You're learning."

"You don't have kids. How are you so good at it?"

"I'm not an expert by any means." Still, he flushed pleasantly at the compliment. "I'll heat up dinner. And how about a drink?" The thought of imbibing on a Monday felt ridiculously rebellious.

He really did need to get a life, didn't he?

Logan said, "Yeah, thanks."

"We might as well live dangerously, right?"

"Sure," Logan agreed with a rumbling laugh.

Seth tried very, very hard not to think of what Logan would say if he talked dirty to him.

Chapter Nine

SETH MUTED THE TV as another batch of commercials blared before the post-game. Logan had been surprised when Seth had suggested watching the Monday night football game with their dinner. Now they were relaxing on the couch, bellies full of chicken and cheesy potatoes. They'd moved on from beer to an after-dinner scotch.

Logan sipped his drink, enjoying the smooth burn. Seth could apparently afford the fancy stuff, and Logan wasn't complaining. Instead of a harsh, hollow aftertaste, he was left with a spicy richness that made him think of his grandma's fruitcake.

On the silent TV, dogs played basketball in a commercial for insurance or some shit. It was snowing, and if he squinted, he could see it piling up on the deck through the sliding doors. The gas fireplace made the room perfectly warm.

He definitely needed to get a tree and stuff before the boss lady came for dinner. And Logan had to admit the room would look great all done up, even if it was just for show and not a real family's decorations.

Seth had gone quiet, although it wasn't awkward. It was weirdly nice, sitting on the big couch and listening to the hum of the flickering fire.

"I need to—" Seth cut himself off, taking another swallow of scotch and swirling the ice in his glass. "It's ridiculous."

"Uh... What is?"

"Oh, sorry. My brain won't shut its trap, and I'm used to talking to myself."

"About what?"

"Everything. Oh, you mean now?" He chuckled and rubbed his face, his five o'clock shadow making a scratchy sound against his palm.

"You don't have to tell me." Although Logan was strangely eager. "Unless you want."

"Maybe it'll do me good to get some advice."

"I dunno if I'm any good at that. That's Jenna's department."

Seth swirled the ice in his glass, smiling. "Whether we like it or not."

"Heh, yeah." Normally Logan would bristle at the slightest criticism of Jenna, but Seth's smile was nice. What was the word? Affectionate. "Well, go ahead if you want my dumbass advice."

After frowning, Seth said, "I came out to my family twelve years ago because I couldn't hide anymore. I couldn't pretend Brandon was just my roommate and that I hadn't met the right girl yet. I hated lying so much."

He stared toward the TV, but his eyes were unfocused. "The lying started to feel more sinful than being gay. And here I am, over a decade later, and I still feel guilty for wanting to…" He sighed. "You know."

Logan frowned. "Huh?"

"Uh, physical needs."

"Are you talking about getting laid?"

Seth looked at him and laughed. "Yes, I am. I can't even *say* it. It's not that I don't like…sex. I do! Very much."

"Okay." Logan swirled his own ice cubes and watched Seth from the corner of his eye. Seth was wearing slacks and a dress shirt. He'd removed his tie, rolled up the sleeves to his elbows, and slouched a bit, his legs parted.

Logan thought about how firm Seth's ass had felt the day

before when they'd gotten cozy for the asshole ex, and now he was thinking about Seth having sex. With another man. Not just hand jobs or hard screws with a nod and thanks after. But full-on sex with kissing and all that. *Real* sex.

It was weird. Also weirdly hot.

Getting off with men had never been about that for Logan—about hotness or whatever. Not the way it was with women and how beautiful they were, how sexy. He couldn't remember thinking of a guy as *sexy*.

He glanced at Seth and the sprawl of his legs, and the way his shirt was unbuttoned at the top exposing his throat.

Until now, apparently.

Gulping his scotch, Logan stared at the TV and some replay of a hard tackle. Seth was quiet again, so maybe he'd drop it and—

"I loved Brandon, and he loved me. Until he didn't." Seth shook his head like he was still in shock, a little smile tugging on his mouth. "And since finally seeing him again, I've realized I truly don't love him anymore. That I'm not *in* love with him. Which is good."

Logan nodded, trying not to stare at Seth's full lips. "It is." That asswipe didn't deserve Seth.

"I dated a few guys before him, but nothing serious. I never…" He flushed light red, shifting and tapping his fingers on his glass. "I didn't do much at all with the other men. I felt like I should be in love. You know—to—to have sex."

Logan tried not to gape. "*Why?*"

Huffing out a laugh, Seth rolled his eyes. "I know. It's stupid. But it was drummed into me at church and at home. That sex was only for marriage. Since Brandon and I couldn't get married back then, I made this…deal, I guess. With myself. With God. I needed it to be an expression of love, and then I was allowed."

"Religions sure fuck up a lot of people. Uh, no offense."

Seth laughed, tipping his head back for a moment, showing

his long throat. "None taken, I assure you. It really is ridiculous, the knots I've tied myself in all these years. Why should I feel guilty for, for...*getting laid?*" He said it like they were cuss words.

"You shouldn't."

"No, I shouldn't! I'm a grown man. I can do what I please." Seth was fidgety now, all worked up. Logan imagined Seth's cheeks would feel warm to the touch.

Logan frowned. "Are you drunk?"

"No!" He laughed again. "A little tipsy, maybe. It's nice. I'm tired of being miserable and alone. Why am I punishing myself by being celibate? Why do I think if no one loves me I don't deserve sex? It's not a sin to have sex if there's no love. Is it?"

"Definitely not. All that sin crap is bullshit."

"It is, isn't it? Why should I sit around here waiting for...what, exactly? Prince Charming? Mr. Right?"

"Are you telling me you haven't gotten your rocks off in over a *year?*"

Seth drained his glass and thunked it onto a coaster on the wooden table. "That's what I'm telling you. Been afraid to try dating again." He screwed up his face. "The whole...rigmarole of it. It's exhausting to contemplate. Now there are these apps, and I'll probably do it all wrong. Do you use them?"

Before Logan could answer, Seth inhaled sharply. "Although you and your wife didn't break up, she..." He covered his mouth before dropping his hand, face even redder. "I'm sorry. I didn't mean to draw a comparison. That was incredibly thoughtless."

"It's okay." Maybe Logan should have felt worse, but Veronica was gone. He felt like shit most of the time for a lot of reasons, and he was so *tired* of it. "Like I told you, our marriage was a bad idea from the start, and it was already over. I can't change any of it. But hey, you can get back out there. Back on the horse." He needed to take his own advice.

"Right." Seth repeated, "Right," murmuring almost to himself, "I need to conquer my fear."

Man, Seth really *was* wound tight. "It'll be like riding a bike."

"Seeing Brandon yesterday, I was terrified." He shook his head, exhaling a little huff of air and half-smiling. "I'm sure you could tell."

"I might have picked up on it."

Seth shifted to face Logan, his right leg bent on the leather couch, his eyes bright and earnest. "But you helped me. Having you there... None of this is real, but Brandon doesn't need to know that. Seeing him, it feels like I crossed a raging river, and I'm finally on the other side. You know what I mean? If I run into Brandon and Peter again, I can just smile and wish them well, and that's that. I'm over the hurdle. I can't tell you how liberating that feels. Thank you."

Satisfaction flowed through Logan. He was so fucking useless most of the time, and being needed warmed his veins even more than the scotch. "You're welcome." He shrugged. "I like helping you," he said without thinking. It was the truth, and as Seth beamed at him, his blue eyes so damn sincere, an idea popped into Logan's head.

A crazy fucking idea.

He might be no good to anyone most of the time, but getting off? That he could help with. Maybe it was the beer and scotch—although he'd barely had three fingers—or Seth talking about sex, but the idea rocked through him with a bolt of adrenaline.

Maybe Seth would turn him down flat, but... Shit. Logan really, *really* wanted to help make this all better. Wanted Seth to look at him again like he was special and *good*.

Before he could lose his nerve, he blurted, "Here's another deal for you. I'll help you get off. Get over your hang-up about it."

Seth's eyes widened, and he stared, his mouth opening and closing. "You'll... What did you say?"

Logan shrugged even though excitement pinballed through

him. Maybe this was stupid, like most of his ideas, but his dick was coming alive at the thought. "We could mess around. But if you don't want to—"

"I didn't say that." Seth licked his lips, leaning closer over the space between them on the couch. His eyes were bright, the earnestness replaced by clear hunger. "But you're straight. Aren't you?"

"So? Doesn't mean I don't want to just get off sometimes. Men are less complicated. We know what we want. Don't have to worry about feelings and all that shit. It's easier."

Seth stared at him. Holding up a hand, he squeezed his eyes shut, then opened them. "You're telling me... Are you saying that you have relations with other men?"

"You mean sex? Sure, once in a while. In the Marines, you'd help a buddy out. Or in the bunkhouse at the rail yard sometimes. Sometimes do it quick in a bathroom. If someone gives me a look and offers to suck my dick, I'm not gonna say no."

"I..." Seth was staring at him like he had two heads. "I never would have guessed. Huh. *Huh.*" He was quiet a moment, biting his lip. "Have you ever done it? Been the one doing the...?" He waved his hand.

"The sucking?" At Seth's red-faced nod, Logan answered, "A few times when I was in Iraq. Fair's fair. But it's mostly hand jobs, or I'll fuck someone's ass if they want it. Like I said, it's just about getting off." He shrugged. "Not that there's anything wrong with sucking cock. I don't look down on you or anything."

Seth's eyebrows rose. "Ah. Good to know. So... Have you ever been...on the bottom?"

"No. That would be way too... No. Not into it." He could admit he'd never tried, and that the idea of being fucked was way too...much. *Too gay,* although he didn't say that out loud. There wasn't anything wrong with it. It just wasn't for him.

And maybe he'd thought about it sometimes, and he'd been

curious once or twice, but hell no. Letting a guy do that would be… Hell, he didn't know what, but it was better to keep it simple with men.

"What about kissing?"

He screwed up his face. "No. That's too…" He took another gulp of scotch, warmth spreading through him. "I'm probably sayin' this shit all wrong. With guys it's just quick and easy."

"But you're not gay."

"Exactly." Now Seth was getting it.

"Or bi?"

Logan scoffed. "Isn't that just being wishy-washy or pretentious?"

"No." Seth's brows drew together, and he was quiet a few moments. "You know, it's perfectly valid to be attracted to both men and women. Bisexuality is real." He clasped Logan's shoulder, a current of heat sparking down all the way down to Logan's fingertips. "It really is okay."

"Sure. Nothin' wrong with it. That's just not me. I'm straight. I've been with women since I was fifteen. I love fucking them. The stuff with guys is different. Separate."

"Huh. I read something about this. Men who have sex with men, but who don't necessarily identify as gay or bi or somewhere on the LGBTQ-plus spectrum."

"Spectrum?" Logan echoed. He had no clue what Seth was talking about. He was straight, and sometimes he got off with dudes. He didn't need to get all fancy or hippie or whatever about it.

Seth's hand was still gripping Logan's shoulder, and he looked down at it like he wasn't sure how it had gotten there. He didn't move it, though, and Logan didn't complain. The grasp was warm and strong. Logan's dick sure liked it, and he rubbed the heel of his hand over himself through his jeans without thinking.

Seth's gaze zeroed in on Logan's crotch, his Adam's apple

bobbing. "Are you…? Do you want to…?"

"Yeah." It was the first time in months he'd been turned on, and he realized maybe it wasn't so strange for Seth to have gone more than a year. Maybe he'd felt as dead inside as Logan. But now, Logan's blood was pumping, and he wanted release.

Even more than that, he wanted to help Seth.

Seth said, "I think this is the most surreal conversation I've ever had. Wouldn't it be strange? For us to…"

"Why? It's just getting off. Doesn't mean anything. We're guys. Sometimes I just need to bust a nut. Don't you?"

"I…" Seth licked his lips, staring between Logan's face and his crotch. "You know what? Yes. I usually analyze everything to death. Analysis paralysis," he muttered. Then, louder: "Yes. Sometimes I need to get off. Damn it."

"Ohh. Watch your language," Logan teased. His heart raced, lust building in his veins. He could see it on Seth's face, that determination and growing confidence, and it turned him on big time.

With a grin, Seth shoved at the coffee table so there was enough room for him to drop to his knees in front of Logan. Seth was breathing shallowly as he muttered, almost to himself, "I'm going to do this. I want to do this. There's nothing wrong with this." His gaze was locked on Logan's crotch.

Logan unzipped his jeans and shoved them down with his skivvies, yanking his left foot free so he could spread his legs wide. He gave himself a few tugs as Seth watched like a starving man.

"Go to town," Logan said.

Seth started without touching Logan's dick at all, running his palms up and down Logan's hairy thighs and dipping his head to nose around his belly. His breath was hot, but sometimes he blew it colder over the tip of Logan's cock, sending shivers through him. Seth's hands weren't as callused as some men's, but they were big and definitely rougher than a woman's. Not better or worse, just different.

When he drank alcohol, it usually took a while for Logan to get fully hard, but shit, Seth knew what he was doing for a guy with hang-ups. Foreplay was something Logan identified with women. In his experience, most of them liked to take their time. There was no foreplay with men in a bathroom stall or getting off at the bunkhouse.

But hell, as Seth ducked farther and licked at his taint, Logan sure as shit wasn't going to complain. Seth circled his blunt nails over Logan's thighs, and goosebumps spread. Logan was rock hard. Damn, it really had been too long.

When Seth finally sucked him into his mouth, Logan moaned loudly. It was so tight and wet, and Seth was doing something with his tongue behind the head that had Logan practically hitting the ceiling. "Fuck, you're good at this," he muttered.

Seth pulled off with a spit-soaked *pop* and smiled up at him, his hands spread wide above Logan's knees, thumbs stroking the soft flesh of his inner thighs. He wasn't just smiling—sunshine was shooting out of him like laser beams, and Logan had to smile back. Seth ducked his head again and sucked him deep.

Even though he'd already said way more than he usually would to another guy—grunts and nods were all it took most of the time—Logan found himself wanting to see that smile again. Seth was a good man. Maybe he could be an actual friend, and clearly he needed the ego boost. Plus, he sucked cock like a *champ*.

As Seth licked up and down his shaft, spit dripping into Logan's pubes, Logan said, "You're fuckin' born for this." He could feel Seth smile around him before sucking hard, hollowing his cheeks.

Logan jerked up his hips involuntarily, and Seth briefly choked before he pressed harder with his hands, fingers digging into Logan's hips.

Logan grunted. "Sorry."

Apparently all was forgiven since Seth was still sucking him like there was no tomorrow. Logan moaned, all the tension draining out of him. The bad tension, anyway. The good kind had pleasure sparking through him.

He could see their reflection in the dark, wide windows, and it gave him a jolt to see himself like that—legs spread and breathing hard with Seth sucking him off. Watching the reflection, he ran his hand over Seth's head, caressing his thick hair. Seth seemed to like it, making happy little noises.

Shit, Logan *loved* that. He wanted to make Seth happy. He mumbled, "Gonna make me come so hard. You want it?" Some guys didn't like swallowing—not that Logan blamed them. But he had a feeling about Seth, and sure enough, Seth gazed up at him, eyes eager as he gave a little nod, his mouth still stuffed with Logan's dick.

The way his lips stretched wide around Logan's meat, his blue eyes looking like he was begging for it, had Logan's belly tensing, his balls tight. "Yeah, you want my cum, don't you?" Not thinking, he reached out and traced a finger around Seth's wet, swollen lips. "Gonna swallow it all?"

Seth reached down to massage Logan's balls, their eyes locked, his nostrils flaring as he slurped harder. The tight tingling in Logan's nuts surged into an orgasm, and he shot down Seth's eager throat with a groan, fingers tangling in his thick hair.

"Fuck yeah," he mumbled.

Seth pulled off Logan's twitching cock, gasping, his chest heaving. White semen dribbled out of his mouth, and Logan impulsively swiped at it with his finger and fed it to him. Eyes closing, Seth sucked his index finger the way he had his cock. The sight had Logan pulsing again, a final few drops escaping his softening dick.

Seth's cock was anything but soft, tenting his dress pants. Logan leaned forward and urged him closer, tugging Seth up fully on his knees. "Come on, get it out."

Breathing hard, Seth blinked at him, shoving down the gray pants and his boxers until his cock sprang free. It was cut and thick, straining, almost purple and leaking. Logan wrapped his palm around it and stroked, spreading the liquid from the tip.

Balancing with a hand on Logan's thigh, Seth moaned low in his throat and curled forward against him. Fiery, wet breath tickled Logan's neck under Seth's open mouth. In his left hand, Seth's dick was an iron rod, hot and ready to blow.

Seth whimpered. "Oh. *Oh*, I..."

"What does it take to get you to swear?" Shit, Logan wanted to find out. He wanted Seth to truly let go—wanted to help him get there. Seth was good. He deserved it. "You're close, aren't you?"

After a few more strokes, Seth's fingers dug into Logan's thigh so hard they'd leave bruises, and with a cry, he came. It whipped through him like a gunshot, his body rigid as he spurted over Logan's hand. It was warm and sticky, dripping on Logan's knuckles.

Logan let go of him and relaxed back, arms at his sides. Seth followed, slumping against him, his face pressed to the side of Logan's neck. Their harsh breathing and the drumming of Logan's heart filled his ears.

He blinked at the muted TV, where the post-game guys were apparently talking about passing stats according to the graphic on the screen. Logan waited for Seth to move, even though he liked the warm weight of him.

Logan was about to run a hand through Seth's hair, but he stopped himself. This wasn't how it went with guys. *It's just getting off. Doing us both a favor. A bonus to our deal.* Logan was about to nudge him when Seth sat back on his heels, breathing heavily, his face flushed. He smiled again, that grin full of sunshine and puppies or some shit.

Logan had no clue what to say, but then he was biting back a moan as Seth dropped his head and sucked Logan's hand clean, his tongue dipping into the V between fingers, lapping up his own jizz.

It probably should have been gross, but a fresh coil of desire unleashed in Logan's gut. He was reaching out again to touch Seth's head, the urge to sink his fingers into that soft, thick hair too much to resist, when Seth pushed to his feet, yanking up his slacks.

"You're right. I needed that. Thank you." Seth looked like he wanted to say more, but after a few seconds he grabbed their glasses off the table. "Another round?"

Logan nodded, watching him disappear toward the kitchen. For a few moments, he could only sit there with his legs spread and his dick out, Seth's spit drying on it. He ordered himself to move and managed to get his foot back through the leg hole in his underwear and jeans before tugging them up and zipping.

Seth whistled softly as he came back in. "Do you think they'll trade Williams?" He held out Logan's glass.

Logan took it. "Huh?" As Seth got settled on the far end of the couch, stretching his long legs out to cross his ankles on the chaise, Logan tried to remember a single thing about Williams and the Patriots. "Dunno." It was the truth, at least.

"I don't think they have the depth without him. It might give the team a short-term gain, but in the long run? Bad move." He un-muted the TV, and the talking heads filled the surround sound.

"Yeah." Logan nodded and repeated, "Yeah."

What the fuck is my problem? Snap out of it.

Seth seemed fine, engrossed in the football talk on the TV while Logan's heart thumped. He felt like he'd been riding roller coasters, his stomach and head all swoopy. All he could think was:

That was one hell of a blow job.

Chapter Ten

LOGAN WAS RIGHT—CASUAL sex was *fantastic*.

As he showered the next morning, Seth found himself grinning. He was positively giddy, thinking about Logan filling his mouth—salty and *male* and powerful.

He tugged at his hard cock, tempted to go downstairs and wake Logan by sucking him again. Rubbing against him and feeling his body, kissing him—

Seth squeezed his shaft painfully. He needed to stay in control. Because, fine, perhaps he hadn't quite gotten the hang of the *casual* aspect yet of the sex they'd had. It had been incredible to taste Logan, to be filled with him, and Logan had clearly enjoyed it, shooting down Seth's throat in long, ropy spurts.

But, *oh*, to then feel that callused hand around his...his *cock*, had made Seth tremble. Embarrassed, he laughed at himself, reaching for the shampoo. Even after all the years of sex with Brandon, he still hesitated to even think of explicit words.

It was ludicrous that he could perform all the acts but then blush to think of his penis as his *cock*. He took hold of it again, stroking, a shudder running through him as he remembered the dirty things Logan had said.

Seth and Brandon had never talked much during sex. Over the years they'd settled into a routine, and it had been good. Seth had always loved going down on Brandon. But now, a new world of possibilities was opening. He inhaled deeply, the steamy air and hot water loosening his muscles. All the things he and Logan could do…

This is just casual, though.

Right. It was only "getting off," as Logan had put it. Seth let go of himself and rinsed the shampoo from his hair. He couldn't get carried away. But how he'd ached to kiss Logan, to feel that stubble against his face and breathe him in. It would have been crossing a line, since Logan said he only kissed women. He'd been clear in his boundaries.

It had taken all of Seth's will power to peel himself off Logan and stand, to act normal and offer him another drink. He'd longed for Logan to take him in his strong arms and just hold him in the afterglow, but that was clearly beyond the parameters of their arrangement.

Seth's knees had been shaking so much he was surprised he'd been able to walk to the kitchen without tripping. He'd splashed scotch over the new gray quartz counter and had stood there deep breathing for a long minute before going back into the great room and feigning casualness with football talk.

He and Logan had a deal, and Seth would hold up his end. He still couldn't believe Logan had sex with men even though he said he was straight. It certainly wasn't Seth's place to label anyone else's sexuality, but he wondered what it would be like if they didn't live in a society teeming with toxic masculinity. Growing up, any boys who didn't fit the traditional mold were deemed lesser and called the F-word.

What was the incentive for a man like Logan to acknowledge bisexuality? Growing up in a working-class family in the Albany suburbs, joining the Marines out of high school, then working most of his adult life on the railway… Likely not the most positive, open-minded environments.

Seth laughed harshly, closing his eyes as he stood under the hot water. Of course he knew what that was like. He'd grown up trying so hard not to be different.

But he'd never been attracted to women, and it had proved impossible to compartmentalize his attraction for men, or his love and affection for them. Logan apparently only felt those kinds of tender feelings for women, and who was Seth to question that?

Logan did say he'd topped men occasionally. *What would it be like?* Seth shuddered, boldly touching himself, trying to push aside the automatic guilt that flared. Was it really less of a sin to have sex when you were in love? Why shouldn't he be able to fantasize?

Taking a deep breath, he let his mind go, letting the explicit words flow, along with matching images.

What would it be like to have his cock in my ass? He's nice and thick. He'd stretch me open, pound into me, fuck me so good—the way I need it.

Seth's breath caught as he jerked himself hard, already splattering the gray granite tiles white as he imagined Logan coming inside him, whispering deliciously filthy things in his ear.

As the guilt threatened to return, he shoved it away. He murmured, "Why shouldn't I feel good? Why shouldn't I enjoy sex? I don't have to be in love to get off. Why would God have made orgasms if we weren't supposed to use them? Have them. Whatever."

He laughed derisively and shut off the water. "I really do talk to myself too much."

On the fuzzy bathmat, he rubbed his head with a towel. It was fortunate that he'd masturbated and taken the edge off. He needed to keep his cool around Logan and remember that the sex was only about physical pleasure. Logan did those things with strangers and didn't have any feelings involved. That's what it was supposed to be.

Yes, Seth was going to conquer his fear and stop making sex such a big deal. He was on the other side of the river. Maybe he should install Grindr on his phone and hook up with some random guy.

But he shuddered unpleasantly at the thought, reaching for his bathrobe and tying the belt tightly around his waist. Although he'd only known Logan less than a week, he trusted him—unlike the unknown men he might meet online.

Taking that bold step and kneeling between Logan's legs to suck him had been terrifying—and exhilarating since Logan had made him feel safe.

Just as he had standing on the street in Saratoga Springs, big and strong at Seth's side, helping him face Brandon and the others. Of course Logan was only being kind—only holding up his end of their deal for a fake relationship—yet his support had felt genuine.

Maybe it was his friendship with Jenna that allowed Seth to trust her brother so quickly. Yes, they had an arrangement, but that didn't mean they couldn't be genuine friends. Seth had seen Logan vulnerable and shaking in the garage when he'd exerted himself too much, and he'd shown Logan his own vulnerability.

You can only be friends. You're not allowed to want more.

He wiped condensation from the mirror and picked up his electric razor, staring at his reflection. He looked the same as he did every morning, and he laughed at himself softly. Had he expected to look different? He and Logan had shared orgasms, but that was all.

Logan was sleeping on the couch as he had every other night since he'd moved in. *Temporarily* moved in. Nothing had changed between them, no matter how much Seth had wanted to bring him up to bed and sleep naked together, touch him from head to toe, rub against his hairy body and muscles. Kiss him for hours.

They had a deal, and *that* wasn't part of it. Seth wasn't allowed to fall for Logan. This was only pretend. He nodded to his reflection.

No ifs, ands, or buts.

He dressed, his pants enjoyably warm from the trouser press in the corner of his room. He chose a dark tie with a subtle purple diamond pattern and surveyed himself in the closet-door mirror.

After fiddling with his hair, he realized he was acting like he was going on a date or something, not to the office. Yes, Logan was downstairs. No, Seth didn't have to impress him with the sharpness of the crease in his pants.

The coffee maker had started brewing automatically, and Seth inhaled gratefully as he went downstairs and rounded the corner of the sitting room. He stumbled to a halt, blinking at Logan standing there by the fridge. Shirtless. Thank goodness he was wearing track pants, although now that Seth knew what his cock looked—and tasted like—he could imagine it so easily…

"Morning!" Seth said too cheerily and loudly.

Logan leaned a hip against the counter. "Morning." A mug in one hand, he smiled tightly. "Hope it's okay that I helped myself."

"Of course! Make yourself completely at home." Seth stood there across the island, trying to think of something else to say. He came up completely blank. Logan looked back at him, and an awkward silence built until Logan turned away.

He poured another mug of coffee and held it out, and Seth forced his feet to move. "Thanks!" His tone was still too cheery. Their fingers brushed, and the instinct to kiss Logan swelled. *Uh, no. He's not your boyfriend. No sleepy-sweet morning kisses.* Seth drank a mouthful of coffee even though it was too hot.

Stop looking at his chest.

Logan laughed uneasily and crossed his arms. "Scars are ugly, I know."

"Huh?" Seth blinked up at him, then back at his chest. He realized there were marks snaking through the dark hair on Logan's sternum. He'd been too distracted by the reddish discs of Logan's tight nipples to even notice. "Oh! No, not ugly at all. I didn't notice them."

He forced his gaze away, wincing at his false tone. He really hadn't noticed, but Logan would think he was lying, not ogling his nipples. It was still dark outside, and in the window's reflection over the kitchen sink, he could see Logan's broad back, which wasn't any less distracting.

Seth asked, "What are you up to today?"

Logan nodded toward the sink. "I'll put up the backsplash tiles and grout it all."

"Oh! Right." Seth had chosen the pale blue glass tiles so long ago he'd almost forgotten about them. "Hope I still like them."

"It'll look good." Logan scratched his chest, the sound of his nails on his hairy flesh drawing Seth's attention despite himself. His pecs were wonderfully furry. Not too much, not too little. Just right.

You're not Goldilocks. Stop it.

"Great! Thanks. Did you have breakfast? There are eggs in the fridge. Please help yourself."

"Cool. Um, thanks." Logan turned and opened the fridge, poking around the shelves.

Seth went to the pantry and blindly reached for something. *Casual. Be casual.* He blinked at what he was holding—baking soda. Quickly putting it back, he picked up a box of gingersnaps and read the nutritional info. From the corner of his eye, he could see Logan leaning against the island again, the fridge door closing with a soft *thwack*.

After a moment, Seth could sense Logan's gaze on him. His neck went hot, and he imagined he could feel Logan's eyes roaming over his body. Which was ridiculous! So Seth glanced over, telling himself Logan would definitely not be looking at him.

But he *was*.

And when their eyes met, they both startled and turned away, Logan returning to the fridge as Seth came out of the pantry and grabbed his coffee and gulped.

Seth cleared his throat. Casual. This wasn't a big deal. Logan bent over the crisper drawer, the track pants stretching over his rear. Seth's balls tightened, desire coiling deep in his belly as he imagined pushing inside Logan's body.

"Okay, I'd better get on the road. Have a great day!" Seth ran for it. He could buy breakfast. And lunch.

"Hey, are we cool?" Logan asked as he turned from the fridge.

Seth stopped and faced him. "Hmm?" His heart drummed. "Uh-huh. Great. Thanks again for helping me…get over the hump. So to speak."

Logan smirked. "Anytime." He sipped his coffee. "Well… Have a good day at work."

"Yes! I will. Thanks. Uh, you too!" Seth gave a wave because he was a complete dork. He escaped to jam on his boots, throw on his coat, and slip his way to the driveway through the fresh snow. He turned on the SUV's engine in the garage and waited a minute while it warmed.

The guy who mowed his grass also came in winter to plow the long driveway, and it was freshly cleared. Seth threw down salt on the pathway so Logan wouldn't slip and got on the road, his pulse racing for a good few miles.

A peppy Kelly Clarkson Christmas song played on the radio, and for once, Seth didn't turn the channel. Instead, he upped the volume with the button on the steering wheel, pressing with his thumb.

His mind wandered to Logan—and masturbating in the shower. A thrill shot through him at the memory of the stretch of his lips around Logan's shaft, and then bringing himself off this morning.

"It's okay," he said aloud, interrupting Kelly. "I had casual sex, and this morning I…*jerked off*, and it's all okay. I'm allowed. There's nothing wrong with it."

The plows and salters had been out, and the drive into work

was smooth. Especially since Seth spent it grinning to himself, thinking about seeing Logan again that night. Wondering if they'd get off again.

"Casual sex is awesome." He repeated his new mantra, tapping the wheel as another pop holiday song came on.

He was still grinning when he pushed open the glass door to the office. Becky gasped excitedly when she saw him, practically bouncing in her chair behind reception, her red hair swirling in waves.

She exclaimed, "Seth Marston, you sly devil! It's always the quiet ones."

Seth's grin froze as he jolted to a stop. Matt had said he'd contain the rumors at work, but it was Tuesday, and apparently the containment could only last so long. "Uh..."

She crooked her finger and beckoned him closer to her desk. "Don't worry, I haven't told anyone."

Seth resisted the urge to snort in derision. "Thanks." If everyone didn't already know about his fake engagement, they would soon.

Becky whispered, "Strong work bagging Jenna's hot bro. I didn't even know he was gay!"

He's not, despite the fact that I sucked his cock last night and then he gave me a hand job. Just thinking the words sent a secret little shiver through him. "Uh, yeah, we just hit it off. Anyway, I should get to it. Have a great day!" He rushed away before Becky could launch into a real cross-examination.

Seth was normally in before Jenna, but he skidded to a stop as he rounded the corner of their pod. She sat at her desk, blotting at her pants above her knee with his Tide pen.

She glanced up, clearly exasperated. "Honestly, how does this baby manage to get spit up on my *leg*?"

"It's a talent." Seth laughed, and it came out too high. Looking at Jenna, strange guilt boiled up in him.

I had your brother in my mouth last night.

Her brows drew together. "Everything okay?"

"Uh-huh! Why wouldn't it be?" He yanked out his desk chair, the wheels knocking into his foot. He could still feel Jenna's curious gaze on him.

"Is Logan behaving himself?"

A strangled laugh brayed out as visions of Logan spread-legged—hard and leaking—danced through Seth's mind. "Uh-huh."

Jenna groaned. "God, don't tell me he's leaving his sweaty gym socks out or farting."

This time, Seth's laugh was genuine, and he looked over at Jenna, who was wincing. He lowered his voice. "I assure you he's being a model guest. No dirty socks or passing gas."

She laughed and whispered back, "Okay, good. To be fair, I haven't lived with him since he was a teenage boy, and you know how gross they can be. Not that you were."

"Of course not." He lifted his chin haughtily. "I've never even broken a sweat."

"You know, you're so neat and orderly I can almost believe that."

Matt's shaggy head appeared atop the partition. "What are we whispering about?" His eyebrows rose. "Caper?"

"Yes!" Jenna hissed. "Keep your voice down."

Matt leaned closer and murmured, "Don't worry. This is all under control."

"Easy for you to say!" Seth rolled his eyes. "But it should be fine. New furniture's coming today. We still have time to get everything in place."

Matt asked, "How's the boy toy?"

Heat washed through Seth like a tidal wave, and he jerked his eyes to the computer screen, the words jumbled and meaningless. "He's not my boy toy."

Matt huffed. "You'd better fake this better for Angela. I'm just saying. What are you going to make her for dinner?"

Dread joined the hot swirl of guilt and embarrassment. "I have no idea." Seth shook his head, his voice raising. "I have no idea!"

"Shh!" Jenna and Matt hissed in unison.

Matt winked. "I'll get Becky on the case and find out what Angela's favorite foods are. Don't worry, man. You got this." He pumped his fist and mouthed, "*Caper!*" before disappearing behind the partition.

Sighing, Seth hoped Matt's confidence wasn't grossly misplaced.

AS HE PULLED into the driveway, a fresh layer of snow crunching under the tires, Seth was momentarily puzzled by the warm glow of lights from inside the house and the silhouette of a man on the walkway leading to the front door.

His heart skipped as he blinked at Logan, who paused in his shoveling to give a wave. The garage door stood open, and Seth eased in and killed the engine.

The moon had emerged from behind clouds, and at the end of the driveway, Seth could see that the distant mailbox was crammed full, flyers poking out the end, the flap unable to close now. He should just empty it. He knew what was likely inside, and not looking wouldn't change a thing.

Yet he turned onto the walkway, breathing through the tightening in his gut and focusing on Logan—which sent a spiral of jittery excitement through him.

We had sex yesterday. Is it going to happen again today? Does he want me the way I want him?

Out loud, Seth said, "You don't have to shovel. Leave it for me."

Breath pluming in the cold air, Logan said, "Happy to do it."

Seth stopped a few feet away on the walkway. He cocked an eyebrow. "Really? *Happy?*"

Logan chuckled. "Believe it or not, I am. I like working. Feeling useful." In the yellow glow through the front window, his cheeks were ruddy.

"It's not too much exertion?" It had honestly been frightening when Logan had been unable to catch his breath that day in the garage.

This was clearly the wrong thing to say, since Logan scowled and muttered, "Nope."

"Okay. You should wear a hat. You'll catch a cold." *Great, act like his mother. That's really sexy.* But should he be attempting to be *sexy?* They were only friends. Barely that—still mostly strangers.

Although the little quirk of Logan's crooked smile was already becoming familiar, and Seth wanted to see it again and again. Wanted to see everything. Wanted to learn all the shapes and sounds of Logan.

Logan's laugh was throaty, and the sound sent lust spiking through Seth. Logan pulled his black woolen hat from his pocket and tugged it over his ears. "You're the boss."

Seth laughed, although unease prickled his skin. "Let me get the other shovel and help." He didn't want Logan to feel like they weren't equals.

"I just have the steps to finish." Logan squinted at the driveway. "Didn't think there was enough fresh to warrant shoveling all of that as well. But I can if you want."

"No, no. Like you said, there's not enough. The SUV gets through it no problem, and if there's too much, a guy comes to plow the drive."

Logan nodded, then bent to push a shovelful of light snow off the walk. "I'll be done in a minute. Why don't you check out the backsplash?"

"Oh! I almost forgot. Thank you." Seth climbed the few steps and stamped his boots before going inside. On the indoor mat, he tugged off his boots, carefully stepping onto the hardwood in his socks and trying to avoid the wet spots.

After hanging up his coat, he padded through the still-empty sitting room and into the kitchen, gasping softly. The pale blue subway tiles gleamed, brightening the space immeasurably and making the white cabinets really pop. It all looked so clean and crisp and inviting, and Seth was suddenly eager to cook. And not just prepackaged stir fries and bacon and eggs. This was a kitchen he wanted to spend time in.

Grinning, he admired it, running his hands over the shiny gray quartz counters. The rhythmic scrape of the shovel on the walkway outside was strangely soothing. Seth had been rattling around the half-finished house all alone for more than a year, and having Logan there helping and doing things for him made Seth feel…

It was silly, but it made him feel cared for. Comforted and peaceful, even though it was only part of their deal. It wasn't *real*. It was only temporary. Soon enough he'd be shoveling his own walkway and he'd be alone again.

His smile faded, his pleasure over the finished kitchen diminishing. Yes, he'd still make better use of it and cook for himself in the new year, but a hollow void cracked through the swell of comfort that had filled him.

"Enough of that," he muttered to himself. Logan was with him now, and he'd make the best of it.

Before long, he had chicken breasts cooked and pasta boiling, and he was grating an old hunk of Parmesan after cutting off the questionable bits. The sauce would have to be jarred, but it was a decent organic brand. He smiled to himself as he listened to Logan come inside the house and take off his winter gear.

"Something smells good," Logan said as he rounded the corner.

"The boiling water?" Seth joked.

"Yep, that must be it."

"The kitchen's so gorgeous I had to start cooking immediately, even though I'm not much of a chef. Thank you. I can't tell you how much I appreciate it."

Logan shrugged, but his smile was definitely pleased. "Glad you like it." He rubbed a hand over his cold-red face, the scruff rasping. The sound went straight to Seth's groin. Logan wore a sweatshirt over his jeans, and he pulled it over his head, his T-shirt riding up and exposing his belly and the dark hair that pointed down to what was under his waistband.

"Do you drink wine?" Seth asked Logan too loudly. "I have a nice Pinot. Well, I think it's nice. Hopefully."

"Sure. I'm not fussy."

Seth busied himself grabbing the bottle from the pantry. "I should get a proper wine rack. Instead of keeping the wine beside the Bran Flakes."

Logan filled the pantry door with his broad shoulders. "Should be easy enough to do. Where do you want it? I'll get the dimensions and ask Pop what he thinks. He was here today supervising." He stepped closer, peering around Seth at the corner of the pantry. "If he tells me what to do, I could probably build one pretty easily."

"Oh, you don't have to do that!"

Logan shrugged. "I want to."

They stood a foot apart, and Seth suddenly could barely breathe. When he did, he inhaled the faint fresh scent of Irish Spring soap. Then he was imagining Logan naked and wet in the shower, lathering himself, sudsy and slippery...

"Seth?"

The timer for the pasta beeped in the kitchen, and Seth plastered on a smile as Logan backed out of the pantry to let him by.

Seth hurried to place the colander in the sink and dump the pasta into it.

He asked Logan, "Do you want to open the wine? I think the glasses are in that box in the corner. Still need to get all the cabinets sorted."

"Sure. And yeah, I figured you'd want to organize it yourself. I'm not the best at that shit. Not like Jenna. And you seem like you enjoy things…neat."

"That's a generous way to put it." Seth shook his head and stirred the bubbling sauce. "Hard to believe I've lived with this half-empty disarray for so long."

Soon they were in front of the TV, watching *Brooklyn Nine-Nine* and laughing. The pasta was hearty and tasty enough, and the red wine went down too easily for a weeknight. Seth clucked his tongue as he splashed a drop of sauce on his gray shirt.

"You don't usually change into sweats or whatever when you get home?" Logan asked from his end of the couch, the middle cushion between them.

"Oh, I usually do, yeah." He dabbed at the spot.

"Well, you don't have to do anything different because I'm here. It's your house."

"Right." He laughed softly. "I suppose I'm not used to having anyone here, so I'm in 'guest mode' or something."

"Well, make yourself at home," Logan joked.

After dinner, Seth did go upstairs and change into a tee and sweatpants, as well as thick, fuzzy socks since his feet were perpetually cold in winter. He also spritzed himself with a woodsy cologne he hadn't worn in ages and fussed with his short hair as if he were going on a date. In his own living room. With an almost-stranger he'd had his mouth on the day before.

Situation normal.

They watched a new Netflix show on home renovations that seemed well-timed, and Seth turned on the fireplace. It was cozy and weirdly comfortable to hang with Logan in near silence aside from the odd comments from both of them on paint and sofa choices.

Logan had changed into his sweatpants too and didn't wear a shirt. Which was perhaps slightly distracting, if Seth was being honest.

Around ten, Seth paused a new episode and said, "I guess I should get to bed."

"Right. How'd you sleep last night?"

"Uh, good! Good." The mention of last night had Seth on red alert, memories sparking fresh lust. He tried to watch Logan from the corner of his eye. Was Logan simply asking an innocent question? Sitting there shirtless and sprawled and sexier than he had any right to be?

Logan held a glass of water, and he toyed with it, his hand moving up and down, gathering condensation. "Yeah, I find getting off helps. With sleep."

"Uh-huh!" Seth all but squeaked.

"But if you want to go straight to bed—"

"No, I'm good. I mean, I can… We can… If you want…"

The rumble of Logan's laughter was warm. "C'mere."

Seth forced himself to move slowly instead of launching at Logan like an attacking predator. Their knees knocked as he settled himself, and before he could formulate a sentence, Logan was cupping him through the cotton with a strong hand, and Seth was almost instantly hard.

He lifted his hips so Logan could tug him free, and he concentrated on breathing and staring at the paused TV, their reflection moving over the image of a rundown bungalow.

The urge to turn his head and shove his tongue down Logan's throat positively burned, but he kept his lips pressed together tightly, his nostrils flaring as pleasure built.

"Doesn't have to be a big deal," Logan murmured, his voice

gone gravelly. He rubbed at himself—at his *cock*—through his sweatpants as he stroked Seth, pausing to spit on his palm a few times.

That's probably how he does it in bathroom stalls, with just spit.

For some reason it excited Seth, the rough drag of Logan's callused hand and the dirtiness of using spit. The rawness of it. It was illicit somehow. Seth leaned into him, Logan's left arm flexing between them as he stroked Seth.

"Not awkward? Using your left hand?" Seth asked. The strokes were so measured and sure, so skillful.

"I'm left-handed."

"Oh!" Seth's breath caught, turning the sound into a long moan. "*Ohhh.*" It felt so good, and Seth was going to come soon, and he wanted Logan to feel as good as he did.

Taking a shaky breath, he spit into his right hand, licking it a few times before reaching toward the bulge in Logan's sweats. "Should I...?"

"Fuck yeah."

So there they sat, hands down each other's pants, knees and elbows bumping as they brought each other off. Their harsh inhalations and exhalations filled the air, heads leaning closer together as their movements became more frantic.

Seth wanted to devour Logan, inhale him and feel that rough stubble on his lips and face, taste tomato and garlic on his tongue and kiss through their orgasms.

But he didn't cross those last several inches. Logan didn't want that. He'd set his boundaries, and even though Seth had Logan's throbbing cock in his hand, the spongy, flushed steel in his grasp so alive and powerful, that was as far as he could touch.

Still, as Seth came, spurting over Logan's knobby knuckles, he imagined that kiss, closing his eyes and letting himself go, his head thrown back and spine arching.

Logan wasn't far behind, and his groan as Seth milked him

was delicious. Pulling his sticky hand free, Seth wiped it on a stray napkin. They breathed hard, and Seth mumbled, "Thanks. That was…"

"Yeah."

"I… Thanks." Before he could stop himself, Seth nuzzled at Logan's cheek. Not kissing him, but almost…

Logan inhaled sharply, shuddering. Then he cleared his throat and sat up straight, breaking contact. "All part of the deal, right?"

It was like a splash of cold water, and Seth tucked himself into his sweatpants, nodding. "Right. Yes. Okay, good night!" He balled up the napkin in his fist and made a hasty retreat.

All part of the deal. Nothing more.

He repeated the words to himself like a mantra as he went to bed and stared at the ceiling far too long.

Chapter Eleven

"SHOOT!" SETH TIGHTENED his arm around the cardboard box full of wine bottles, feeling it slip as he turned the key in the lock.

His front door sprang open, and he almost sprawled flat on his face. He would have if not for Logan's strong hands on his arms. Logan took the box, easing it onto the floor by the mat. "Close one. You almost cussed."

Seth laughed as he closed the door, the warmth of the house beckoning. Not to mention Logan. A pang of longing filled him—the urge to pull Logan into a hug, to kiss him hello the way he would a lover. A partner. He had to remind himself that this was all pretend.

Well, aside from the orgasms.

Those were very, very real. The night before, Seth and Logan had eaten Thai delivery in the great room while watching TV. After some time for digestion, Seth had blown Logan, on his knees between Logan's legs, glad of the thick throw rug.

Logan hadn't offered to do the same yet, and Seth hadn't asked. He was getting off powerfully just with the touch of Logan's rough hand, the hot puff of his breath on Seth's cheek, the press of their thighs and shoulders when they sat close. In those moments, Seth could almost forget that it was only a bargain between them.

"Table's here," Logan said.

"Oh, thank goodness!" There had been an unexplained delay, and Seth had devised a backup plan. "Glad we won't have to throw together an IKEA special."

"Me too. It looks great. Boss lady'll love it."

Today was the big day when Angela came to dinner, and Seth had taken a few of his banked personal hours to pick up the groceries and start cooking. His stomach tightened. "I can't believe Angela Barker is actually coming to my house for dinner."

It was time to stick to business and remember their deal and why they were doing this in the first place. It was time to be professional and keep his head about him.

"You'll do great. Jenna said that floppy-haired guy got the dirt on Angela's fave food?"

"Matt, yeah. His girlfriend is the office manager, and she knows everything. And Jenna looked up recipes that should fit the bill."

"Bet she gave you a very specific shopping list too." Logan's lips quirked into a smile.

Oh, how Seth wanted to kiss that mouth. Wanted to get completely naked with Logan and feel the whole press of his body, skin-to-skin from head-to-toe. He wanted to make Logan moan and sigh and be *happy.* Seth wanted to take that heaviness shrouded around him and make him smile all the time.

"Gee, how'd you know?" he joked, and Logan smiled wider.

And *fine,* maybe it was more than lust sparking in Seth. But he had to keep it in check, because affection and *feelings* weren't on the menu. Logan identified as straight, and he'd made his boundaries clear.

Even if he'd ended up caressing Seth's hair when Seth had gone down on him again, groaning before he'd reached out, as if he'd been giving in somehow. It didn't mean anything, and Seth needed to remember that this was all simply part of their deal.

He nodded to the wine and grocery bags as he yanked his feet free from his winter boots. "Pricey Bordeaux and rib-eye steaks. Guess I'd better figure out how that grill out back works."

"You ain't used it before?" a gruff voice asked, feet shuffling toward them in cheap slippers.

"Mr. Derwood!" Seth felt nervous and embarrassed that he'd just been thinking inappropriately about Logan. "I didn't realize you were here."

The man grunted. His shoulders were stooped and his face lined, belly large and fingers stained with tobacco. He wore track pants and a striped sweater. Seth had been shocked to learn he was only in his sixties. Bill said, "Got yer wine rack in."

"Oh! Thank you so much."

Logan added, "Hope it's okay. And I wasn't sure how you wanted to do the decorations and tree, so I won't be offended if you move stuff."

"I'm sure it's all wonderful. Thank you again."

The sitting room now held two wingback chairs by the window with a small table between them, a glass coffee table separating a new beige couch that had been in stock at one of the local stores. The area rug was a fluffy white, navy, and tan.

These items had been delivered the day before, and it was nice to have the space filled. Seth honestly wouldn't really use the room much, but the back of the couch served as a good separator between the front room and the kitchen.

A ceramic Christmas tree lit with golden lights now sat on the table between the chairs, a real pinecone and fir candle arrangement on the coffee table, red holly berries bright and cheerful. Seth had to touch the berries to see if they were real since the plastic was so convincing.

On the new dining table off to the right beside the kitchen, there was a similar holiday centerpiece. It suited the big rustic table, and Seth found himself smiling.

"The chairs really do fit well, don't you think?" he asked Logan, heat rippling through him as he remembered standing in front of the store window, Logan's hand on his rear and that sexy whisper…

"Imagine I'm saying something really dirty."

Logan's father was right there, and Seth was officially out of control. He didn't even hear Logan's reply, but assumed it was an agreement. The wine rack had been built into one end of the island, a criss-cross of wood painted white that matched the cabinets perfectly.

"Wow," Seth breathed. "You built this?"

Logan shrugged. "Sure. Pop told me what to do. You've lost some storage space in the island, but with the cupboards and huge pantry, I don't think you'll miss it."

"This is perfect. Thank you so much." He turned to Logan's father. "Mr. Derwood, I'd like to pay you for your consultation."

"Sure. I'll stay for dinner and have a steak."

Seth froze. "Uh…" He glanced at Logan, who seemed equally at a loss for words. First there was Angela to impress, although maybe she'd appreciate the family aspect? But Seth and Logan also had to pretend to be a couple, and what would Logan's father say about *that*?

Bill laughed, a rough, rasping bark, his shoulders shaking. "Just messin' with ya. You don't want me around at your fancy dinner. Besides, I don't wanna watch my boy pretendin' to be a fairy."

Seth jolted. Wait, when had Bill discovered the plan? He stammered, "Oh, um—I… Well…" He looked to Logan, who shifted uneasily and jammed his hands in his pockets, his neck flushed red.

Logan mumbled, "I didn't think Jenna was telling you about that part."

Bill snorted. "Jenny didn't need to tell me. I'm not deaf. My ears are one of the few things not breakin' down. You're all not as clever as you think you are."

Seth had to chuckle ruefully. He certainly couldn't argue that point. A line of tension between his shoulder blades made his neck ache, and he rubbed at the nape, wishing he could disappear.

He supposed "fairy" wasn't the worst thing Bill could have called him. Logan was a wall of tension, and Seth needed to say something, but his tongue felt too thick.

"Look, you seem like a decent fella," Bill said. "Been real good to my Jenny. And Logan." He grunted. "None of my business what you get up to. Don't make sense to me, but…" He grunted again. "In my day, folks didn't…" He raised weathered hands and lowered them dismissively. "Look, you need to season that grill. Got oil?"

"Uh, yes." Seth nodded and hurried into the pantry, relieved at the abrupt change of topic. He imagined that in Bill Derwood's day, most "folks" stayed locked away in the closet. Still, at least the man hadn't said anything truly hateful. Hadn't called Seth an abomination.

He fetched his winter gear and headed toward the back of the house, carrying his boots so he didn't track snow and salt on the floors. He jolted to a stop as he entered the great room. The decorations in the sitting room were nothing compared to the veritable explosion of Christmas here.

"Goodness," Seth breathed.

Logan had strung colored lights and garlands across the back wall along the metal divider in the arched glass above the sliding doors and blinds. More candle/holly/fir displays sat on the side tables and coffee table, red bows neat and bright.

The *pièce de résistance* was a massive pine tree standing between the TV and black fireplace, strung with colored lights, garlands, and ornaments, dangling silver icicles making it positively shimmer. A lit silver-gold angel sat atop, and beneath, wrapped presents crowded.

Seth deeply inhaled the fresh, woodsy smell, gazing around in wonder. The room had never seemed so cozy and warm—so much like a *home*. And suddenly he was blinking back tears.

For so many years, he'd told himself Christmas wasn't for him. That he didn't deserve it somehow. Standing in front of the tree, surrounded by holiday glitter and color, he ached down to his bones for this home to truly be his and not only for show.

Yet it wasn't.

The charmingly clumsily wrapped presents were surely empty. Only window dressing for the life he was pretending was real for Angela's sake. It was *all* window dressing—the new furniture and decorations, and Logan himself. Come the new year, Logan would be gone, the decorations would come down, and Seth would be alone again.

"Is it not good?"

Seth hadn't heard Logan's approach, and he jumped, managing an awkward laugh, glad that he'd kept the tears from falling. Not meeting Logan's gaze, he forced a smile, looking all around the room. "It's fantastic!"

"Yeah? Jenna told me what to do, so…"

When Seth made himself look at Logan, Logan was watching him warily. Seth was able to smile genuinely this time. "It really is wonderful. Thank you."

"Okay. Cool." Logan carried his own boots, his father shuffling up behind him.

Bill sat heavily on the far end of the sofa and groaned as he bent to tug on his boots. Logan made a step toward him, but his father snapped, "I can do it!"

So Seth and Logan stood awkwardly by the sliding door, waiting. Seth said, "I'll shovel a path," and escaped outside. He'd left a spare shovel on the porch and went to work gladly.

Even if this was all for show, at least his house would be finished. His grill would even be seasoned! And at least he'd gotten over his hang-up about casual sex. Hadn't he? Even if he craved more with Logan, he wasn't going to get it, and that was simply the way it was.

Yes, in the new year, Seth would start dating. He'd install the apps and go out with a bunch of men, and maybe he'd eventually meet someone who wanted more with him. Something real. In the meantime, he could enjoy the holidays with Logan, couldn't he?

Well. After tonight's dinner and the weekend retreat tomorrow. After they convinced Angela they were madly in love. Piece of cake.

Fortunately, Mr. Derwood was a wealth of information on barbecuing, and he seasoned the grill and taught Seth how to use it, giving him cooking times and techniques. Seth took out his phone and tapped notes, his bare fingers icy. Logan finished shoveling the rest of the back deck, even though there wasn't really a need.

Time was marching on, and Logan drove his father home while Seth set the steaks marinating and prepped the creamy, cheesy scalloped potato ingredients. When Logan came home— came *back*—he mumbled an offer to vacuum and mop, keeping his gaze anywhere but meeting Seth's eyes.

Brandon had wanted a sound system wired through the main floor, and Seth had reluctantly agreed. He'd never actually used it, but after a while, he went to the stereo set back in a little alcove between the dining room and great room and turned on a Christmas channel on one of the streaming networks.

Judy Garland's rich, soulful voice filled the main floor. As Seth obsessed over the thickness of his potato slices and ensuring consistency, Logan fiddled with a fresh pad on the steam mop. It seemed very likely it was his first encounter with such a device, but he didn't ask for help.

It was all very…domestic, and Seth tried to pretend it didn't make his heart swell.

But this isn't real. Logan is your fake boyfriend. Remember that.

"This is a pretty song," Logan said. "A little sad, though."

"Oh, the mention of 'muddling through' in this version is nothing compared to the original lyrics. Most depressing Christmas song ever."

"Really?" Bent over the mop, Logan grumbled something under his breath.

Seth had to laugh. "Are you ready to declare defeat and ask me how to get the pad on?"

Logan glared, but there was no heat to it. He stood back with his hands on his hips. The black Henley that stretched over his chest and arms clung to his muscles. He looked like he belonged on the back of a motorcycle rather than steam mopping.

He's doing it for me.

Seth reminded himself that it was all part of their deal as he showed Logan how to release the mechanism and slip on a new pad. To distract himself from Logan's muscles, he rambled on.

"Yeah, the original version of 'Have Yourself a Merry Little Christmas' posits that this Christmas might be our last, so enjoy it while we can. Which isn't untrue, but it was less 'seize the day and grab happiness' and more a 'life sucks and then you die' vibe. They rewrote it, and then it was tweaked again for Sinatra's version. That's the most common one. All happiness and sweet nostalgia."

"Huh. That's interesting."

Seth stood and handed over the mop. "You're being kind. I used to love all things Christmas, and apparently still retain useless, boring facts in my brain."

"It's not boring." Logan bent to plug in the mop by the edge of the kitchen, dark denim accentuating his spectacular backside. "Maybe you can love Christmas again."

"Maybe." He went to the pantry and stopped short. "What's this?"

Logan looked embarrassed, scratching his head and fidgeting. He switched off the mop. "I know you bought a fancy dessert, but I thought the boss lady might like homemade. Might taste like crap. Probably does since I made it."

Seth stared at the dark cake sitting on a stand under a glass dome. It looked like chocolate, and sure, it was a little lopsided, but that only made it more charming. "I… It's perfect. Thank you. I didn't know you could bake."

Logan scoffed. "I can't."

"Clearly untrue since I'm looking at the fruits of your labor."

"It's an easy recipe." He shrugged, toying with the mop handle, running his rough hands over the molded plastic.

Seth's groin tightened. He wanted those hands on his body. *Stop thinking about sex!*

"It was our mom's favorite. We always had it for Christmas. She said pie was for Thanksgiving, and cake was for Christmas, but not that gross fruitcake. She said chocolate was way better. I used to help her with it when I was a kid."

Guilt for his inappropriate thoughts flared as Seth watched Logan smile, a sad little lilt of his lips, his eyes distant, looking lost in a memory. Seth said, "I'm sure it's delicious."

"Yeah. She'd always give me one of the beaters to lick while she kept the other. We'd get chocolate on our noses and chins trying to get it all."

Stop thinking about Logan licking something else! This is an innocent story! Seth cleared his throat. "I can't wait to try it. Thank you." There was a battered metal box sitting beside the cake stand, which had to be Jenna's. Seth stepped forward and picked it up, opening it to find lined index cards inside separated by tabs in neat block letters reading: *Salads, Appetizers, Mains, Sides, Cookies & Bars, Various Desserts,* and *Cakes!*

"Cake was her favorite," Logan said from the door of the pantry.

Smiling at the exclamation mark, Seth thumbed through the cards. The recipes were written in neat, looping cursive, and some were stained with faded remnants of tomato sauce or drops of oil. He knew which cake recipe Logan had made when he came to it, the ink faded in places and chocolate stains abundant, the corners ragged from use.

Seth reverently held the recipe and imagined Logan bent over a mixing bowl creaming butter and sugar. For an insane moment, he thought he might burst into tears, and he didn't really know why.

"Uh, sour cream is the secret ingredient," Logan said.

"Right!" Seth replied too brightly. "It sounds delicious!" He scanned the ingredients. "My mom used applesauce in just about everything she baked." His throat was too thick again. "Still does, I'm sure." He hadn't let himself even glance at the mailbox when he'd come home, though the flyers were probably littering the snowy ground now.

Seth carefully returned the recipe card to the *Cake!* section. He ran his fingers over the metal box, which was a dull silver with a faded, mishapen daisy painted on the side.

"Made it in shop class in ninth grade," Logan said sheepishly.

"It's lovely. Truly."

He shrugged. "Mom stored the recipes she called 'keepers' in it. Her frosting's the best. Oh, here." He disappeared, the fridge door opening before he returned with a small bowl, which he thrust out. "There was extra. Try it."

Seth stared at the bowl of chocolate frosting, swirled ridges hardening from the fridge. "Should I just...?" He lifted a finger.

"I can get you a spoon if you really want," Logan said dubiously.

Laughing, Seth scooped up a finger-full and sucked it into his mouth. He closed his eyes and moaned. "Oh my goodness. That is incredible." He licked his finger, opening his eyes.

Logan watched him with a hooded gaze, his voice gravelly as he said, "Yeah?"

"Um…" What would Logan do if Seth kissed him right now?

"You've got…" Logan motioned at Seth's mouth, and Seth licked the side of his lips, his groin tightening. Then he dipped his finger in the bowl again and sucked it clean, his eyes locked with Logan's, their breathing harsh in the quiet of the pantry, the air thickening as they leaned closer—

Beep-beep-beep!

They sprang apart, and Logan barely kept hold of the bowl. He backed out, and Seth followed to jab at the timer on the counter. "First part of the potatoes is done!" Seth exclaimed too loudly. "Better get back to work. Showtime's in a couple hours." He had to keep his wits about him.

"Right. You worried about it?" Logan asked as he returned to the mop, the bowl of leftover frosting back in the fridge.

Seth certainly had been earlier, and now it rushed back. He tried to shrug it off. "A little, I guess. It's fine. I should get moving so I can change before Angela and Dale get here." She'd invited her assistant along to make it a foursome for dinner, which made sense.

"Oh, shit. What am I supposed to wear?" The mop was hissing again, and Logan peered down at it suspiciously.

"Just a dress shirt and slacks? Maybe a tie?" Seth asked hopefully.

"Uh…" Logan experimentally pushed the mop, seeming pleased when the wet pad slid across the floor. "I have a set of nice clothes I wear to job interviews somewhere. Haven't needed to dress up, so I probably shoved them in one of my bags. I put all my stuff in your room, by the way. Pillow and blanket too. Do you have an iron?"

The idea of not having an iron was like not having a refrigerator, but Seth only nodded. "I do. And a trouser press. I'll show you after we finish here."

Soon they had Logan's slacks pressing, and Seth ran the iron over the cheap white dress shirt. He wished Logan could wear one of his, but his shoulders were too broad. Logan said, "Got it!" as he extricated a crumpled tie from a duffel bag.

"Er... Would you like to borrow one of mine?" *Please borrow one of mine.*

Logan laughed. "Sure. Boss lady has expensive taste. In the closet?"

"Yes, there's a rack."

A low whistle sounded. "Is there ever. You have a shit-ton of ties."

"I suppose I do. Here, let me see. Put this on."

The dark green tie had silver highlights, and it complemented Logan's hazel-y eyes. As Logan fiddled with the knot, Seth found himself reaching up and gently knocking Logan's hands away. He fixed the knot and straightened Logan's collar, Logan's breath puffing across Seth's face.

"There," Seth said, his voice hitching. He cleared his throat. "Suits you."

"I'll try not to spill on it. And don't worry—it's going to be fine." Logan squeezed Seth's shoulder, sending warmth spiraling through him. "We can fake it."

The warmth fled, and Seth backed away, nodding. He bumped into the wall. "Yep! I'll go check on the potatoes."

He escaped to the kitchen, all beautiful and gleaming now thanks to Logan, and tried to focus on the meal. Yes, it was time to be professional. This was for his career, and Logan was right.

We can fake it.

Chapter Twelve

"IT IS SUCH a treat to be in a real-live *home.*" Angela tinkled with jewelry as she walked, her sparkly earrings Christmas wreaths this time with diamonds and rubies and emeralds—or really shiny fakes, but Logan figured they were the real deal.

She'd also changed from her high-heeled boots into a pair of red-soled stilettos that tapped the wood floors with her confident strides through Seth's sitting room and into the open kitchen.

Fiddling with his tie, Logan stared at the shoes, trying to re-member what they were called. When he looked up, he realized Angela had noticed. Laughing awkwardly, he said, "Uh, nice shoes. Are they French or something?"

"You have an eye for fashion, huh?" Angela beamed. "The gays often do! They're Loubou-*tin.*"

Dale cleared his throat, looking like he wanted to say some-thing, but after a second, he just smiled without teeth. Since Seth was by the kitchen island looking like a deer in the headlights, apparently already freaking out having the boss lady in his house, Logan needed to say something.

So because he was a moron, he said, "My wife wanted a pair of those. She saw them on TV or something."

Angela's shiny red lips formed an O before she tilted her head sympathetically. "I understand she passed."

He choked down his irritation at the wording and nodded. "Uh, anyway."

Seth asked too loudly, "Can I get you both a drink?"

"I'll have a G and T," Dale said—whatever that was. He'd arrived wearing a dark suit but had left the jacket of it hanging with his coat.

Angela was still fixed on Logan. "I think it's remarkable that you've been able to find happiness again. And with a man! Love is love."

He nodded, not looking at Seth. Not thinking about how much happier he really had been the past week or so. "Thanks." He thought of Veronica again, guilt bubbling up.

Seth toured Angela and Dale around, and Logan was pleased that they complimented the holiday decorations. He had to say that the tree looked damn good, tall and glittery with colorful lights and balls and everything. It made the great room really cozy, especially with the gas fire burning. He'd debated between a star and angel on top, and decided Seth was an angel type of guy.

Once Angela and Dale had their cocktails, complete with fancy stir sticks, Seth put out trays of little appetizers on the great room's coffee table, and they sat there talking about BRK and Angela's kids and cheerleading. Angela was like one of those old toys that you wound up, and Logan was more than happy to nod and smile and let her yammer on. Seth and Dale seemed to be too.

After finishing a beer that Seth had poured into a glass for him, Logan shrugged into his coat to go fire up the grill, more than happy to escape the small talk. Angela had informed them the driver was arriving at nine since it was a "school night," and Logan figured the guy would be right on time. He had to make sure dinner wasn't late, and even though Pop had taught Seth the basics, he'd asked Logan to handle the barbecue.

"So you're the manly meat griller?" Angela asked with a weird wink.

"Yep." Logan had decided to just agree with everything she said.

She took a bite of a cracker with cheese. "Do you find the bisexual men are usually like that?"

At the sliding door, Logan shoved his feet into his boots. "Sure!" He escaped outside and turned on the gas, hoping the snowflakes drifting down wouldn't get any thicker. He probably should have grabbed his gloves, his fingers going numb, the freezing air harsh.

His lungs hitched, and he fought back a flare of panic before exhaling in a plume of frost. He could still breathe. Everything was fine. It was all in his asshole head.

Bisexual.

Logan poured more oil, brushing it onto the grill. It was fine that Angela had assumed it about him. Shouldn't bother him if she thought that. It wasn't him—he'd always been straight. But it was fine.

The oil sizzled on the metal, and he poured more, sloshing too much and getting it over his freezing hand. Snowflakes caught on the oil and melted.

Sure, he and Seth were getting off. And Seth wasn't the first dude Logan had hooked up with. But that didn't make him *bisexual.* That was for pretentious college kids trying to be adventurous or some shit. Didn't apply to him.

He brushed on more oil, drops splattering all over the place. Maybe he was looking forward to being alone with Seth later, but it didn't mean anything. Seth was awesome at sucking cock— which made sense since he was a real gay guy. Logan was only doing him a favor, but there was nothing wrong with enjoying it.

"How's it coming?"

Logan jumped the way Jenna did when Pop came up behind and tickled her. Seth said, "Sorry to sneak up," as he closed the sliding door behind him, his parka unzipped. He rubbed his bare hands, blowing into them. "Should it be smoking like that?"

"Shit," Logan muttered. "Nah, bit too much oil. But it'll burn off." He'd messed up a simple job. *Typical.* "Sorry."

"It's okay. I'm sure you've got it all under control. You manly creature, you."

Logan adjusted the barbecue's shelf, his smile hurting his cheeks. "Right. I guess that's me."

Seth took Logan's shoulder, strong and comforting and weirdly warm, even through the bulk of Logan's jacket. "You okay? I know Angela is a bit…much with all her questions." He smiled, and gritted out, "And I'm pretty sure she's watching us now. It's like she's never seen a same-sex couple in their natural habitat." He dropped his hand and whispered, "Not that we're…"

Logan murmured, "I get it." He could feel Angela's gaze on them as well. Dale was probably bored shitless. Giving Seth a wink and a sly smile, Logan drew him closer, his arm slipping under Seth's parka. He spread his hand on Seth's waist and nuzzled his cheek.

Seth's laugh was a little high-pitched. He whispered, "Should I pretend you're saying something really dirty?"

Logan chuckled as he leaned back. "Always." There were fat snowflakes caught in Seth's dark hair, and Logan automatically brushed them away. Seth glanced up at the dark sky, and when he lowered his head, there was a flake right on his lower lip.

And Logan kissed it away before it could melt, barely a little press of his mouth on Seth's. It was nothing—only a split second—but Logan couldn't believe he'd just done it.

Chest too tight again, he dropped his hand from Seth's back as he turned to the grill. He said too loudly, "Meat."

Seth seemed frozen in place, more snow catching in his hair, the lips that Logan had just kissed parted. Blinking, Seth said, "What?" Then he nodded. "Steak. Yes! I'll get the steak. We need to—yes, right. Dinner! I'll get the meat." He whirled around and almost tripped in his unlaced boots. He waved, and Logan realized Angela was definitely watching them.

She was smiling like a maniac, her hands pressed to her chest and shaking her head. Was she going to cry or some shit? As Seth opened the door, Logan could hear her exclaim, "Sugar, it's so beautiful to see you two together. Like I always say, love is—"

The glass door slid shut, cutting her off. Logan fiddled with the grill, his heart pounding. It was all part of the act. Kissing Seth like that wasn't anything. They had a deal. And Angela was eating it up, so it was working. That promotion was as good as done. Logan breathed a little easier. He wanted Seth to get the promotion. Seth deserved good things.

And in the new year, Logan would unfuck his life. He'd figure out a way to get a job, and he'd take care of Connor. He wasn't sure how, but first things first. He had to concentrate on helping Seth. This was something he could accomplish.

Seth returned with the steaks. "So far, so good. Thanks again for all this. I know it must be…" He motioned with his hand. "Anyway, thank you."

"All good," Logan said, focusing on the grill and the steaks, getting the temp just right. "We've got this." He bumped Seth's shoulder, and Seth leaned back into him.

Once they had dinner on the table, Angela and Dale praised the food, and Logan had to say it was all delicious. He had to stop himself from shoveling it in too fast, and said, "The potatoes are amazing."

"Thanks, hon," Seth said with a smile from the other end of the table, and Logan smiled back. A Christmas carol played softly in the background, sung by one of those big church choirs with pretty voices.

Logan's phone buzzed. "Shit, sorry." He grimaced as he pulled it from his pocket to switch it off. "Uh, sorry for the language too."

Angela laughed, almost a cackle. "*Shit,* sugar, I've heard far worse." She winked. "Might've said worse too. Go ahead and check it. Might be your boy."

"Oh. Right. Yeah. Says he did well on his last exam." Logan snorted. "And that the joke I sent was stupid." He quickly typed back: *Good job. And that joke was hilarious.* Connor's immediate reply was an eye-roll emoji, but for some reason it didn't feel like he really meant it. Logan smiled and slipped the phone back in his pocket.

Angela swallowed a bite of steak. "He's thirteen? Get ready for that attitude for years to come. All our jokes are lame and we're clueless. They've got all the answers."

Seth laughed. "That sounds about right with Connor."

Logan smiled at Angela tentatively. "So it's not just me who doesn't know anything?"

"This is all part of having a teenager, trust me. My girls think they know every darn thing there is to know."

"So how do you stay patient?" Logan asked.

Angela lifted her glass. "Lots of Merlot. But really, it's hard sometimes. You just want to shake them and stop them from making mistakes you can see coming a mile away. I remind myself that it's my job to love them through all their mistakes. Hug them when they need it, and especially when they think they don't. Because they sure need all the hugs and patience we can give them. Even when they're bein' assholes. Especially then."

Logan's throat suddenly tightened thinking of Connor's regular scowl and crossed arms, how he kept himself an angry little island. Logan had to get through to him. He had to make it better. Nodding, he said, "Thank you," to Angela and meant it.

"Connor's a real challenge, but Logan's doing a wonderful job," Seth said. "Parenting isn't easy. I'm so proud of him." He smiled at Logan, and it was probably just bullshit for Angela's sake, but damn if Logan didn't want so badly to make Seth proud for real.

"Sugar, you just have to keep trying. I was probably the same as a teenager, although my daddy had the patience of Job." She smirked. "Momma, not so much." Her face softened. "But with Connor's momma gone, it must be real hard on him. Especially at Christmastime."

Logan nodded, pushing his roasted squash and parsnip around his plate. "First Christmas without her."

Seth cleared his throat in the silence and said, "But we're determined to give him a wonderful holiday. The retreat will be the perfect start."

"It's going to be fabulous," Angela said. "Isn't it, Dale?"

Dale nodded and actually spoke more than a few words. "There'll be sleigh rides and snowman-building contests. Sledding and skating. Crafts and lots of food, and there's a big indoor pool as well. A Santa's coming with toys during lunch. We think the children will be thrilled."

"Wow," Seth said. "How did you plan all this last minute?"

Angela winked at Dale. "Dale's my little miracle worker. Don't ask him how the sausage gets made—just enjoy the taste. Speaking of taste—Seth, you and Logan have hit it out of the park."

"Oh, thank you," Seth said. "I'm so glad you're enjoying it."

Logan noticed Dale's smile seemed a little tight, a twitch in his cheek before it smoothed out again. How the sausage was made probably involved a fuck-ton of work for Dale with no complaining.

Seth added, "Logan's dad helped with the grilling. I admit I'm a newbie."

Angela beamed. "Isn't that one of the best things about family? Passing on traditions and recipes and old-fashioned how-to. Imagine how much would be lost if gays were all cast out? Everyone needs family. I've said it before and I'll say it again."

She lifted her wineglass for a toast, and they all followed suit. Logan could tell Seth's smile was fake, although he wasn't sure how he knew. Probably because Seth's family were shit-bricks, and it must suck even more at Christmas.

Angela said, "Here's to Seth and Logan and your lovely little family. I can't wait to meet Connor this weekend." After she drank, she added, "And Logan, a little birdie tells me you baked your momma's famous chocolate cake for dessert?"

"Oh, yeah. I hope it doesn't suck." He gulped too much of the red wine, which was a little sweet and went down easy. "I mean, if my mom had made it, it definitely wouldn't suck. But I followed the recipe exactly."

He wondered what she would have made of all this with him pretending to be Seth's boyfriend. The only image that came to mind was her lopsided grin and the devilish spark in her blue eyes. She would have played along really well.

"It's going to be delicious," Seth said. "I may or may not have tasted a tiny little bit of the frosting. Mmm." He gave Logan a wink, and then seemed shocked by himself, his cheeks going red.

It was *adorable*, and Logan grinned.

"So, what do you do on the railway?" Angela asked him.

The warm, cozy feeling exploded like a grenade. Logan squeezed his fork, the reminder that he was a total failure slamming him back down to earth. He should have just lied again, but for some fucked-up reason, he found himself saying, "Actually, I had a bad accident last year. I can't do that work anymore. I'm looking for something else, but…" *But I'm a useless sack of shit.*

She gasped, and Dale made sympathetic noises. Angela said, "I'm so sorry to hear that, sugar! Are you all healed up now?"

He didn't feel like he'd ever be, but Logan said, "Mostly."

"Logan's a veteran as well," Seth said. "He served a tour as a Marine. I really think more should be done to support vets in finding employment."

"Thank you for your service," Angela said to Logan very seriously. "And I could not agree more, Seth. Dale, make a note to look into job opportunities for Logan."

Oh, fuck no. "I don't want charity!" He shifted on Seth's new wooden chair, barely stopping himself from shoving back from the table. "I can do honest work for honest pay." His face felt hot, and he wasn't going to be able to breathe in a second.

But Angela didn't seem bothered by his outburst. "I assure you it wouldn't be charity. I expect damn hard work from every one of my employees. Or from anyone I recommend to business partners. I'm making connections in Albany, and you never know what jobs might come up. This is how it works. Nothing wrong with getting a foot in the door. Then it's up to you to walk through it and not get tossed out on your butt. I make no bones about inheriting my company from my daddy on a silver platter. But I've worked my tail off to expand it and make it even more of a success. I will continue to work hard. It ain't charity."

Logan realized he was gripping the edge of the table, and he exhaled, sitting back and dropping his hands. "I... I see what you're saying. I'm sorry."

"Don't be." She gave him a kind smile. "And don't be a dumbass with too much pride either."

Logan had to laugh. "That's good advice."

Seth laughed too. "Words to live by." He added, "Logan's quite handy and has experience as a contractor. He built that wine rack into the kitchen island."

"I was admiring that!" Angela exclaimed, and it didn't seem like bullshit.

"He finished the kitchen as well and helped with all the decorating," Seth said, and Logan supposed it was true.

"What a beautiful home you boys have built together." Angela lifted her glass again. "Here's to your first Christmas here as a family, and many happy and healthy years to come."

Logan drank, not meeting Seth's eyes. Wishing—just for a crazy minute—that it could all be true.

Chapter Thirteen

"WELL." SETH CLOSED the front door and leaned against it. "We did it."

They'd stood shivering in the doorway waving as Angela's driver had backed down the long drive and out onto the snowy street. Logan rubbed his hands, enjoying the warmth and the relief. He loosened his tie and pulled it off over his head.

Seth laughed softly. "Been dying to do that, huh?"

"Yep."

"Thank you. I know it couldn't have been easy tonight. And that cake really was delicious. I just might have another piece to celebrate our success." He pushed off the door, and Logan followed into the kitchen, pleased that Seth liked the cake so much. With a smile, he watched Seth pour a glass of milk and then lift the carton in question.

Logan said, "A celebratory glass of milk? Not scotch?"

Seth wrinkled his nose. "Milk goes way better with cake. You want?"

"Sure. Cake too. Glad you like it."

"Mmm." Seth cut off two big wedges and ran his finger along the dull part of the knife, licking up the frosting. "So creamy. Sweet, but not cloyingly so. It really is an excellent cake." His tongue darted out to grab a stray bit of chocolate from the corner of his mouth. "Logan?"

"Uh-huh." He realized he'd been staring as Seth licked his

finger clean. "Um, thanks."

They stood by the island, eating cake and sipping milk, a Christmas song filling the air with a gentle melody about snow and mistletoe. Logan didn't want to think about it too much yet, but he couldn't help saying, "That was nice of her—about jobs. Might not lead to anything, but…"

"But it just might! I think we have every reason to be optimistic. If anyone can get something done, it's Angela Barker."

Logan watched Seth lick milk from his upper lip. *We.*

Seth frowned at him. "I know you're afraid to hope, but I really think you can look on the bright side here."

"Yeah," Logan said. "We'll see. But thanks." He ate a big forkful of cake and gulped his milk, wiping his mouth with the back of his hand. "Should turn off the lights outside."

His socks were quiet on the hardwood as he returned to the front door and flipped the switch. In the sitting room, he leaned over the golden little tree in the window, switching it off. He could see the car tracks down the driveway being filled in already with fresh snow, the mailbox in the distance with a fluffy lid of flakes.

"Oh, that reminds me," he said, walking back into the kitchen. He opened one of the drawers on the island where he'd stuffed the mail. "When I came in earlier, I noticed the mailbox was overflowing. Probably mostly fliers and crap, but here you go." He dropped the pile on top of the island with a *thwap* and took his last bite of cake.

Seth was frozen with his fork halfway to his mouth, staring at the mail with a strange expression. Logan watched, swallowing his cake with a gulp. He realized it was *fear* on Seth's face, clear in the shallow breaths he was taking and the way his gaze was locked on the mail as if Logan had dropped a big hairy spider there.

"What is it?" Logan asked. He eyed the fliers and letters, trying to see the problem and wanting to fix it. He didn't like seeing

Seth like this. Not at all.

Seth tried to smile, ripping his gaze away and blinking at Logan. "Hmm? Oh, nothing." His voice was high and tight.

"Bullshit. Tell me what's wrong." Logan looked at the mail again. He still had no fucking clue what it could be. "Are you expecting bad news or something?" Most mail these days was junk anyway. Did anyone still write bad news that wasn't delivered online or over the phone first?

Seth closed his eyes for a moment and exhaled heavily. He shook his head and pushed away his plate before reaching for the pile. Part of Logan wanted to move closer and touch him—maybe squeeze his shoulder or something—but he stayed put. Best not to crowd him.

"It's silly," Seth mumbled. He stood straighter and determinedly leafed through the flyers, a few envelopes sprinkled throughout. His hand froze, and his bitter smile sent a shiver of dread down Logan's spine. Seth lifted the square, red envelope.

Logan could see the delivery address had been crossed out, and *return to sender* had been scrawled across the front in huge letters. It looked like a Christmas card or something. He couldn't make out who it had been sent to.

Seth answered the unasked questions. "My parents." He flicked through the mail, drawing out two more identical red envelopes. He held them up. "My brother and sister." Dropping the three cards on the island, he added, "I don't bother trying with my grandparents or my aunts and uncles and cousins anymore. But every year I still send these three. Hoping…"

"Fuck. I'm sorry." He should have just left the mail alone. *Stupid.*

Shaking his head, Seth attempted a laugh. "It's the definition of insanity, right? Doing the same thing and expecting a different outcome?" He ran a fingertip over one of the red envelopes. "The cards have always come back on the same day, as if my family has marched to the mailbox together to return my pathetic little olive branch in tandem disgust." His gaze ran over the pile of mail. "Not sure which day it was this year. I haven't checked the mail for two weeks. Last year…"

After a few dull thuds of his heart, Logan quietly asked, "What?"

Seth picked up one of the envelopes, staring at it. "They came back on the twenty-third. I'd almost convinced myself it would be the year my family kept the cards. It would be the year that maybe we could find a way to have some peace between us. Even if they'd just kept the cards, at least I'd be able to believe they don't wish I was dead." He dropped the envelope back to the counter with a soft slap.

"I'm sure they don't wish that." They were fucking assholes if they did. Even more than Logan had thought.

Seth laughed, and Logan hadn't realized how much he liked the usual gentle baritone of Seth's laughter until he heard this ragged bark that set his teeth on edge.

"Oh, they definitely wish I was dead."

"I'm sure—"

"No, *I'm* sure. Here, I'll prove it." He pivoted and strode to the stairs, thumping up them without waiting to see if Logan was following. Which he was, his pulse racing. This was all so wrong, and maybe he could still fix it.

In his bedroom, Seth flicked on the overhead light and marched to his dresser to open one of the top drawers. He pulled out a square leather box, dark brown and expensive looking. Logan waited in the doorway, wary. He should have kept his damn mouth shut and just left Seth alone.

Seth was practically shaking with tension or maybe fury. Logan wasn't sure. He only knew he hated it.

Whipping around, Seth held out a folded piece of paper. "Here." It sounded like he'd swallowed sand.

Logan didn't have a choice but to come inside and take the paper, which was bent a bit at the edges and seemed to have been read many times. When Logan unfolded it, the crease down the middle was deep. It was typed, which he wasn't expecting for some reason. He blinked at the words that ran in a narrow column down the page.

MARSTON, SETH
October 2, 1981—December 24, 2006

Seth Michael Marston passed away suddenly. Seth was raised in the loving arms of Christ by his parents, Mary and Stephen; grandparents Doris and John, and Sarah (reunited with Christ 1998) and Michael; alongside his loving siblings Christine (David) and Paul (Bethany).

Seth tragically chose the abominable path of the devil, sinning without shame And choosing the wicked homosexual lifestyle. He broke the hearts of his family, who weep for his loss and take solace in Jesus Christ our Lord.

There will be no service. Memorial donations gratefully accepted at The Church of Christ's Grace in Macon, Georgia.

Logan stared at the words, first with confusion, then disbelief. Then the horror slammed into him, his throat painfully tight. He had to swallow twice before he whispered, "They wrote your obituary?" The paper shook in his hand. "Jesus fucking Christ."

Seth laughed harshly. "Indeed. They published it too, in the local paper. I'd have never thought they'd want a soul to know the truth, but this way, I guess they were in control. They probably knew rumors would run rampant, and this way, they were the righteous victims. And I think they expected me to be so humiliated and ashamed that I'd repent my sins and beg forgiveness. But I didn't. Couldn't."

"Shouldn't!" Logan stared down at the hateful words dressed up in religion. "This isn't what Christians should do. Jesus wouldn't do this."

Seth smiled thinly, taking the paper back. "I don't think so either. There are many accepting churches out there, but mine wasn't one of them, to put it mildly. *Everyone* knew—all my old friends, extended family. No one ever talked to me again."

He folded the piece of paper back into the box and closed it away in the drawer. "I think maybe they still expect me to beg forgiveness and repent. Crawl back to them."

Logan wondered why Seth hung onto that piece of paper at all, let alone in a fancy box like it was something precious, but he kept his trap shut. "That's fucked up."

Tense from head to foot, Seth nodded. "I'd been living in Atlanta with Brandon for three years after college. In a studio apartment. I mean, I thought they might piece it together when they came to visit one summer, but apparently not. So I decided that year to tell them all when I came home for Christmas."

He paced a few steps, his fingers digging into his arms where they were crossed. "I told them I was gay and in love with Brandon. That I knew I'd never be able to change, no matter how much I prayed. That… That I didn't *want* to change. That this was the way God made me."

Seth jerked his shoulders in a shrug. "The next morning, my dad and my brother dragged me out of the house. Threw my suitcase after me. Then my mom gave me that piece of paper with the obituary they'd written. My sister and grandparents were there too. They watched from the porch. Everyone was crying and praying. They turned their backs on me and locked the door. That was it."

"Unless you changed your mind?"

"Right. Obviously that's not going to happen." He paced again, shaking his head. "And every year I send them Christmas cards and tell them about my life as if I think it will make any bit of difference. They're bigots. They're not going to change. But I keep hoping anyway. I'm an idiot. Pathetic."

"Hey, stop that." Logan stepped closer. "You are not. Don't be mad at yourself. Be mad at them. They're the assholes." *Fucking cowardly pieces of shit who don't deserve you.*

Seth stared at him, and as the silence stretched out, Logan was afraid he'd gone too far even though he'd choked down most of what he'd wanted to say. Then Seth lunged toward him, clutching at Logan painfully. Trying to breathe, Logan didn't know what to do, standing there with his arms at his sides and Seth attached to him.

He'd never *hugged* another guy—at least not like this. There was no back-slapping, and it went on and on, Seth hanging on like his life depended on it, his arms in a vise around Logan, face pressed against Logan's neck, wet and warm.

Shit, he was *trembling,* and Logan wrapped his arms around him. "Shhh," he murmured, since that's what he would have done with Veronica or one of his old girlfriends. Not that Seth was a woman, but he was upset and clearly needed comforting.

They were practically the same height, and Seth was stooped with his face in Logan's neck, still clinging to him. Logan didn't think he was crying, just hanging on real tight. Instead of slapping Seth's back, Logan stroked it tentatively and said, "It's okay."

"I'm sorry," Seth mumbled, his breath hot on Logan's neck. "Thank you."

"Don't worry about it." They were pressed together, and Logan had to admit it felt good. Warm and solid. They stood there, and it probably should have been really awkward or weird, but...it wasn't.

"I need..." Shaking, Seth kissed Logan's throat, his hands tightening and sliding down to his hips. Sparks flared as Seth rocked their bodies together. "I want..." He exhaled sharply. "Shit."

It was the strongest curse word Logan had heard from Seth,

and it sparked something in Logan. He couldn't fix Seth's terrible family, but this? This he could do.

He smoothed a palm down over Seth's ass. "You want me to fuck you?"

Logan could hear and feel the sigh of relief that washed through Seth. "Yes. Please. Please do that."

Seth didn't seem able to say the words, but Logan had the feeling he liked hearing them. That it was what he needed. "That's what you want? My cock inside you?"

Almost whimpering, Seth nodded against Logan's neck, rutting his hips forward.

"How do you want it? Want it rough?"

Groaning, Seth broke away. "Yes." He opened a drawer beside the bed and took out a bottle of lube and an unopened box of condoms, dropping them on the neatly made bed. He jerked off his clothes with shaking hands and left everything in a pile on the carpet.

Logan was still kicking off his slacks as Seth yanked down the duvet and crawled onto his hands and knees on the sheets. Struggling with his skivvies, Logan realized he was hard as rock, lust roaring in his veins. His breath was short, but his chest didn't hurt.

He squirted lube all over the place, managing to get some on his fingers before kneeling behind Seth. He stared at Seth's firm, amazing ass and grabbed hold.

"Fuck, you're hot." The words were out before Logan could stop them. A distant voice hissed that there was something different about this than the other times he'd gotten off with guys.

He and Seth were completely naked together, and although he'd fucked guys before, it had never been on a bed. He'd never said any of them were hot.

"Please," Seth begged, his head hanging low, body shaking.

"You want my cock? Want me inside you?" Logan's words

made his own balls tingle and tighten. With guys there usually hadn't been any talking aside from maybe a "thanks, man," once they'd gotten each other off.

But the way Seth moaned and let go, the words turning him on and giving him what he needed—what he couldn't say—that made Logan crazy horny.

"I'm going to fuck you so hard, baby." *Baby? Where the hell did that come from?*

Seth cried out, pushing back against Logan's hands and widening his knees. "Please."

When Logan had fucked guys before, the men had usually prepared themselves, or they'd just used spit. Hadn't always been a lot of options in Iraq or the bunkhouse. But now he was tentative, pushing the tip of one finger inside Seth, not wanting to hurt him. *Never* wanting to hurt him.

Seth squeezed around Logan's finger, and holy shit, he imagined what that would be like on his dick. *Amazing.* He pushed in farther, making sure his finger was dripping with lube. "You like that?"

"*Yes.*"

Logan was dying to bury himself in Seth, but he went slowly, eventually easing in another finger as Seth trembled. Then another.

"Please just do it. I need it." Seth moaned as Logan inched in. "Need you."

Logan tried to ignore the way those two words made his chest feel light and his dick even harder. "You want it now?" He could not screw this up. He asked again, "Rough?"

"Yes, yes—like that."

After unrolling a condom and slathering on lube, he spread Seth's ass and inched into him. It had to hurt, although Seth didn't complain, only grunting and groaning along. Logan tried to soothe him with gentle touches over his head and shoulders.

Whimpering, Seth bore down, muttering encouragement Logan couldn't quite make out—more noises than actual words. Then he clearly pleaded, "Harder."

"Fuck, you're so tight. So good." Logan thrust fully into him, making it rough but glad of the lube. He didn't want to risk really hurting Seth. "You like that? You wanna come on my dick?"

"Yes," Seth panted. Sweat beaded between his shoulder blades already, and Logan bent to lick his salty skin. Seth said something else he didn't hear, and Logan lifted his head. There had been an urgency in his tone.

"What did you say?" Was he going too hard? He slowed his thrusts, running his hand over Seth's head, fingers sliding through that thick hair. "You okay?"

"Yes!" It came out almost like a sob. "I said I'm a queer. It's what I am." He pushed back against Logan, turning to look over his shoulder with wild, defiant eyes, his cheeks red and hair sticking up. "It's what I am. I'm not sorry. I'll never be sorry. Even if they never talk to me again, I can't be sorry."

"That's right, baby. Fuck them. They're the ones going to hell, not you. You're perfect like this." To punctuate his words, Logan pulled almost all the way out and slammed back in, their skin slapping together.

Sweat dampened Logan's forehead, and he breathed hard, his chest tight, but not in the danger zone. Even if it was, he wouldn't stop. He was going to give this to Seth. He was going to fuck him and make him come harder than that piece of shit Brandon ever did.

Holding Seth's hip with one hand and reaching below him with the other, Logan stroked Seth's straining cock. He was leaking, and Logan smeared the liquid with his thumb, muttering, "You got more of this for me? You want to come? You like being fucked like a dog? Baby, you take my dick like you were born for it."

"Yes!" Seth gasped, his whole body jerking. "There. That's—"

Logan angled to get more pressure on just the right place, and Seth unloaded with a shout, shaking and clamping down. Logan jerked him through it, Seth's cock throbbing and twitching. He loved the feel of it in his hand, so alive and strong but vulnerable at the same time. It made his balls ache. He shoved his face onto the side of Seth's neck, lips open and pressing, feeling a wild pulse.

Seth's arms gave out, and he collapsed to his elbows, breathing loudly, his ass still up in the air, beautiful and tight. Logan took hold of his hips, still going hard, chasing his own orgasm.

"Fuck, you feel so good," he muttered. "Going to come hard. Seth…" Holding Seth's hips, he unleashed, wishing there was no condom so he could come inside him until it was dripping out.

"Fuck," he groaned, the pleasure so pure and deep he twitched, Seth squeezing around him perfectly, more intense than any sex Logan could remember.

He breathed heavily, but his chest felt loose and easy. He ran his hand down Seth's spine, kissing the top knobs before easing out as gently as he could, both of them moaning. After he got rid of the condom in the bathroom, Logan wet a washcloth and returned to the bedroom.

Seth was sprawled on his belly, boneless. Normally, Logan would have tossed the cloth and said thanks before leaving. He stood at the foot of the bed, the overhead light bright on Seth's flushed skin, his long limbs lean and strong.

Even though he'd gotten off, the urge to touch remained. Logan's fingers itched. He was crawling beside Seth on the bed before he could talk himself out of it. Gently, he wiped Seth's asshole, then urged him to roll over. He cleaned what he could with the cloth, and Seth's eyes flickered open, a sweet smile tugging up his lips.

"Thank you." He trailed his fingertips over Logan's cheek, and Logan turned his face into that touch, letting himself be drawn down.

Then Seth kissed him.

Their mouths met before Logan could process it. The stubble on his chin rasped against the hint of Seth's, but their lips were soft, pressing together like they fit just right.

Like they'd kissed a thousand times, like it made perfect sense to breathe the same air, tasting sweetness that was more than chocolate cake. This was nothing like the peck by the barbecue with Angela watching.

Their mouths opened, but as their tongues met, Seth jerked and shoved Logan away, scrambling back. "I'm sorry!"

Blinking, Logan tried to focus. His pulse raced, and he wanted nothing more than to roll on top of Seth and taste him completely. Kiss him until they couldn't even breathe, rub their naked bodies together and pull the covers over their heads.

But Seth was staring at him like he was seeing a car accident, and Logan's chest seized up tight, a dagger of pain returning.

Seth ran a hand through his hair, clutching at it. "I'm so sorry. That wasn't part of the deal."

Right. The deal.

"No." But… Fuck, Logan had never kissed another man before tonight, and now he wanted to kiss Seth more than anything. *Needed* it. Maybe it was gay, or bi, or whatever the fuck, and right then, he didn't care. He didn't care that Seth was a guy. All he cared about was kissing him again.

Before Logan could even try to find the right words to say any of that, Seth was up and tugging on his clothes even though it was time for bed. His fingers shook as he did up the buttons on his wrinkly shirt and said, "You've helped me so much, but I think we should keep things strictly business from now on. We just need to pretend through the retreat. A few more days. No more of…this." He shook his head, gaze on his trembling hands. "I really do apologize. Clearly this was a mistake."

Logan had to say something, but the tightness in his chest increased, cramping pain radiating outward. Seth thought it was a mistake? Hell, he was probably right. Logan's mind spun like an old record player with the needle stuck.

"I hope you'll accept my apology." Seth stood stiffly by the bed. His shirt was even tucked into his slacks.

Logan was still naked, and he needed to reassure Seth that he wasn't angry. That he...he was... *Glad*. But that made no sense. He'd always been straight—he'd never *liked* a guy. It was just supposed to be casual, but now Seth was so shaken, and Logan wanted to make it right.

"It's okay," he said, because he was useless.

Seth nodded tightly and walked out of the room. *His* room, and now Logan was sitting there naked on Seth's bed trying to figure out what the fuck was happening.

He had no clue where to begin, so he stumbled up and yanked on his clothes. Seth was downstairs. "Baby, It's Cold Outside" echoed up from the speakers they'd left on before it was switched off.

In the silence, Logan tiptoed into the bathroom adjoining the guest room, closing the door. He leaned over the sink and splashed his face with cold water.

This was all supposed to be fake.

While he leaned against the counter, taking deep breaths and trying to understand, he heard a door close. Peeking into the hall, he saw it was to Seth's bedroom. Should he go knock? What the fuck was he going to say? Maybe he should give Seth time alone. Seth seemed to want it, so he shouldn't push.

He crept downstairs. The great room was lit by the Christmas tree—soft blue, green, red, yellow, and pink lights that reflected on the tall glass windows. Logan pressed his forehead to the sliding door, watching the snow drift down and inhaling the fresh pine in the air.

Everything was silent. Peaceful. But in his head, he heard Seth on a loop.

"That wasn't part of the deal."

"Clearly this was a mistake."

It was after midnight when Logan accepted that Seth wasn't coming back down. Should he go up? They should probably talk about it, as much as Logan dreaded the thought. Would Seth be glad if Logan went up and got into bed with him?

He huddled under the blanket on the couch, closing his eyes and trying not to think about kissing Seth, wishing he knew the right thing to do for once in his damn life.

Chapter Fourteen

S ETH TOLD HIMSELF again that he needed to stop talking.

He'd been nattering on during the entire drive to Connor's school, Logan mumbling agreements every so often as Seth sermonized about global warming, the abysmal state of world politics, and a recent scandal involving one of the judges on a baking show. As if Logan cared in the least about baking shows!

Although he had made that cake.

As Seth exited the freeway, his belly flip-flopped, a sweet spike of warmth filling him. That adorably lopsided, delicious cake that had been Mrs. Derwood's favorite. That Logan had baked it for him filled Seth with such gratitude and affection, which was insane since it had all been for show.

It was only part of the deal. Nothing more.

It felt like more, though. Just like last night had. Seth's bottom was sore, but in a pleasing way that gave him a forbidden thrill every time he shifted on the heated seat. It had been so long since he'd experienced sex like that. He'd been abstinent for over a year, but even before that with Brandon, the fire had petered out long before.

With Logan, he'd felt consumed. Mastered and taken care of, *known* in a way that made him want to weep with pleasure and gratitude. Logan had called him *baby,* and Seth had felt loved, even though he knew it was impossible. But he could fool himself in the moment.

Then he'd gone and ruined it all by kissing Logan. Logan had been kind not to shove him away. Kinder than Seth deserved after breaching their agreement. Logan had said no kissing, and Seth had to remember that none of this was real.

The whole idea had been to engage in casual sex to get him over his hang-ups. Not to saddle Logan with his family issues and have a sort of breakdown. Seth should have been ashamed of how he'd unloaded all of it on Logan and then begged for sex.

Yet when he remembered the hot growl of Logan's voice in his ear, it thrilled him.

"Baby, you take my dick like you were born for it."

"It's coming up on the right," Logan said in the here and now.

"Okay!" Seth replied far too loudly, his voice pitched up and cheeks feverish. He made the turn onto the curving drive to Rencliffe, the bare trees standing sentinel, fresh snow clinging to their branches, the sun peeking out from clouds.

The drive had been plowed and salted, and when they reached the gothic buildings, the closest lot was full of vehicles and parents picking up their sons.

Seth parked and climbed out of his SUV, walking in silence next to Logan, their boots crunching in the snow. Seth stopped short. "Oh, wait. Would you rather I stayed in the car?"

"Nah. Connor will probably be nicer if you're here." Logan's hands were in the pockets of his leather jacket as they walked on, and Seth thought he should really be wearing a hat.

Before he could stop himself, he asked, "You brought winter gear, right?" *I sound like a nag.* "Just don't want you to be cold this weekend," he added lamely.

"Yep," Logan said. He lifted his chin. "There he is."

Connor waited under a vast stone arch, his arms crossed and shoulders hunched. He wore a bright red ski jacket that was too short in the sleeves with a striped scarf that looked handmade. A stuffed duffel bag sat by his boots. As Seth waved, a pretty woman appeared, saying something to Connor.

She called, "Good afternoon, Mr. Derwood! Happy holidays."

"Hey," Logan replied. "Thanks. Um, you too, Ms. Patel."

She smiled at Seth, clearly waiting for an introduction. There was an awkward silence for several moments until she said, "Hello, Mr...?"

"Oh! This is my—" Logan cut off, floundering. "Seth."

"Seth Marston." Seth stuck out his hand. "I'm a friend of Logan's."

"Mira Patel." Her hand was soft, but the grip strong. To Logan she said, "Could we have a quick word?"

Logan gave Connor a sharp glance, frowning, then nodded and followed her inside the school. Seth smiled at Connor. "You must be glad school's finished." Then he remembered Connor had been threatened with expulsion. "For the holidays, I mean. I'm sure your exams went very well."

Connor shrugged, his arms still crossed. He needed a hat too, his ears red from the cold. Seth adjusted his own beanie, wondering if it would be weird to offer it.

"Did everything go well?" Seth asked tentatively. *Please don't let this boy be expelled.* Seth could imagine how devastating it would be. And what on earth would Logan do? Seth had promised he and Connor could stay until the new year but had been too swept up in—well, in Logan and the amendment to their deal—to really think about what exactly Logan would do come January. Or even how he and Logan and Connor would spend Christmas.

He felt queasy at the uncertainty of it all and prayed Angela would come through with some kind of job connection. And in the meantime, he had to focus on getting through the weekend retreat.

Connor rolled his eyes. "Yeah. I got an A on every exam."

"That's wonderful! Congratulations. Logan will be so proud. I'm proud too, although I know I just met you."

The surly veneer cracked a bit, and Connor smiled slightly. "Thanks."

"We'll have to celebrate this weekend in Lake Placid. What's your favorite treat?"

"Dunno."

"Well, we'll think of something. Thank you again for agreeing to this. I can't tell you how much I appreciate it."

"Sure." Connor shrugged, but gave Seth a bigger smile.

So perhaps he liked feeling useful. Who didn't? Seth vowed to find ways to encourage it. As Logan returned, Seth exclaimed, "Connor tells me he aced his exams!"

Logan grinned—a real smile that lit up his worn face. "I know. He can come back in the new year. Good job." He clapped a hand on Connor's shoulder and said exactly what Seth was silently urging him to. "I'm real proud."

"I told you I could do it," Connor said, but without heat.

"You did," Logan agreed.

It was possibly the friendliest exchange between them that Seth had witnessed. He hoped it boded well for the weekend. "We'd better get going. The bus leaves the office at two."

Angela had allowed everyone attending the retreat—which was nearly all staff except those who had unchangeable travel plans—to leave work at noon to collect their families and luggage. As they drove into Albany, Seth peppered Connor with questions about his schoolwork, and Connor seemed willing enough to answer, warming up to the topic of computer science.

"You still like robots?" Logan asked.

"Yeah," Connor answered warily. In the rear-view mirror, Seth could see his gaze narrow and shoulders hunch. "It's not just kid stuff, you know."

Logan opened his mouth as if to bite back a response, then snapped his jaw shut. When he spoke, his voice was even. "Yeah, I remember that amazing robot you built."

"That wasn't from scratch or anything. I had instructions from the internet." Still, Connor seemed pleased.

"You got it to wake up your mom one morning, and she screamed so loud I dropped the coffee pot."

The tentative peace was shattered, Connor visibly retreating into his shell. "Surprised you were even there that morning."

Logan opened and closed his mouth again, pressing his lips together. This time, he stared out the window and said nothing more, probably thinking silence was better than an argument.

Seth flipped on the radio, and "I Saw Mommy Kissing Santa Claus" filled the SUV. Cringing, he jabbed the button on the wheel with his thumb, changing the station until he found one playing regular music. It was "Highway to Hell" by AC/DC, a song that had been forbidden to him growing up.

He sincerely hoped they were on a highway to a far better destination this weekend.

AT THE GREAT Adirondack Lodge, Santa had come early. The man himself greeted the BRK Sync buses, passing out Lindt balls with a hearty "Ho-ho-ho!" In the early dusk, Lake Placid was a winter wonderland, its quaint, shop-lined main street aglow with holiday lights and wreaths, the snowbanks still fluffy and white and not splashed with mud and grime yet.

The lodge sat at the foot of the main street on the icy shores of Mirror Lake, the actual Lake Placid apparently nearby, but outside of its namesake town. The Olympic center was across the street, and Logan motioned to it.

"Pop would love to come here. The US beat Russia in hockey at the 1980 Olympics. One of his favorite moments in life."

"Oh!" Seth said. "Yes, I've heard of that. We should take a look tomorrow. What do you say, Connor?"

Through a mouthful of chocolate, Connor mumbled, "What-ever."

He'd sat in the back with some other kids on the two-and-a-half-hour bus trip. Logan had offered Seth the window seat, and he'd stared out at the snowy landscape, trying not to think about the occasional touch of Logan's thigh against his, and how their shoulders brushed, the leather of Logan's jacket smelling rich and enticing. Logan had leaned back and closed his eyes, although he hadn't seemed to actually sleep.

Not that Seth had been sneaking glances at him or anything.

They trooped into the lodge, where a hotel staff member went through the list and handed out room keys. It took a while, and Seth was aware of the curious glances from his colleagues as he stood next to Logan. Connor had his face buried in his phone again, and Jenna was busy bouncing crying baby Noah while Jun wrangled Ian.

A shiver zipped down Seth's spine as Logan leaned in, his strong hand finding the back of Seth's neck above the collar of his unzipped parka. Logan whispered right in Seth's ear, his lips almost brushing.

"People are real curious, huh?"

Seth nodded, not trusting himself to speak without squeaking.

Logan chuckled. "Pretend I'm saying something funny."

Of course, in Seth's mind he'd heard the echo from that day they'd run into Brandon, and he laughed slightly hysterically as he tried very hard not to think of Logan saying anything dirty. Now more people were looking at them, and Seth caught Angela's eye across the crowd. A grin splitting her face, she waved and winked.

It's all an act. All part of the deal. Now play along!

He did, he and Logan laughing at nothing and acting like they were engrossed in some secret conversation. Connor shot them the odd frown and eye roll, but Seth supposed that played right into their ruse, as most teenagers were embarrassed by their parents.

For a moment, as the hotel woman called out, "Marston family!" Seth let himself imagine what it would be like if Logan really was his fiancé and Connor their son. He had to catch his breath at the swift punch of longing and cursed himself for being a fool.

Their room was on the third floor of the lodge, and they rode the elevator in silence, Connor's thumbs still flying over his phone screen. Once inside the room, he suddenly came to life.

"I get my own bed!" Connor launched himself at the bed by the window, throwing his duffel on top and then sprawling on the mattress. A little saying from childhood came to mind, and Seth half-expected Connor to add, "*No take-backs!*"

Standing in the entryway, there was a bar fridge, microwave, and coffee machine to the right, then a bathroom, and beyond that, the beds were to the right in the room, a long dresser with TV atop to the left.

Seth and Logan eyed the near bed uneasily. It was a queen, at least, but still. Seth shifted and cleared his throat. "I'm sure we can get them to bring up a cot."

Connor looked over his shoulder where he was sprawled on his belly, screwing up his face. "Wouldn't that seem weird if you guys are supposed to be getting married?"

"Well…" Seth was going to say no one had to know, but considering his luck, Angela herself would be in the hallway as the cot was wheeled in. "Good point."

Connor glared at Logan. "What, you think it's catching or something? I've slept in the same bed with Jayden. It's no big deal." He rolled his eyes. "I'm sure Seth isn't going to try anything."

Logan unzipped his leather jacket and opened the mirrored closet in the narrow entryway. "Obviously. It's fine," he said gruffly. "Of course we can sleep there."

It was interesting to Seth that after using the other F-word when they first met, now Connor was implying Logan was the one with homophobic issues. Seth gave the kid the benefit of the doubt that he'd been thoughtless that first night, lashing out blindly. He just wished Connor would stop attacking Logan. He wanted to scold him, but would that be overstepping? Surely it would.

"Better get changed for dinner. It starts early."

Logan and Connor stared at him. Logan glanced down at his jeans and Henley. "Changed into what?" Alarm creased his handsome face. "Was I supposed to bring something fancy?"

"No, no. I'm sure the dress code is casual." He was wearing his usual dress shirt and tie with slacks. "I'll probably be the one overdressed. I should change."

He bustled around, unzipping his small suitcase and hanging up the clothes he'd brought. Logan sat on the bed and flipped on the TV, going through the channels while Connor was back into a game. Seth had brought a forest-green cashmere sweater that he thought would look good over dark jeans. Yes, that would do nicely.

He almost took the clothes into the bathroom to change but decided that would seem ridiculously prudish and likely strange to Connor. Not that Connor had so much as blinked, entirely engrossed in his game and paying Seth no mind. After taking off his tie, Seth began unbuttoning his shirt.

Logan was watching.

Butterflies flapped in Seth's stomach. It was from the corner of his eye, but yes, Logan was *definitely* watching. Seth pretended he hadn't noticed, trying not to fumble with the buttons. He sucked in and peeled off his shirt, puffing out his chest a bit. Hoping he didn't look like a fool.

Standing in his boxers, Seth hung up his shirt, looping the tie over the neck of the hanger. He could feel the heat of Logan's gaze on his bare skin like a caress. Without meaning to, he thought of the night before, being on his hands and knees for Logan, being filled by him.

He remembered the rough caresses of Logan's hands on his flanks, his hips, his thighs. His…

Cock.

Oh good lord, Seth was getting hard. He bit the inside of his cheek, still facing into the closet. Thinking of his old cat Agatha did the trick, the ache of missing her flushing out the burst of lust. He finished dressing quickly and escaped into the bathroom to splash cold water on his cheeks.

Dinner was a buffet of comfort food—definitely not fancy. Which was actually a relief, and Seth dug into the mac and cheese with gusto. He, Logan, and Connor sat with Jenna, Jun, and the boys, and Jenna kept up most of the dinner conversation.

Matt and Becky were at the next table, and Matt gave Seth a thumbs-up and mouthed, *"Caper, caper, caper!"* Seth promptly spilled gravy on his sweater and excused himself to the bathroom to blot at it with a paper towel.

When he re-entered the corridor off the hotel restaurant, Jenna was there bouncing a fussy Noah. She groaned. "I just want to eat all the carbs and go to sleep. Kids are exhausting."

Seth whispered, "Don't complain about motherhood too loudly with Angela around. Actually, that's not fair. She had good advice for Logan last night."

Jenna stepped closer. "How did it go? You barely answered my nosy texts." Since Friday was her temporary day off from the office, this was the first chance Seth had had to speak with her privately.

He whispered, "Really well, I think? Seemed to, at least. She was all smiles."

"And Logan performed?"

It was an innocent question, but Seth's brain immediately supplied the memory of Logan *performing* extremely admirably in Seth's bed. The echo of grunts and moans and slapping skin filled his head, and he swore his butt twinged. "Uh-huh!"

Jenna groaned. "Oh no. What did he do? What aren't you telling me?"

"Nothing!"

"You're a terrible liar, Seth."

He rubbed his face. "I know! That's why I should never have agreed to any of this!" But the thought of not getting to know Logan the past week or two was a gut-punch, shocking in its sudden severity. Seth exhaled shakily. "But I'm glad I did. Logan's been terrific. Really."

Jenna raised her eyebrows. "Yeah? Okay, good. You guys seem to be faking it really well. I almost believe all the longing glances between you two."

It truly shouldn't have hurt—but, oh, it did. Seth told himself it was ridiculous, yet his heart ached anyway, and he could only manage a strangled half-smile. He hadn't even realized he and Logan had been glancing at each other during dinner, and especially not with longing.

Part of him wanted to insist that it wasn't fake at all, that the sex he and Logan were having *had* to mean something. Of course he couldn't say that to Jenna since she had no idea her brother was anything but straight. At least not that Seth was aware, and there was definitely no good way to casually probe to see if she had an inkling.

Jenna touched his arm. "It seems like you guys have become friends? I'm so happy about that. You're both wonderful people, you know that?"

His smile this time was genuine. "So are you." He hugged her briefly, careful not to squish Noah, who had settled. "And yes, I'd like to think we've become friends through this deal. Logan's so hard on himself. He and Connor both."

"Hopefully this weekend will be good for them. And you." She glanced around. "We'd better get back. Angela's probably going to make a 'BRK is one big happy family' speech any minute."

Sure enough, Angela did just that. Seth clapped in the right places and nodded and smiled as he tried not to look at Logan. It was a relief when they could escape back to their room after a performance by a local choir.

"Santa Claus is Coming to Town" was stuck on a loop in Seth's head as he changed into his flannel pajamas. He was aware of Logan's gaze and looked up as he finished the buttons on his top. Logan stood by the side of the bed in his black boxer briefs.

And nothing else.

"Oh," Seth murmured without meaning to. Connor was in the bathroom, so it was just the two of them for the moment. Seth looked down at his plaid PJs. He felt stupidly prim and over-dressed.

"I should probably…" Logan unzipped his duffel and pulled out a plain gray T-shirt. He pulled it on, covering his sexy, hairy chest. "Ugly, I know."

Seth jolted, realizing he was staring, and that Logan meant the scars. "No. Not at all. That wasn't…"

Connor re-emerged, wearing an oversized T-shirt and boxers. He yawned widely as he shuffled by, pimple ointment dotted over his face. He huddled under the covers and didn't bother saying goodnight.

In their bed, Logan crawled over to the left side, which was against the wall separating the bedroom area from the bathroom. Seth stretched out on the edge of the mattress, in danger of rolling off and cracking his head on the side table. He reached up and snapped out the light, murmuring, "'Night."

"Sleep well," Logan whispered from behind him. Only inches separated them, and Seth imagined he could feel the heat of Logan's muscular body.

He could still feel it an hour later, sleep stubbornly elusive. As gently as possible, Seth rolled over, facing Logan. In the white glow of the digital clock on the side table, he could see the lines and shadows of Logan's face, and the rise and fall of his shoulder as he breathed softly.

When Logan opened his eyes, Seth had to bite back a gasp, his heart skipping. They stared at each other, and Seth's body responded, his breath shallow, blood flooding south as he got shamefully hard. He reminded himself Connor was in the other bed and that even if he wasn't, this connection with Logan wasn't real.

They stared at each other, only inches apart. It would be so easy to lean a bit closer, to kiss Logan again and breathe him in, just for a minute before they slept. He could feel the heat from Logan's body and wanted to climb into his skin…

Seth rolled away, squeezing his eyes shut as he curled on the very edge of the bed. He swore he could sense Logan watching him, and willed himself to think of something else—anything else!—so he could sleep and this night would be mercifully over.

Chapter Fifteen

A THUD AND muffled curse woke him, and Logan was instantly alert. He sat up, blinking at Connor near the foot of the bed in the gloom, hopping on one foot.

The alarm clock on the table between the beds gave off enough light to see. It was just past seven. Beside Logan, Seth curled away from him under the comforter. Logan could see enough of his slack face to know he was still asleep.

Connor was in his swimming trunks and a concert T-shirt from a rapper Logan could remember him blasting from his room when he and Veronica had argued.

Connor whispered, "I'm going swimming with some other kids." He nodded to a folded piece of paper on the bureau by the TV and said defensively, "I left a note," as if he was expecting Logan to get mad. His chin was jutted out. Always ready for a fight.

Logan smiled and nodded. "Have fun," he whispered. "You've got your card?" He tugged at the neck of his tee, not used to waking up wearing anything but his skivvies.

Connor eyed him warily but held up the plastic key card. With his other hand, he waved awkwardly, then tiptoed into the foyer. In the mirrored closet, Logan could just make him out sliding on his flip-flops and easing open the door. The yellow light from the hallway flared bright, and then was gone as Connor closed the door silently.

Logan sat listening to Seth's steady breathing and cute little murmurs as he shifted onto his back. His lips were parted, and he drew up one arm over his head. What would he do if Logan woke him with a kiss? Would he like it? Or would he get all uptight?

Would I like it?

He'd never thought of another guy as "cute" before. There was something about Seth that gave him all these weirdly…soft thoughts. Not that Seth wasn't manly. He was. Even in his grandpa button-up plaid pajamas. Logan wanted to unbutton him and rub his hands over Seth's hairy chest, roll on top of him and kiss him awake, feel the scratch of his stubble…

The wall was to Logan's left, and he carefully crawled to the bottom of the bed so he could go piss and stop thinking about stupid shit that would ruin everything. Sure, Seth had kissed him after they fucked, but then he'd seemed horrified. Maybe it was because he didn't want to kiss a loser like Logan.

After switching off the bathroom light, he opened the door and crept back out—and almost banged right into Seth. Seth jumped back, and they both laughed. Weak daylight was glowing around the edges of the curtains now, and Logan could see Seth's spiky bedhead.

And his morning wood tenting those plaid PJs.

Seth's eyes went wide like someone in a dumb movie, and it was so damn *cute*. He was probably about to make some stammering apology, and Logan couldn't remember the last time he'd simply *liked* someone so much. He laughed again, and Seth blinked at him, a hopeful little smile tugging on his lips.

Logan wanted to take care of him. He wanted to say a bunch of stuff, but he had no clue where to start—he'd always been crappy at words. But fuck, he burned with it, and he was moving, pushing Seth against the striped wallpaper. Dropping to kneel at his feet.

Seth gasped, his hands clutching at Logan's shoulders.

Being on his knees, looking up at Seth—at his chest rising and falling quickly under the buttoned-up PJ top, his tongue licking his lips—made Logan horny as hell. He rubbed his cheek against Seth's hard dick through the soft flannel.

It had been years since Logan had returned the favor of a blow job. It had been rushed, and yeah, he'd liked it. He'd enjoyed the power of it, even though he was the one kneeling.

But with Seth, it was so much more. Seeing buttoned-up Seth come undone made him excited and stupidly proud. It made him want to do anything—everything—to give Seth what he needed.

Maybe it was what Logan needed too.

He tore down Seth's pajama bottoms and swallowed him as deep as he could, loving how Seth bucked his hips and gasped again. Logan choked and pulled back, keeping the head in his mouth as he breathed through his nose. He sucked hard, tonguing the slit. He probably wasn't very good at it, but Seth didn't seem to mind.

In the hush of the room, their grunts and groans seemed really loud, and it made Logan's dick rock hard in his boxer briefs. He loved the way Seth was holding his head now, his fingers flexing, digging in one second, and then rubbing the next.

It was probably weird, but he loved how Seth was still buttoned in his pajama top while underneath he was bare, getting his dick sucked. He tasted musky and male, and Logan licked desperately, taking him too deep again, spit dribbling out of his mouth as he choked.

His head spun, whole body tensing as he sucked like his life depended on it. Making Seth come felt like the most important thing in the world.

Logan fondled Seth's balls, and that did it. He shot his load with a rumble of moans and whimpers, palming Logan's head. Logan swallowed as much as he could, not caring about the bitter taste, sucking him through it until Seth's trembles turned to jerks and it was obviously too much.

Logan released Seth's dick, and his mouth felt messy, his lips swollen. He pushed to his feet, and Seth reached for him, rubbing Logan's shaft through the cotton of his skivvies.

Seth was wrecked, his mouth open and face bright red in the pale light. Logan moaned, thrusting against Seth's palm, leaning against the wall, his hands on either side of Seth's face.

He'd only have to lean in a few more inches and they'd be kissing.

And *fuck*, Logan wanted to kiss him for real. Wanted to shove his tongue into Seth's mouth and kiss him until they couldn't breathe. Would Seth freak out if he did? He groaned as Seth pulled him out of his shorts, and—

The slide of a key card in the door echoed as loud as a gunshot, and Logan stumbled back. He and Seth stared at each other in horror, everything feeling like slow motion as the door handle went down.

Logan dove back into the bathroom, kicking the door shut and crossing the tile floor so Connor couldn't hear him panting. The T-shirt was too tight on his neck, and he tugged it off.

He heard Connor say, "I forgot my goggles. We're diving for pennies."

"Cool!" Seth said, his voice really loud and fake, but farther away. He was probably back in bed with the covers up.

"Um, yeah," Connor said, and Logan could picture his face creased in his *"you're a weirdo"* expression that was usually reserved for Logan. After a few moments, Connor said, "Later," and all was silent again.

Slumping against the towel rack, his head against the tile wall, Logan exhaled. He was still achingly hard, and he automatically reached down to stroke himself, shoving his underwear to his hips to free himself.

The bathroom door opened, and Seth appeared, wearing his

pajama bottoms again, the top still buttoned neatly. They stared at each other, and Seth opened his mouth to say something, probably an apology or whatever, but then snapped his jaw shut, gaze flicking from Logan's face to his dick in his hand. Even though he'd just come—the taste of it lingering in Logan's mouth—Seth's eyes went dark, and he licked his lips.

Spreading his legs, Logan jerked himself. The scars on his chest surely looked too ugly in the bright light, but Seth didn't seem to mind judging by the way he stared.

As he worked himself, Logan watched the hitch in Seth's breathing. It made him so hot the way Seth looked at him like that.

He wanted to talk dirty and get Seth hard again—because he bet he could, without even touching him. But words were all twisted up in Logan's head, and he could only grunt, the slap of his hand on his dick echoing.

Maybe none of this had been part of the casual sex addition to their deal, because as Logan came, he arched his back, his toes curling on the tile, displaying himself for Seth in a way that was very, very gay—or bisexual or whatever the hell people wanted to call it. Sure as shit, none of it felt *casual*.

Breathing hard, he slumped against the towels. They stared at each other.

Finally, Seth said too loudly, "You want first shower? We should get ready for breakfast. Time to put on a show, right?"

Logan had been panting so much his voice was raspy. "Yeah. Don't worry, we'll fool everyone." He tried not to be embarrassed about the show *he'd* just put on.

Under the hot blast of the shower, he wondered who the fuck they were actually fooling.

"No. No way." Seth crossed his arms, staring down the hill. "We're going to kill ourselves."

Logan laughed. "That's half the fun of sledding." He'd climbed up without his chest hurting, and even after the awkwardness of breakfast—trying to make boring small talk and not think about getting Seth's dick in his mouth again ASAP—he was excited to sled. It had been years.

They stood at the top of a big wide hill outside of town. There were lots of people sledding, locals and BRK staff climbing up on the sides of the slope and then blasting down the middle. It was a mostly cloudy morning, the snow thick around their boots.

They wore wool hats and thick gloves, and Logan had looped a red scarf around his neck over his leather jacket. Jenna had knit it for him, and she and Jun, Ian, and Connor were all decked out in more of her creations in all sorts of bright colors. Noah was being cared for with some other kids who were too young or didn't want to sled.

She nudged Seth playfully. "Come on, where's your Christmas spirit?"

"Since when is Christmas spirit about hurtling down an embankment and breaking our necks?"

"The spirit of Christmas is giving," Jenna said. "And you'll be giving us a huge amount of amusement to watch you sled down this hill, Southern boy. Preferably screaming all the way."

Connor laughed. "Savage." Jenna gave him a wink, and he grinned.

"You're supposed to be my friend!" Seth huffed. "What if there's an avalanche?"

They all laughed, and Jun said, "We're at the top of the hill, and this isn't a mountain." He pointed in the distance at the jagged gray peaks, snow covering the Adirondacks. "Those are mountains."

"Feels like a mountain," Seth muttered, holding up his round plastic sled. "And we're supposed to ride down on *this?*" He rubbed at the back of his neck.

Logan's smile faded as he realized Seth was actually nervous. More than that—he was afraid. "Hey, it's okay." He stepped closer and squeezed Seth's shoulder through his puffy parka. "You can walk down."

Seth groaned. "I'll look like such a wimp in front of everyone. And we're so…high. It didn't look this high from down there."

Shit, was he afraid of heights? Logan said, "I'll walk down with you."

"But you want to sled." Seth sighed. "I'm being a big baby."

"You're not." He rubbed Seth's back up and down, up and down, and Seth leaned closer to him. "We'll walk down together."

"Or sled down together," Connor said, looking at them with his forehead creased like it did when he was trying to figure out some hard math thing. "Logan knows what he's doing. Right?"

It was possibly the first time Logan had ever heard Connor say anything like that. He tried not to be too happy since the kid would probably be telling him he was an idiot in a minute. Logan was still rubbing Seth's back, and he thumped it now.

"I do. Jenna and I grew up with these flying saucers."

"Flying?" Seth shuddered. "No flying, please." He kicked at the plastic. "There's no way two of us can fit."

"Oh, you totally can," Jun said. "My brothers and I used to get four of us stacked on one."

Logan positioned his sled near the edge and flopped down, getting his butt wedged in at the back. He spread his legs. "Come on."

For a second, Seth just stood there, his face going beet red, breath clouding out in little bursts. Then he mumbled something under his breath, looking up as if saying a prayer.

Gingerly, he squatted and got into place, and Logan yanked him back so he was snug between his thighs. Logan had worn his long johns with waterproof pants over top, and the material squeaked as Seth squirmed into place.

The pom-pom of Seth's beanie was in Logan's face, so he hooked his chin over Seth's shoulder. "Lift your arms over my legs." Now Logan could wrap his arms tightly around Seth's middle. "Lean back into me and keep your feet up. That's really important, okay? Feet up."

Jenna bent with her hands on Logan's shoulders, and Logan said, "No spin."

"Okay, okay," she grumbled. "Don't worry, Seth. Logan'll take care of you. We're coming right behind!"

Logan tightened his arms, pressing his cheek against Seth's, the skin freshly shaved and warm with Seth's blush even in the cold air. "Feet up!"

Then they were sailing down the hill, the wind whipping, Seth's feet jutting up perfectly straight in the air like a solider obeying orders. The world fell away and everything was the two of them locked together, soaring so fast.

Adrenaline spiked, and Logan made a "Wooooo!" noise as they flew down. Seth dug his gloved hands into Logan's thighs, making little gasping, squeaking noises that were so fucking cute Logan could hardly take it.

They slowed at the bottom, sliding along the flat ground toward a tall snowbank that had been built up to make sure no one went into the thick pine trees beyond. They skidded to a stop, breathing hard, the shouts of Jenna and Jun and the kids echoing as they neared the bottom as well.

"See?" Logan said, squeezing Seth with his arms. "All in one piece."

Panting, Seth leaned back against him, his hands gripping Logan's knees. "That was... Goodness. Wow."

The others skidded near, Connor spinning and tumbling out with a laugh. More people were coming down all the time, and they needed to get out of the impact zone, but Logan wished he could just stay all snug with Seth for a while longer.

Jenna held up her hand for Jun, who tugged her to her feet. She grinned at Seth. "Well?"

"It was absolutely terrifying." He turned his head to look at Logan, his blue eyes lit up. "Let's do it again."

They all laughed, climbing up the hill and zooming back down several more times. Seth didn't want to go down alone, and Logan was happy to share his sled.

When they were tired out, it was time for hot chocolate and donut holes set up near their bus on folding tables. Dale really had thought of everything. Logan wanted to tell him he'd done a real good job, but wondered if it would seem like kissing ass since Dale was supposed to be finding work for him.

As he poured hot chocolate into a paper cup from a big plastic container, thumbing down the spout, excitement skittered through him. Would Dale actually be able to get him a job? Obviously Logan had to do an interview and prove himself at whatever it was, but if he could actually get money coming in, it would be such a relief.

He popped a sugary donut in his mouth. It would be more than a relief to have a job again. It would feel so damn good to not be useless anymore. He could get a place and stop freeloading off Seth, and save money for Connor and be worth something again.

Although he had to admit that the thought of moving out of Seth's house wasn't as happy as it should have been. Probably because even with a job, he'd never be able to afford something as nice as Seth's place. And with Connor at school, he'd be alone most of the time. But that was fine. Maybe he and Seth could still hang out. Maybe...

Shoving another donut in his mouth, Logan told himself to stop being such a moron. He might not even get the job even if Dale could help him, and that was a big if anyway. And he and

Seth… It was stupid to think about. They had a deal, and that was it. It was temporary.

"I thought you were just faking it with Seth?"

Stomach dropping, Logan gripped his paper cup a little harder and took a gulp, burning the roof of his mouth. "I am."

Holding his own cup, Connor was watching him suspiciously, his eyebrows almost meeting. "Really?"

"Of course." Logan forced a laugh.

"Because you look at him the way you looked at my mom, back at the beginning. When I thought maybe things wouldn't suck."

Logan tried to figure out what Connor was saying. It didn't make any sense. "When you thought… But you hated me from day one."

Connor looked down at the donuts, shrugging. "You weren't so bad, I guess." He picked out a chocolate one and ate it.

"I…" Logan had no clue what to say. "Oh. Thanks?"

Connor huffed, eating another donut and mumbling, "Anyway, Seth seems into you. But you're just pretending. Right?"

"Don't talk with your mouth full." Logan glanced at where Seth stood off with Jenna and Jun, drinking their hot chocolate and laughing about something.

Connor rolled his eyes, licking crumbs from his lips. He looked up at Logan, apparently waiting for an answer.

Heart thumping, Logan chugged his hot chocolate, wiping his mouth after. "Guess we're both good actors." Sure, he and Seth were screwing, and they were into it, but that's all it was. That was the deal—casual.

"Guess so."

Logan tried to think of something to say. "You looking forward to lunch with Santa?"

There was that familiar scowl. "I'm not some little kid."

"I know. But it's Christmas. My mom used to say we all get to be kids at Christmas." He hadn't thought of that in years, and for a moment, he missed her so damn much.

This was Connor's first Christmas without Veronica, and he wanted to tell him that it would be okay, and that it would get easier over time. Or at least it would be different. It would still hurt like hell sometimes, but not all the time.

But he didn't say any of that because Connor was already gone with a handful of donut holes, off to hang with some kids around his age. Shit, Logan really needed to get presents for Connor to open. Jenna would surely be getting some for Christmas Eve at her place, but they'd be at Seth's on Christmas morning.

And shit, he needed to get Seth a present too. More than one. With no money, he'd have to borrow from Jenna and Jun, and what if he didn't get a job after all? He was suddenly afraid he'd puke up hot chocolate all over the snow.

"Okay?" Seth asked as he walked up. "Don't tell me all that sledding has made you green around the gills and not me." He squeezed the back of Logan's neck over his scarf, and Logan concentrated on deep breaths, a stab of pain in his chest flaring and then easing.

He almost said he was fine and shrugged Seth off but let Seth ground him until he could give him a real smile.

Chapter Sixteen

"WELL, IF THAT isn't the moony face of a man in love!"

Seth jolted as Angela's twangy voice rang out from alarmingly close by. He realized he'd been too busy staring at Logan rolling the base for a snowman. And at Logan's firm backside as he bent over to perform said task, his short leather jacket riding up, jeans clinging to his butt and thighs.

Squirming, he tried to laugh. "Guilty as charged." He raised his gloved hands. *Ha, ha, ha. Hilarious.*

The pom-pom on Angela's fuchsia beanie wobbled as she joined him at the railing of the large stone patio where Seth stood watching the snowpeople being created in all shapes and sizes on the hotel's back lawn.

Ice covered the empty lake beyond, but Seth assumed it was still too thin to skate on since they were skating later at the Olympic center. Sunlight beamed down, glaring off the snow, the sky having cleared to a perfect blue, the air absolutely frigid.

"It really is festive here," Seth said, nodding at the decorations strung between light poles.

"It is. I love the holidays. I think no matter what your background, you should be able to enjoy Santa and Rudolph if you want. It's a treat to get all the snow, even if it's colder than a penguin's pecker."

Seth laugh-choked, coughing hard. "That's one way to put it."

Angela laughed. "I speak it like it is." She eyed Connor in the distance where he stood with crossed arms, watching Logan roll the massive snowball, little Ian joining in beside Logan. Connor was saying something.

Angela snorted softly. "Probably telling his daddy he's doin' it all wrong."

Seth laughed ruefully. "Most likely. Connor can be a handful." He was acting like he hadn't just met the boy and guilt nagged at the deception. Still, he had gotten to know Connor a bit and would be spending the holidays with him. He rolled his eyes internally. *As if that makes this lie less of a whopper.*

"Logan was his stepfather, right? His biological father's not in the picture?"

"Not much at all. He lives in Florida and is hardly in touch."

She shook her head, pom-pom waving. "That'll really do a number on a kid, especially after losing his momma."

"Yes." Seth thought of his own parents. He'd been grown, but it had undoubtedly done a number on him to be rejected and ignored.

"It'll be good for him once you and Logan are married. Give him stability. I realized I plumb forgot to ask about the wedding details when I came for dinner. When's the big day?"

Uh-oh. Was she angling for an invitation? Seth stammered, "Um, well—you see—uh, I—" He snapped his jaw shut, feeling his ears go hot under his wool hat.

Well, *now* he had Angela's attention. Her sculpted eyebrows met. "Is there a problem?"

"No! It's just… I need to find a church."

"Oh! Surely there are some open-minded houses of worship up here? New York State doesn't get much bluer. Heck, you might be pleasantly surprised by some of the churches in Texas. Not all of 'em, I grant you, but I suppose that's true everywhere." She sighed heavily. "I'll just never understand why we can't love our fellow man the way the good lord made 'em."

"I'm sure my parents would have some thoughts on the matter." Seth cringed as soon as he said it. "Anyway, I'm sure we'll find something soon." He fiddled with the fringe on his plaid scarf. "So we're going skating later, right? Can't wait!"

But Angela didn't answer, instead watching him with clear sadness, her mouth pulled down. "Your parents aren't supportive of you and Logan?"

"No. Well, they don't know Logan exists. It's been years since I had any contact with them. One Christmas, I told them I was gay and had a boyfriend, and they showed me the door." He shrugged, going for careless and surely failing.

"Oh, sugar." Angela squeezed her gloved hand over his where Seth gripped the balcony railing, the icy stone cold even through insulated leather. "That just breaks my heart. I hope you know you're not alone."

Seth nodded, a lump in his throat almost choking him. Come January, he *would* be alone again. Sure, he'd see Jenna at work, but he'd come back to his finally finished house every night and there'd be no one else. Not even Agatha.

He missed her with a sharp pang. He'd felt too guilty about "replacing" her, but he really had to get another cat. And after saying it aloud, he realized he *did* want to find a church.

He found himself saying, "After my family turned their backs on me, I stopped going to church. I should have found a place in Atlanta, but I told myself I had a private relationship with God. And I do, but it would be nice to find a congregation where I could be myself." He shook his head. "I'm sorry. I don't know why I'm telling you all this."

Angela winked, her long lashes heavy with mascara. "Because I'm a nosy broad."

"I'm not sure whether I should agree or not."

She laughed throatily. "I get plenty of people blowin' smoke up my backside. Now tell me about your ideas for your department. No pressure, even though I'm putting you on the spot."

"Oh! Right. No problem." For a horrifying moment, his mind was completely blank. But he watched Logan rolling another snowball with the kids and caught his breath. "I'd start with tweaking our initial approach."

They stood by the railing discussing Seth's ideas, Angela asking sharp, intelligent questions before she was called away by Dale. Before she left, she winked at Seth and told him HR would be in touch in the new year about his promotion, and he almost did a cartwheel right there on the snow-covered stone.

When they all trooped over to the Olympic center for skating, he couldn't wipe the grin off his face. Logan leaned in, his breath gusting warm over Seth's cheek. "What's got you so happy?"

Everything. The promotion. You.

"Pretty sure I got the job," Seth whispered.

Logan grinned, and his craggy face was beautiful in a way Seth had never imagined when they'd met. It seemed impossible it had been less than two weeks ago. As Seth lined up for skates, he checked his math.

Yes, eleven days. But that was another reason why whatever this was between them was only casual. They barely knew each other, and they'd made a mutually beneficial arrangement.

A successful one! Seth had apparently snagged the job, Logan might get a job out of it himself, and he'd had a place to stay while helping Seth get over his hang-ups about having sex without being in love. Seth was surprised to not feel particularly guilty about the hookups.

That's because they aren't just hookups.

His traitorous mind immediately supplied images of Logan on his knees that morning with his mouth full of... Well, of Seth. He shivered with pleasure just to think of it—and what had followed. Seeing Logan touching himself had been shockingly electric. The silence between them during the act had made it feel even more secret and special.

Although now Seth could imagine what Logan would say about it.

"You liked seeing me jack myself, hmm? Bet it makes your cock hard to think about watching me. Want to watch me again? Or do you want to get down on your hands and knees so I can fuck you and come—"

"Size?"

For an awful moment at the head of the line, Seth could only think about penises. Then he managed, "Eleven and a half," and the bored girl behind the counter thunked a pair of skates on top. Seth added, "And a ten and a half, and a six. Please."

The skate pairs were tied together by their laces, and he carried them hooked over his fingers to where Logan and Connor waited on one of the benches lining a white wall.

He was very glad his parka went to mid-thigh, and he forced his mind back to the present. Skating. With countless children present. No sex going on, casual or otherwise. He jammed his socked feet inside the skates and focused on lacing them.

"You need to tie those tighter," Logan said a minute later. He and Connor had their skates on already and were standing waiting. Logan knelt at Seth's feet to retie the laces, which was so sweet, yet spectacularly unhelpful in regards to Seth's partial erection.

The black skates were big and clunky and apparently made for hockey, although Seth wasn't sure how exactly they differed from figure skates. As he stood, he clutched Logan's arm. "Whoa. I don't know if I can walk in these, let alone go out on the ice."

"You've never skated before?" Connor asked.

"I'm from a small town in Georgia. I think there might have been a rink, but I never went there." Too busy with countless church activities.

Connor said, "It's just like walking, but you know. Faster or something."

"Right. No problem." Seth squared his shoulders and walked assuredly. There. He could do this.

His confidence evaporated the moment the thin blades touched the ice. He clung to the boards beside the entryway, where others waited behind him to get out on the rink. His knees shook, and he took a baby step forward, trying just to get out of the way.

He immediately overbalanced and landed on his knees and bare hands. He'd stupidly left his gloves with his shoes since it was chilly in the arena, but quite comfortable compared to outside.

"Whoa!" Logan was there, his hands also bare as they grabbed around Seth's waist and lifted him to his feet. Seth leaned too far back against Logan, his skates making little slicing motions. But Logan was a rock behind him, chuckling softly as he pushed Seth to the safety of the boards and the railing around the rink.

"You're like Bambi," Connor laughed, his eyes crinkling.

"This was a mistake. I can't do it." Seth gripped the wide top of the boards. His whole bottom half felt out of control, although at least his inappropriate erection had vanished.

Other people whizzed by, everyone circling the rink counter-clockwise. On the loudspeaker, someone sang about rocking around the Christmas tree. "You guys go ahead. I'll wait on the bench. Just help me get there."

Logan laughed too, taking Seth's hand after prying it loose from the boards. "Come on. One lap around."

Connor nudged Seth's other side. "We won't let you fall. If you do, you'll take us all down." He nudged Seth again. "Let go."

Saying a quick prayer not to break any bones, Seth released the boards and took a tiny step. Then another. Connor's small hand took his right, and with Logan on the left, Seth tentatively walked across the ice. He had their hands in a death grip, but they didn't complain.

The skates hurt his feet, and his thighs burned from the strain of keeping steady, but he was making progress. Jenna, Jun, and Ian whizzed by with a wave, Ian between them.

"I'm like the five-year-old," Seth grumbled. "Except Ian's much better at this."

"It's okay," Connor said. "We all have to learn stuff sometimes. Try pushing off some." He demonstrated, gliding on his right foot and pulling Seth along. "It's actually easier to go faster."

Seth tried to mimic the smooth stride, almost pitching over onto his face. They patiently pulled him upright, and he tried again. And again. And again. As the Madonna cover of "Santa Baby" played, Seth was practically skating.

"I'm doing it!" he exclaimed, and then pitched forward, overcorrected back, and smacked onto the ice on his butt, yanking down Logan and Connor too with gravity's help.

The three of them sat on their rear ends laughing, families skating by around them. "I'm sorry!" Seth shook his head. "Oh my lord, how am I going to get up?"

Connor was already on his feet, and Logan rolled to his knees and pushed upright. He said to Connor, "Dunno. Maybe we should leave him here."

Connor blinked as if surprised to be in on a joke with Logan. He shrugged with forced nonchalance. "I guess. We can pick him up again after a few laps. He'll still be here."

It made Seth's heart so glad to see them bonding, even if he was the butt—no pun intended—of the joke. He harrumphed theatrically. "Go on. Abandon me here to my fate."

Matt and Becky skated by, and Matt howled with laughter, pointing at Seth, Becky rolling her eyes.

"Nah," Connor said, and they took Seth's hands again, pulling him to his feet and keeping him steady. "It's more fun with you."

Hand-in-hand, the three of them set off again, and Seth managed half a lap before slipping and pulling them down in a heap of laughter.

DINNER WAS OVER, but it seemed Angela had one more activity planned. Or least Dale did, as he instructed volunteers in setting up two rows of chairs in the middle of the open space in the dining room as hotel staff cleaned up the buffet tables.

Beside Seth, Logan eyed the game setup suspiciously. "What's this, musical chairs or some shit?" He took another sip of red wine.

The room still smelled like roast beef and gravy, and Seth was stuffed. Connor had gone off with the other kids for a screening of *Home Alone* in a conference room, Angela promising them bean bags and candy and a popcorn machine.

"Logan!" Dale trotted over with a smile. "Been meaning to tell you that I sent your resume to Bob Ricci. He owns a statewide contracting company that's done some work for Angela in New York City. He's going to call you later this week after Christmas. He's eager to do more work for Angela, so unless you royally screw up the interview—and I mean *royally*—he'll have a job for you in January. He said he's starting a new office renovation in downtown Albany. It's perfect timing."

"Wow." Logan shot to his feet and stuck out his hand, pumping Dale's vigorously. "Thank you."

Seth grinned, barely resisting the urge to hug Dale for making this happen. Logan was beaming with joy, and Seth's heart clenched to see it.

Logan said, "I promise I won't take a dump on his desk at the interview."

Dale tipped his head back and laughed. "You remind me of Angela. You both say exactly what's on your mind. And remember, even though she got your foot in the door, you're the one who's going to walk through." He nodded to Seth. "Merry Christmas. It's been a pleasure meeting you both."

Seth stood to shake his hand, and he and Logan shared a grin when Dale left. Seth squeezed the back of Logan's neck, wanting to pull him close and kiss him, wanting to whirl him around in celebration even though Logan was probably too heavy for him to lift.

At the next table, Jenna bounced in her chair, she and Jun giving them a thumbs-up since they'd clearly overheard Dale's news. Ian had gone to the movie, and Noah was with a hotel sitter for a few hours. Jenna had been sniffing her glass of wine loudly, apparently savoring every sip.

Logan sat back down heavily, smiling in a daze. "I might have a job."

Seth squeezed his wrist, almost taking Logan's hand. "You'll nail the interview. I know it."

Of course, if Logan got a job, there'd be no reason for him not to move out in January like they'd agreed. That splashed cold water on his happiness, although Seth really did want Logan to get the job. He wanted Logan to get…everything. Absolutely everything.

He wanted to share everything with him.

We made a deal. Casual. No feelings. Stop making it into more.

Folding his hands in his lap, Seth tuned back in as Angela stood by the rows of chairs holding a long branch with red ribbon tied on it and a sprig of berries dangling off the end as if it was a fishing rod.

Waving the branch, she said, "Y'all know what this is, right? We're going to play a fun little game for the grown-ups. It's like musical chairs, but whoever's left standing gives their sweetie a kiss under the mistletoe. Don't worry, BRK is a family company and this is strictly PG. Maybe PG-13 if someone's feelin' saucy. Maestro?"

"Have a Holly Jolly Christmas" filled the air, and couples rose to circle the chairs, some clearly reluctant, others skipping along.

Seth laughed as Matt dragged Becky up, but his smile froze as
Angela pointed right at him.

She shouted, "Come on now! We need some diversity up
here!"

Jenna and Jun tugged on Logan and Seth's arms. Jun muttered, "If we have to do this, you have to do this."

They made their way to the double row of back-to-back
chairs. Seth gave Logan an apologetic smile, and Logan shrugged,
smiling back as they joined the group circling the chairs.

The silence was sudden, followed by shouts and laughter as
they scrambled for the chairs. Logan and Seth ended up a few
apart, but both safely seated. Left standing, Miriam from IT
pulled up a man Seth presumed was her husband and kissed him
soundly as Angela held the mistletoe over their heads with her
branch.

Everyone applauded, and the song started again, Burl Ives's
kind voice telling them to have a cup of cheer and kiss under the
mistletoe. The game went on, Seth's heart racing as they circled,
waiting for the shock of silence to dive for a chair.

When he missed, it was Matt who grabbed it before him, his
shaggy hair flying. He whispered, "Caper!" with a big grin. Logan
stood and joined Seth, and Angela whipped the mistletoe over
their heads with eagerness she didn't try to hide.

"Now let's hear it for our lovebirds!" she exclaimed.

Everyone clapped and hooted, and Seth felt like he was blushing all the way down to his feet in his leather shoes. Fidgeting,
Logan's smile was too tight.

Seth laughed nervously and stepped closer, giving Logan a
lightning-quick peck on the lips. More clapping, and Seth waved
and laughed, ready to escape back to the table.

Then Logan was blocking his way.

Then Logan was taking Seth's face in his work-rough hands.

Then Logan was kissing him.

Then Logan was kissing him for *real*.

Not a peck. A genuine kiss—sweet and soft and sure all at the same time, pressing their lips together like there was nothing else in the whole world but the two of them. Nothing casual about it.

Head spinning, Seth clutched at Logan's waist. His heart was thunder in his ears as the kiss went on, their mouths fused and his knees actually going weak. Logan smelled like musky earth and pine, and Seth melted into him.

When he gasped for air, he realized the thunder wasn't only his heart—it was stomping feet and palms on tables, a swell of applause and support from everyone in the room. Seth's skin prickled with the heat of so many eyes on him, but Logan's warm gaze was the only one that mattered.

What's happening?

Seth couldn't look at anyone as he and Logan returned to their table. His heart pounded, his body thrumming with adrenaline and stubborn joy. And when Logan tugged his wrist, Seth followed him out of the dining room and into the elevator. Neither of them spoke, staring straight ahead.

The kiss had felt so real. But Logan was probably regretting it, fleeing to their room because he was done with this charade.

The hotel room was dimly lit and silent as the door shut behind Seth with a *click*. His heart thumped as Logan turned to regard him seriously in the narrow entryway. Logan opened and closed his mouth, frowning.

Then he kissed Seth again, this time his tongue thrusting past Seth's lips as he grabbed him. Seth could only moan, meeting Logan's tongue, wet and insistent, tasting of gravy and wine and perfection.

"Want you," Logan muttered against Seth's mouth, their kisses broken only by little gulps of air.

"Oh!" He hummed with desire, and as Logan dropped to his knees like he had that morning, Seth thumped back against the door, already hard, and—

He gasped and jerked up ramrod straight, his fingers digging into Logan's shoulder, staring in horrified disbelief at Connor, who'd appeared by the end of the far bed. They'd left the bedside lamp on before going down for dinner, and it partly illuminated Connor now, half of his face creased and confused, the rest in shadow.

"What are you doing?" Connor asked.

Logan shot to his feet. "What are you doing here?" he asked too sharply. "I thought you were watching the movie."

Jaw tight, Connor said, "Seen it a million times. We decided to go swimming again. I came up to get changed." He still wore his jeans, long-sleeved T-shirt, and sneakers. He asked again, his voice harder, "What are you doing?"

"Nothing!" they answered in unison, as if they were the kids and Connor the adult.

Fists clenching, his shirt sleeves too short, Connor marched toward them, glaring daggers at Logan. "You're lying to him like you did to my mom, aren't you? Aren't you!" His face creased. "I should have known. I thought maybe I was wrong, but I'm not."

Logan seemed stunned into silence. Seth said, "Connor, everything's okay. I know this must be confusing, but—"

"He's playing you!" Connor shouted. "Can't you see that? He's telling you everything you want to hear. He's a liar. Don't believe what he says. He doesn't really like you!" He sneered at Logan. "You're not even gay, but you'll do anything to get what you want. You don't really care about him. Or me. I bet you'll take all Seth's money."

"I didn't marry your mother for her money," Logan said quietly. Seth prayed his restraint would continue.

"Yeah, the joke was on you because she didn't have any," Connor spat. "But you needed a place to live, so you made her think you loved her. It was all a lie, wasn't it?"

"No!" Logan's chest rose and fell with a sharp breath. "I really did love her, and she loved me. We got caught up in a stupid dream of helping each other, and we moved way too fast. We never should have got married. But I didn't lie when I said our vows. It was way too good to be true, but I wanted to believe we could be happy."

Logan looked to Seth, his eyes beseeching. "And maybe I'm being a dumb fuck all over again, but I really like you."

Seth took his hand, squeezing Logan's rough fingers. "I like you too."

Red-faced, Connor gritted his teeth. "But I asked you this morning, and you told me it was all fake!"

"I didn't know what to say," Logan said. "It *is* supposed to be fake. That was the deal."

"And now you're suddenly gay?"

"No." Logan rubbed his face with his free hand, the other clinging to Seth's. "I honestly don't know what I am. Apparently more bisexual than I thought. What I know for sure is that I like Seth more than I've liked anyone in a long, long time."

Connor looked between them, his pimply face creased. He glared at Logan. "But you'll ruin everything! Seth's awesome, and you'll fuck him over!"

Seth kept his voice even. "Okay, let's sit down and take some deep breaths, and we can talk about this."

"He's using you! What's there to talk about? Fuck this." Connor shoved past them with surprising strength, wriggling behind Seth and out the door before they could stop him.

"Shit!" Logan was hot on his heels, and Seth followed, jogging down the carpeted hall past wooden doors.

Connor went for the stairs, and they chased him down and right outside through a fire exit, Seth grimacing as his leather shoes filled with freezing snow that came up to his shins.

"Connor, get back here!" Logan shouted. But Connor ignored

him, running hard through the snow at the back of the hotel, weaving around snowmen and out onto the lake. Seth's lungs burned in the freezing air, but he didn't slow.

"Get back here! Get off that ice!" Logan yelled. "Now!"

"Fuck you!" Connor slid forward, his arms outstretched as if he was on skates instead of sneakers.

Seth tried for a gentler approach. "Connor, please! Just come back and we can talk."

Connor ignored him, continuing away from the shore. Seth wasn't even sure exactly where the land ended and the lake begun.

Logan bellowed, "I swear to God, if you don't get back here now—"

Connor spun around. "What? What are you going to do? I hate you! I'm going to live with my dad in Florida."

"Have you spoken with him?" Seth asked loudly after coming to a stop. None of them had jackets on, and it was too cold to be outside. Connor faced them from about thirty feet away.

After sputtering, Connor insisted, "He's busy! He has a hard job!" In the moonlight, tears glittered on his cheeks even at a distance, a stifled sob making him gasp. "But he's my dad, so he has to love me. He *has* to."

Logan exhaled sharply in a white plume. In a calmer tone, he called, "Come inside and we'll talk about this."

He glanced behind, and Seth realized they'd garnered some attention, faces at windows and a few people in open doors, shivering and watching them.

Logan called again, "Please come back."

Connor sneered. "Afraid of what people will think? They should know the truth. You used my mom and now you're using him too." A fresh surge of rage seemed to erupt. "Go to hell!" He turned and slip-stepped across the ice, the wind having blown away the snow from some patches.

There was no dramatic *craaaack!* or warning sign. One second

Connor was there and the next he disappeared into a pit of darkness with only a splash that echoed in the night.

Seth's heart slammed against his ribs, and he sprinted onto the lake, shouts echoing in the distance, Logan's fingers clutching at his sleeve. Seth lurched forward, shaking off Logan.

"Wait!" Logan shouted. "You'll—"

The ice crumpled beneath him, plunging Seth into the icy depths. The cold punched the breath from his lungs, his limbs locking, muscles rigid. His brain shouted at him to kick and resurface, but his body wouldn't—couldn't—obey.

Lungs burning and body frozen, he sank.

Fingers tugged his hair upward, and he barely felt it. As he broke through the water, he sucked in a deep, desperate breath. Logan was on his belly hauling Seth out, saying something Seth couldn't understand.

Then Logan was gone, and there were other people slithering across the ice on their stomachs, reaching for him and dragging him to safety.

But Connor! Seth tried to speak, but it was only a garbled grunt. From behind him, he heard a cry, weak and high-pitched, an animal sound that sent a shiver through his soul, his limbs jerking in spasm.

People were talking at him, tugging at him, wrapping a blanket around him. Seth's lungs stuttered, and he screamed at his body to cooperate.

Finally, he was able to turn his head to look for Connor and Logan. They weren't there.

Panic rocketed him to his feet. Had he been sitting on the ground? He stumbled back toward the lake, ignoring the voices around him and hands trying to stop him. Didn't they understand? Logan and Connor were out there! Seth had to find them!

Someone grabbed his shoulders, right up in his face. Seth blinked at him, realizing it was Matt. Matt was saying something.

Seth felt like he was trying to get a radio station but was a few degrees off, the words distant and staticky.

"Okay," Matt said.

Seth put everything into focusing on Matt. "What?" he rasped.

"They're okay. You're all safe." Still grasping Seth's rigid shoulders, he looked behind him. "See?"

Blinking, Seth made out the cluster of people beyond, Logan and Connor at the center. Relief coursed through him, and he staggered, shivering violently now, his body finally responding to his commands. With Matt's arm around his shoulders, he stumbled to them. A siren wailed distantly.

There were so many voices, but they were static again as Seth reached for Logan, slumping against him. There was only soaked cotton between them as Logan hugged Seth tightly, his arms trembling. Connor huddled against them, people wrapping blankets around him.

Then paramedics were there with bright lights and very loud questions, poking and prodding. Someone was saying they were lucky they were so close to the hotel and the town, and that they'd only been in the water a very short time.

"I want my mom."

Connor's words cut through the rest of the noise, so horribly plaintive that everyone seemed to stop short. Connor said it again, his anguished wail piercing Seth's heart.

"I want my mom!"

Seth and Logan reached for him together, Connor thrashing for a few moments before collapsing against them, weeping with gasping sobs that seemed far too big for his skinny little body to contain without shattering completely.

Holding him safe between them, Seth and Logan clutched each other with frozen fingers as Connor cried for the mother he'd never have again.

Chapter Seventeen

"WELL, *THAT WAS* quite a scene tonight."

Sitting on the side of the hospital bed, Logan looked up to find Angela standing in the open gap in the curtain around his ER berth. Hands on hips, lips pressed tight, she shook her head gravely, fancy dangling earrings catching the washed-out fluorescent light.

Logan cringed. The last thing he wanted to do right now was act more. "Sorry," he rasped, his throat still dry.

Her face softened, and she reached for his hand, giving it a kind squeeze. "Sugar, I'm messin' with you. Thought I'd lighten the mood. There's nothing to be sorry for. We're all just relieved you, Seth, and Connor are okay."

"Oh. Uh, thanks." One of the worries that had been jabbing at him spilled out. "You're not going to fire Seth?"

She scoffed. "What on earth gave you that idea? You think I have time to find another new director of systems training? Tomorrow's December twenty-third, and I'm flying home when we get back to Albany. Besides, he's the man for the job. No question about it."

"Thank God," Logan muttered, relief pouring through him. He'd still been shivering in his hospital sweatpants and sweatshirt, and now he relaxed a bit. He hadn't fucked it up for Seth after all.

"So what's with the glum face?" Angela let go of his hand and hoisted herself up to sit beside him on the bed, her short legs dangling, leather high-heeled boots knocking together. Logan was only wearing thick socks, but his feet brushed the linoleum floor.

"Dunno. I'm worried about Connor and Seth. Jenna said they're fine. She's been going back and forth. I tried to stay with Connor, but he didn't want me there." Logan ached from it, but it wasn't about him. If Connor needed Jenna right now, that's who he'd get.

"Yep, just getting their walking papers like you have."

"Good. I don't know what's wrong with me."

"I'd say it's a touch of shock."

"Yeah. That's what the doc said."

"Taking an unexpected ice bath will do that. Not to mention seeing your son and your man go under. That must've been the fright of your life."

His son. His man.

A thick, sticky burst of emotion punched him in the gut. Logan wanted it to be true. He wanted a family. *This* family with Connor and Seth.

"I never thought I could love a man like this." He flattened his hand on his chest, almost able to feel the scars through the cheap cotton sweatshirt. "With—with my whole heart." He had to watch his mouth and not give the game away to Angela.

But it didn't feel like a game at all anymore.

He shuddered violently. "I thought they were gone."

Angela slipped her arm around his shoulders with a surprisingly strong grip, and Logan let himself lean into it. Then he found himself talking again, his brain shouting to be careful.

"I can't get it out of my head. Seeing them disappear." He rubbed his hands up and down his thighs, nervous energy pinballing through him. "They were there, and then they were gone. I don't think I was ever that scared before. Even fighting in the desert. Maybe that's just faded over the years. But this was like I was choking. Sometimes I have trouble breathing because of the accident I had, and it was like that, but so much worse. I thought I was gonna die too if they were dead."

Saying it out loud was fucking scary, but it felt good at the same time.

"You yanked out your man and jumped right in after your boy like a big darn hero."

His brain replayed it: Connor being gulped up by the lake, Seth running after him—not knowing to drop to his stomach to spread out his weight since he grew up in Georgia without ice. The bone-deep relief when he'd pulled Seth out and the terror that Connor would be out of reach.

He snorted. "I'm no hero. I'm the reason Connor ran out there in the first place. I messed up. Again."

When Logan had taken a huge breath and plunged into the water to get Connor, part of him had thought it must be a nightmare. The idea of losing Connor—of failing him so badly, of never having a chance to be the dad he needed—was un-fucking-bearable.

Angela squeezed his shoulders. "Show me a parent who says they never messed up, and I'll show you someone crooked as a dog's hind leg."

Logan had to laugh, which felt good. Then the guilt crashed in. He'd fucked up and Connor and Seth had almost died. He shouldn't be laughing.

Angela said softly, "That poor boy, crying for his momma. That's a hurt you can't fix."

"If I'd been there the night she died, maybe I could have saved her. We were breaking up, and…"

Angela sighed. "Life sure can be a kick in the crotch. You wish you could turn back time and make it right somehow. But the only thing you and Seth can do is be there and give him all the love in the world. And I know you will."

Will we? Can we? Logan wanted it so bad, the constant ache inside him surging and taking his breath away. It wasn't only that he didn't want to be alone. He wanted Seth—and Connor. He wanted to make a family with them.

A real one.

"We haven't known each other that long," he blurted, because he was an idiot.

But Angela didn't seem suspicious and only shrugged. "So? I knew my husband was the one the first time I met him. Rosebud county fair, nineteen-eighty-four. I was sweet sixteen."

"Rosebud?"

"Yep, south of Waco. Paul was taking tickets at the Ferris wheel—rickety old thing, let me tell you. My girlfriends refused to ride it, so I went on my own. I was always the adventurous one, and Paul was just too cute to pass up. He was a shy one, but he stammered out a few sentences, and every time I came around the bottom, I waved to him, and he waved back. When my time was up, he let me keep going. I rode that old wheel for an hour, and then the fair was closing, and he took a spin with me. His buddy stopped it at the top, and we sat up there talking—mostly me talking and him listenin'—and I never wanted to come down. When you know, you know."

"I thought I knew with Connor's mom. Veronica." Logan scrubbed his face. "That's a lie. I knew we were kidding ourselves, but I went along. I don't want fuck up again with Seth. It feels different, but what if I'm wrong?"

She shrugged. "Only one way to find out."

Logan was quiet, listening to machines beep and murmured conversations beyond the curtain. "It's happened real fast with Seth." He didn't say quite *how* fast. "But seeing him and Connor go through the ice. Seeing how they could be taken away just like *that*." He snapped his fingers dully. "That's what happened to Veronica." He snapped again.

"Then you know how precious life is. Grab on to the people

who make your heart happy and don't ever let go. And to hell with anyone who doesn't like it."

"Is that what you did?"

"Yes, sir. We waited until after high school to get hitched—I knew, but I was no fool either. It's been *mumble-mumble* years now." She laughed. "But he still listens to me until I'm tired of talkin'. Every word."

"I want that."

"Ain't a thing wrong with that."

But what did Seth want? Logan believed Seth liked him, but it was all so new. What if this really was a mistake as well?

Only one way to find out.

IT WAS PAST midnight when they trooped into the hotel room, all of them wearing the gray sweatsuits from the hospital and cheap flip-flops, their shoes still soaking wet.

Jenna said to come down the hall and wake her the second they needed something, but what they needed was rest. They took turns in the bathroom and changed into PJs.

Logan watched Seth shiver as he buttoned up his grandpa pajamas. He wanted to kiss him so bad. He didn't want Seth to ever be scared or hurt again. Hell, he didn't want Seth to even be cold.

Connor sat up against the padded headboard of his bed, his big tee pulled up to his chin along with the thick comforter. Seth asked, "Should I turn up the heat more?" Connor shook his head. Seth sat on the other bed. "We should get some sleep, huh?"

Connor nodded but didn't move. The lamp between the beds cast a low golden glow. Shivering himself in his T-shirt and boxer briefs, Logan sat beside Seth, brushing against him and the flannel, resisting pulling Seth onto his lap just to hold him.

They sat in silence, Seth giving him a worried glance. Logan figured Connor wanted to talk or he would already be asleep. Or be pretending or something. But he sat up still.

"I miss my mom," Connor whispered. His eyes were still red and puffy from earlier, and he seemed so small in the big bed. Would Logan mess it up if he tried to hug him?

Logan cleared his throat. "I know. I wish I could bring her back for you. I wish I could go back and be there and change it."

After a few beats of silence, Seth murmured, "I thought they said there was nothing anyone could do."

"But I *was* there!" Connor's lip wobbled, tears filling his big brown eyes. "I was up late playing video games even after she told me to turn it off and go to bed. I used my headphones, and eventually I fell asleep with the game still going. If she—what if she called for me? What if she asked me for help?"

Logan shook his head. "With that kind of aneurysm, there was nothing you could have done. It was over in a few seconds." He snapped his fingers. "Like that."

He wasn't sure if it was exactly true—docs could guess, but no one would ever know for sure how long it had taken and if she'd suffered. But he wouldn't let Connor blame himself. Connor was a kid, and he needed sure things. He needed Logan to be sure. What was that saying? *Fake it 'til you make it.*

"But what if it wasn't?" Connor whispered. "What if she laid there with her brain exploding and I didn't hear her? What if she was scared? I was right next door, and she told me to stop playing. I didn't listen, and then I couldn't hear her!" He sobbed raggedly. "Don't you get it? It's my fault!"

"*No.*" Logan was on his feet, and he stood there uselessly for a few moments before sitting by Connor's feet, Connor's knees still pulled to his chest under the covers.

Don't fuck this up.

Logan said, "It wasn't your fault. You didn't do anything

wrong. You know your mom would say the same thing. She loved you more than anything in the whole world. She would never blame you. Not in a million years."

"I wanted her to make breakfast." Connor sniffled loudly, wiping his nose with his hand. "Because I was too lazy to do it myself. I was an asshole. That was why I went to find her. Not because I was worried. I should have been. I should have noticed the coffee pot was still upside-down on the side of the sink from when she washed it the night before. But I was only thinking about myself."

"You're a kid," Logan said. "That's what kids do. You think I appreciated everything my mom did for me? No way. Took it for granted until I joined the Marines. And pretty soon she was gone, and I didn't even get to say goodbye."

Connor blinked at him, fresh tears streaking his flushed cheeks. "Really? I didn't know that."

"Yeah. It sucked. It sucked real hard. I got to talk to her on my CO's computer, but it's not the same. She looked so pale and…small. I couldn't understand how she'd gotten so small, so fast."

Connor shivered. "Mom was all gray," he whispered. "Waxy, like she was fake. But it was her. And then they put a sheet over her like she didn't mean anything. She was everything!"

Logan put his hand over the mound under the comforter where Connor's knees were. "I know. Your mom and I made a mistake getting married, but I'm so glad I met her. And you."

Wiping his eyes, Connor snorted. "Yeah, right. You're just stuck with me."

"That's what family's about. Being stuck with each other." Hand still on Connor's knees, he looked at Seth sitting on the other bed. "And sometimes your birth family sucks and they throw you out like Seth's did. Or they don't take care of you the way they should, like your dad."

KEIRA ANDREWS

Logan held his breath, waiting for Connor to freak out and defend his asshole father. But he didn't. He nodded, sniffling loudly. "My dad sucks." He looked at Seth. "Your family sucks too."

"Yeah," Seth said. "But you know, we get to pick our families too. You and Logan get to pick each other. Your mom brought you together, and you can choose to embrace it." He smiled wryly. "Maybe give each other a break?"

Logan and Connor looked at each other, and they smiled too. Logan's chest went warm and gooey. "Yeah, that sounds like a plan, huh?" He jostled Connor's knees.

"Okay." He wiped his eyes. "Thanks for rescuing me."

Logan thought of how bony and fragile Connor had felt under his frozen hands as he'd pushed him up onto the ice. How breakable. He couldn't let Connor break. Maybe he wouldn't always do or say the right thing, but he was going to try his hardest every day.

He was going to be the best dad he could.

Logan cleared his throat. "Anytime. Although let's not do that again. And let's not... Look, I'm sorry I lied to you about me and Seth. I should have told you the truth, even though it was confusing. Confusing to me, I mean."

He glanced at Seth, who gave him a little smile. Logan went on, his heart drumming. "Because this was all supposed to be pretend, and it doesn't feel like that now. It feels real. And I want it to be real. I really like Seth a lot."

He was still looking at Seth. Seth's smile grew wider, and he was so pretty and sweet, and yep—Logan wanted to kiss him over and over. He wanted to kiss Seth until their lips hurt. Logan smiled back before looking at Connor again.

Connor eyed him with his brows drawn close. "You really mean it?"

"I do. I'm not trying to steal Seth's money or anything like

204

that."

Connor's cheeks went pink, and he looked down. "I know," he mumbled. He snaked one hand out from under the covers and pulled at a loose thread on a seam. "Did you cheat on my mom?" He looked Logan straight in the eyes.

"Never." Logan didn't have to fake the confidence in what he was saying. "I didn't cheat on her. We weren't meant to be together in the long run, but I never even looked at other women." He hesitated. "Or men. I'm a lot of things, and I sure ain't perfect, but I'm not a cheater."

Connor nodded. "I believe you. I think... I think I always knew that." He dropped his head, then blurted, "I'm sorry I called you stupid so many times. I—you're not stupid. I just get so mad." His thin shoulders hunched.

"I get it," Logan said gruffly. "It's okay. How about a clean slate? Like Seth said, we can give each other a break."

"Yeah. Okay." Connor wiped his nose. "I'm tired. Can I sleep now?" When Logan nodded, Connor curled away toward the dark window, the drapes firmly shut.

"We should all sleep," Logan said, getting up and crawling across the mattress past Seth. He shimmied under the covers and stretched out on his back.

Seth got settled and switched off the lamp. "Sleep tight, Connor."

In the darkness, he turned toward Logan, his palm warm and comforting on Logan's chest. He whispered, "How's your breathing?"

"Good," Logan whispered back. *Better now.*

"It was so hard to breathe after being in that freezing water. Must have been worse for you." He rubbed his fingers lightly over the spot where Logan's scars were beneath the cotton.

"Didn't even think about it. All that mattered was you and Connor. You both disappeared. It was only a few seconds, I guess, but it was fucking forever."

Seth shivered, and Logan shifted them until he was spooning Seth, pressed against his back. There was nothing sexy about it—certainly not with Connor a few feet away. But it was just right.

Despite the warmth in the room, Logan could hear Connor's teeth chattering. In the faint light of the clock, Logan and Seth shared a worried look and sat up. Connor was still curled toward the window, his shoulders shaking.

"Still cold, Connor?" Seth asked.

A small, chattering voice said, "Yeah."

Seth met Logan's gaze and pointed down at their bed. Logan nodded, and Seth asked, "Do you want to sleep with us? We're all freezing."

The silence lasted several dull thuds of Logan's heart, and then Connor whispered, "Okay."

He got out of bed and stood hugging himself as Logan scooted over to the wall. Seth pulled up his legs, and Connor crawled between Seth and Logan and got under the covers.

Connor said, "It's too quiet."

Seth reached for the remote and turned on the TV, the screen flickering blue in the darkness. He kept the volume low and switched channels until he landed on *Elf.*

There was something soothing about the soft murmur of the TV, although Logan's brain still turned itself over. There was so much he wanted to say to Seth. They liked each other, but… Now what?

Now you sleep, asshole.

As much as Logan ached to feel Seth in his arms, snuggling under the covers with Connor between them was comforting in a way all its own. As the characters in the movie sung "Santa Claus is Coming to Town," Logan drifted off and let himself believe.

Chapter Eighteen

S ETH HAD WOKEN with Connor's knobby knee in his back and an arm half across his face, and the three of them had grumbled about it being way too hot in the room.

But there hadn't been any real fire to the complaints, and although it was a little awkward and stilted, they'd gotten ready for breakfast in companionable-enough silence, the TV still on and playing the Mormon choir singing carols.

Breakfast was spent smiling and nodding at all the well-meaning inquiries into their well-being, and Seth was relieved when they boarded the buses back to Albany. Connor sat with Ian and buried his nose in the games on his phone, and Seth drowsed next to Logan, their arms brushing.

The fragile peace continued as they drove back to Seth's house after bidding Angela farewell. The next day was Christmas Eve, and the office was closed until the twenty-sixth. Seth was relieved to have the time off, although his stomach fluttered thinking about the conversation he and Logan had to have. And would Connor's quiet calm hold?

It had snowed more, and the midafternoon skies were gray. Seth's long driveway had been freshly plowed by the man he hired. Inside, he dropped his bag and looked around in foolish surprise at the new decor. He blurted, "I almost forgot that it's finished now."

Logan chuckled as he unzipped his leather jacket and hung it in the closet. "Still like it?"

"Yes." Seth smiled as he walked through to the kitchen, flipping on lights. "Definitely."

Connor followed, peering around. "Wow. Looks awesome."

"It was all Logan," Seth said. "He did an amazing job." *Please be nice,* he willed Connor.

Standing in the entrance to the great room, where the decorated pine tree waited, Connor nodded. "It's really good."

Logan's smile was shy and tentative, and Seth wanted to kiss him so badly he felt like a swooning teenager. Logan gruffly said, "Thanks."

"Can I hang out in my room?" Connor asked Seth. "I mean, like, upstairs."

"Of course. We'll order something in for dinner in a few hours. Any requests? Chinese or Thai or pizza and wings? Or anything you like."

"Sweet and sour chicken balls and fried rice would be cool. Can I have Coke?"

"Absolutely," Logan said.

A little while later, Connor locked away upstairs, Seth and Logan took what had become their places on the couch, the middle cushion between them. They watched football, the colored lights of the Christmas tree reflecting on the glass as the afternoon grew dark early.

There was so much to say, but maybe they both needed some quiet before they said it. But Seth got more and more anxious, finally blurting, "If we like each other, does that mean we're—" He tried to find the right words, settling on, "Not casual?"

Logan seemed to have been holding his breath, and he exhaled in a slump of shoulders. "Yeah." He shifted over on the couch and muted the TV with the remote. He spread his hand over Seth's right thigh, and electricity zipped through Seth. "You know how they say 'fake it 'til you make it'?"

"Uh-huh."

"It doesn't feel like we're faking anything now."

Seth slid his arm around Logan's broad shoulders. They were both in jeans and sweaters, and the worn wool of Logan's was soft under Seth's fingers. "You said you want me," Seth whispered.

"Hell yes." Logan squeezed his thigh. "I wanna bust a nut all over you."

Seth had to laugh. "Thank you?"

Logan laughed too, his eyes crinkling beautifully. "I just mean… You get me really hot. I wanna do things with you I never have with a guy." He glanced at the entry to the great room, leaning forward and apparently making sure they were still alone.

Clearing his throat, Logan went on. "What I mean is, I meant it when I said I like you. As more than a friend."

Seth's heart thudded. "And not just for casual sex?"

"No." He frowned. "You don't want that, do you? I got the feeling you're not very good at it." He quickly added, "The casual part! You're excellent at sex."

Now Seth's face was hot, but he said, "Thanks. And yeah. People tell me I should be going on the hookup apps and dating and having fun. But I don't want to hook up with a dozen men. That's not who I am. I want to be with you."

"Yeah?" Logan grinned.

Seth's heart soared. Tracing the shell of Logan's ear with his finger, arm snug around him, he whispered, "I love having sex with you. It's…liberating."

They kissed, moving toward each other in unison, mouths opening and tongues exploring. It was languid and sweet, and Logan rubbed his hand over Seth's thigh lazily. Seth tingled all over but was content to keep it slow and PG-13 for the moment.

"Never kissed a guy," Logan mumbled, nuzzling Seth's cheek. "Turns out it's not so different from kissing a woman." He leaned back. His smile was soft, his eyes vulnerable. "Definitely never fallen for a guy before you."

Seth kissed Logan deeply, tilting his head and wanting to climb right inside his body. With a soft moan, he whispered, "I've fallen for you too, just in case that's not crystal clear."

"Still like hearing it." Logan squeezed Seth's thigh. His face grew serious, and after nuzzling Seth again, he leaned back. "I don't want to fuck this up. I know I rushed into it with Veronica, but I swear it's not my MO. And with her…"

After a few moments of silence, Seth said, "You don't have to talk about it."

"I want to." Logan rubbed his face wearily. "Honestly, I knew it was a mistake. I knew it. She was the one who proposed, and I didn't want to say no. She'd made sure she didn't work as my nurse anymore so there was no unethical shit, but I was still in the hospital. I was fired and none of my friends from the railway had even visited. I felt like garbage, and Veronica was like this angel. And she had insurance, and I was going to be bankrupt from the hospital bills otherwise. We both got swept up in the idea that getting married would fix our problems."

"I understand."

"She was a good woman."

"Of course!"

Logan shook his head, his voice low. "I can't imagine what it was like for him, finding her dead."

Seth couldn't either. Poor, poor Connor. "At least he talked about it. We'll be here to listen and support him."

"I want that. When you two went through the ice—I thought that might be it, that you were both dead and I'd never get the chance to make it right with Connor… Or make it real with you."

Seth could barely breathe as he waited for Logan to finish.

Taking a deep breath, Logan peered at him intently. "The deal was we'd stay until January. Do you—what do you think about that?"

"I think we clearly need a new deal. One involving a lot of very non-casual sex and you and Connor staying here indefinitely. We'll see what happens. We don't need to put any limits or deadlines on it. Except that we'll be partners who don't sleep with anyone else. I know open relationships can be great for some people, but…"

"Hmm." Logan seemed to be pondering it.

The hair on Seth's neck stood up, an icy chill slipping down his spine. Maybe that was a deal breaker for Logan?

"Holy shit, the look on your face!" Laughing, Logan pressed a wet kiss to Seth's cheek. "Sorry. I was just messing with you. I don't want anyone else. I don't do open. Never have."

Seth elbowed him. "Jerk. So I guess we have a new deal?" He removed his right arm from around Logan's shoulders and extended his hand formally. "Boyfriends-slash-partners-slash-whatever we want to call it. Indefinitely. Living together, because why the hell not?"

They were old enough to know what they wanted, and if it was a disaster, so be it. They'd cross that bridge if it ever appeared.

Logan shook his hand firmly. "That's some salty language from you." He waggled his brows. "Makes me want to fuck your brains out."

Seth grinned. "Such a sweet talker."

"Don't pretend you don't like my talk." Lips at Seth's ear, he added, "Later, I'm going to tell you all about how much I want to fuck your tight hole and—"

They both seemed to register the soft thuds on the stairs at the same time, springing apart. They burst out laughing, and Seth felt like a teenager in the best possible way. Connor appeared at the top of the few steps down into the great room.

"What?" he asked warily.

Seth tugged Logan closer on the couch, sliding an arm around him again. "Nothing. Come join us."

"You guys are weird. But yeah, okay." He came and flopped down on the other end of the couch, Logan in the middle. "Hey, can we watch the new season of *Stranger Things*? It just dropped on Netflix. They didn't give any warning."

"Absolutely." Seth nodded at the remote. "It's the button on the top. You'll need to know how to work it since Logan and I have decided you're both staying. Of course, you'll be going back to school in the new year, but we'd love it if you came here on weekends."

"Yeah?" Connor picked up the remote, toying with it. "That's pretty fast. But that's cool." He turned on Netflix and settled back. "Can we order dinner? I'm hungry."

"Are you ever not hungry?" Logan asked, clearly going for teasing.

Connor visibly bristled. "So what?"

"Nothing." Logan lifted his hands calmly. "Sorry. Just trying to joke."

"Okay," Connor mumbled, his pale cheeks going beet red. He fidgeted with the remote, shoulders up around his ears. He blurted, "Mom said I was hungry like it's my job and I'm trying for a raise."

Seth and Logan laughed, and Seth said, "She had your number, huh? Well, don't worry. We'll keep the pantry stocked." Maybe Connor could feel comfortable enough to talk about his mother more.

Connor gave him a little smile. "Cool. Thanks."

Seth knew it would be a long road, but maybe Connor was ready to start healing.

Chapter Nineteen

SINCE IT WAS Christmas Eve and he was at Jenna's kitchen table, Logan should have been concentrating on cutting up the broccoli and cauliflower for the veggie platter.

Not thinking about waking up with Seth that morning. Waking up with Seth naked. Waking up with Seth and making him blush real hard by thinking up new dirty things to say. Morning blow jobs and kissing, and then more kissing.

All the kissing.

"Are you even listening to me?" A big yellow squash in one hand, Jenna turned down the volume on a crappy version of "Jingle Bells" playing through her tablet. Her blond hair was knotted up in a fancy twist, and she wore a Mrs. Claus apron over her velvet blue dress that she complained was too tight but Logan thought was pretty.

He jerked guiltily. "Sorry. What?"

"What's up with you?"

"Nothing," he automatically replied.

She pressed her lips together. "Why did you volunteer to help me instead of going outside to play? What's up? Is it about the job? It was great news that Angela set up that interview for you. Don't tell me your pride is getting in the way."

"No!" Logan sliced into a big hunk of cauliflower. "Trust me, I have zero pride left. I'm grateful for anything I can get." Now Jenna looked sad, and he felt like an asshole. "I don't mean...

What I mean is that I'm grateful to Angela. She's really gone out of her way. I'm not looking that gift horse in the mouth, I promise."

"Okay. You deserve good things, you know." There was a burst of distant laughter outside, and she went to the window. "This snowball fight looks pretty epic. You should get out there with Seth and Connor. Although Jun and Ian probably need the help more."

Pop was in his usual spot in the den watching the game show channel with Noah asleep in his playpen. Logan and Jenna were alone, so now was the time to tell her.

Any minute now.

Turning from the window, she fixed Logan in her sights and said way too casually, "That was quite the kiss during musical chairs. Very convincing. I honestly had no idea you were such a good actor. Seth either, since he's the worst liar in the world."

The pressure built in Logan's chest. He'd borrowed a tie from Seth, and he tugged at it, but then he had to laugh. "How do you always know everything?"

Her eyebrows shot up. "Jun said I was being silly. Wait, are you serious?" She glanced at the door that led to the hall down to the den. Pulling out a chair, she leaned forward, voice low. "You and Seth? For real?"

His heart was booming, but he shrugged. "Yeah."

Her jaw dropped. "But you've never…with a guy. Have you?"

"Just sex. In Iraq, and sometimes at the bunkhouse."

She got up and took a bottle of white out of the fridge, pouring them both big glasses. Logan didn't really like the sweet wine, but he drank it nervously as she sat back across from him, gaze distant.

"Say something," he muttered. "Cat doesn't usually have your tongue." He was trying to tell himself this was no big deal, but it was. It was a big damn deal.

"Oh! Sorry. Processing." Jenna reached over the vegetables and grabbed his hand. "You know I love you and support you a hundred percent."

He exhaled. "I figured, but that's still nice to hear." He squeezed her fingers.

"It must be scary."

"Yeah." He swallowed hard. "It's a big change. I'm not gonna wuss out, though. It—he means too much. Maybe some people won't like it, but tough shit. It's not like I have any friends left anyway."

"The people who matter will support you. The end."

"Even Pop?" he whispered.

Jenna winced through her teeth. "I think so? He's kind of weirdly mellowed. He probably won't love it at first, but he'll come around. He wants you to be happy and settled. He worries about you a lot. More than you think."

"Huh." Logan wasn't sure what to make of that.

She sat back and picked up her wine. "You and Seth! It's perfect. You've both been so lonely, whether you want to admit it or not. And it's not just physical?"

"No!" He shifted in his chair, crossing his arms. Talking about this was the worst, especially with his baby sister. "It's different with Seth."

Her smile reminded him of the moony look she got when she watched rom-coms. "You like him."

"Yeah." He grumbled. "A lot, okay?"

"And before it was only physical with men. Never with feelings involved?"

"Right."

"But why?"

"Because!" He grunted, realizing he sounded like Connor. "It's just… I always thought dating and stuff is what you do with women. Getting off with guys once in a while was separate."

"Okay." Jenna sipped her wine. "But you don't think it's wrong, right? Same-sex relationships."

"No," he scoffed. "I just didn't think it was for me. Turns out I was wrong. Seth and I were only pretending at first, but now…" He picked up the knife and cut the stalk off a broccoli spear.

"You're blushing!" Jenna clapped delightedly. "This is the best Christmas present you could give me."

"You're welcome," he said with as much sarcasm as he could.

"So, you're…bisexual?"

It still seemed weird as hell to think of himself as anything but straight after insisting on it for so long. Fooling himself for so long. He cleared his throat. "Yeah. I'm bisexual." He exhaled a long breath, a knot of tightness in his chest releasing.

"I'll drink to that!" Jenna lifted her glass, and he clinked his against it.

"You'll drink to anything," he teased with a grateful laugh.

"Pumped out a ton of milk this morning, so you're damn right I will. It's Christmas." She took a big swallow. "Are you moving in for real? Is that why Connor's in such a good mood?"

"I guess. We're gonna see how it goes, but yeah. Moving in."

"It's going to go wonderfully! I know it."

"That's what I thought about Veronica."

Jenna pursed her lips. "No you didn't. You knew it was a mistake from day one. But now we have Connor. Everything happens for a reason." She grimaced. "Not Veronica's death. I didn't mean it like that."

"I know. I get it." He looked out the window at where Connor was dodging a snowball and laughing as it hit Seth instead. "I wish she was still alive, but I wouldn't want to give him up." He shook his head. "Never thought I'd say that."

"You were thrust into being a single dad overnight, and it's not easy, to say the very least. You're still learning, but you're what Connor needs."

Logan was starting to believe it. "He'll probably drive me nuts soon enough, but we're both trying. We didn't fight at all today. We've been watching that eighties show on Netflix about the kids and monsters. Seth and I hadn't seen it, so Connor said we should start at the beginning. It's been fun watching together."

"That's great! All you can do is try, and keep trying even when he acts like an asshole. Because sometimes kids are the worst, but they're the best." Jenna's eyes filled, and she laughed. "Sorry, you know how emo I get at Christmas. But if there's any time to start fresh, it's now, don't you think?"

"Yeah. Peace and good will and all that shit."

They laughed, and the oven timer dinged. Jenna bolted up. "Need to check the turkey. Maybe you and Pop should talk?"

"What, *now?*"

"Peace and good will and all that shit."

Here went nothing. Logan took a gulp of the sweet wine and headed into the den before he could chicken out. Better to just rip off the Band-Aid.

Noah was still fast asleep in his playpen on the floor by Pop's armchair, his little mouth open, face so innocent that it made Logan want to pick him up and hold him close. Of course that would wake him, and he had to spit out the truth to Pop.

Pop wore a button-down shirt and dress slacks with his ugly old slippers. They'd always dressed up on Christmas Eve for turkey dinner and midnight mass, then spent Christmas Day in their PJs, opening presents and eating leftovers.

Now that Jenna and Jun went to Jun's parents every other year with Pop and the kids, the routine had changed, and they were skipping church to get a good night's sleep before driving in the morning. Logan was looking forward to a day of PJs with Seth and Connor. He wished like hell he was there now, but first things first.

Rip it off!

Sitting on the edge of a couch cushion, Logan looked at the Christmas tree with its golden lights and the old angel on top tilting to the right. He asked, "People giving good answers?" He nodded toward *Family Feud* on the TV.

Pop grunted. "A few."

Do it. Don't be a shit-brick coward. Just fucking say it. "You know how Seth and me have been living together? I'm gonna keep living there in January. We really like each other. We were pretending at first, but now it's real."

Pop's gray, bushy brows met, and he stared at Logan. "What are you sayin'? That you're a fairy?"

Logan's first instinct was to deny it loudly. He forced a breath, his chest tightening. "I dunno. Kinda? I've always liked girls. Still do. But I think I've liked guys too. More than I would admit."

Pop shoved a handful of pretzel mix in his mouth. He chewed noisily, watching a family trying to guess the most popular answer for "favorite way to wake up in the morning."

There was clapping and exclaiming, and blood rushed in Logan's ears, his heartbeat so loud he could barely hear himself think.

He waited.

Then he waited some more, every muscle clenched, his butt barely on the edge of the couch cushion. Was Pop going to tell him to get out? Was he going to say Logan disgusted him? That he was a disgrace to the family and—

"Like the kid on *Schitt's Creek*," Pop said, rooting around in the snack bowl and coming up with an orange peanut M&M.

"What?" Logan could barely get the word out.

"You know, with Eugene Levy. Rich people get stuck in a small town. Funny show. It's like *shit's*, but it's spelled different."

Logan tried to breathe. "Right. Yeah, I get it. I don't—what about it?"

Pop looked at him now. "The kid on the show. He's whaddya call it—bipan-curious or whatever." He shrugged. "I guess it's the popular thing these days, huh? Seems like it's everywhere now. I don't really get it, but no one asks what I think anymore."

Logan's lungs expanded a few more inches. "I'm asking. What you think." He clenched his hands into fists so hard his nails dug into his palms. "About me and Seth."

Frowning, Pop stared at him again. "So you're saying you two are…" He motioned back and forth with a wrinkled hand.

Part of Logan wanted to deny it all, say never mind and run the fuck away. But he didn't. He nodded.

Pop screwed up his face. "I don't get why you'd want to. You're a good-lookin' kid. The girls have always chased you."

"It's not about that. It's not that I can't get a girl and I'm settling or something."

"Huh." He seemed to think about it. "That makes you happy? Bein' with him? Like *that*?"

"I know it must seem weird to you, but yeah. It does."

Pop grunted, and Logan couldn't tell what it meant. Pop said, "You do seem happier. I was sayin' to Jenny before. The kid too. So I guess that's good. And you said you're going to keep living over there?"

"Yeah. We're going to see what happens. Maybe it won't work out, but…"

Pop grunted again, turning back to the TV. "Won't know unless you try. You could do worse." Then he shouted, "Read the newspaper! Doesn't anyone read the newspaper in the morning anymore?"

Her dress swaying, Jenna appeared with a plate of cookies, having clearly been eavesdropping. "You know who reads the newspaper every morning? Seth. He's very old-fashioned that way. He picks one up on his way into the office."

Logan wasn't sure if it was true, but God, he loved his sister. Pop laughed, a wheezing rasp. "Jenny'll be convincing me Seth's the second coming of Jesus soon enough if she has her way." He grabbed three cookies and took a big bite of one. "Only your mother made better chocolate-chip cookies. God rest her soul."

Jenny sat beside Logan on the couch, squeezing his arm and kissing his cheek. He took a cookie. "These really are just like Mom made."

She beamed. "Thanks." Then she whispered, "That went better than I expected!"

"I keep telling you, I'm not fuckin' deaf," Pop grumbled, biting into another cookie. He asked Logan through his mouthful, "Didn't you make your mom's chocolate cake for the big dinner with the boss lady?"

"Yeah," Logan said. "Everyone loved it."

"You should bring some cookies home," Pop said. "Seth and Connor'll miss out if we eat 'em all."

"I might have made an extra batch for you boys this morning." Jenna gave Logan a wink.

Home.

Settling back on the couch, Logan took a bite of sweet, soft cookie. The front door banged open, Noah woke and wailed so loud Logan thought he must be dying, and cold air reached the den.

"Close the damn door!" Pop shouted as Jenna scooped up Noah, a stamping of boots thudding from the foyer.

Jun, Seth, Connor, and Ian joined them in the den, cheeks rosy from being outside. Seth took a cookie and sat next to Logan with a wince. Logan frowned. "You okay?"

"My slacks are damp, but that's what I get for engaging in a snowball fight."

Logan laughed. "Maybe you should take them off." He realized what he'd said, but it was too late.

"Save that for later!" Pop chortled, his belly jiggling as he laughed at his own joke.

Jun had his mouth full of cookie, but mumbled, "Wait,

what?"

"Pants off!" Ian shouted, yanking down his little slacks and pulling them free, a sock going with them. In Superman undies and his dress shirt, he raced around the carpet, reaching out to jingle ornaments on the tree as he passed by, gold and silver icicles swaying dangerously.

"Everyone's pants on!" Holding Noah, Jenna gave chase, Ian darting around her and squealing his way toward the kitchen.

Seth was bright red to the tips of his ears, and Connor was laughing his ass off. Logan whispered to Seth, "Christmas at the Derwoods. This is what you're getting into. Don't say I didn't warn you."

Still blushing, Seth only grinned. He nudged Logan's shoulder, and Logan nudged back, not ready to get smoochy in front of his family, especially with Pop there. Seth would probably pass out anyway.

Part of Logan still couldn't believe it. Him and Seth. Him and Seth for *real*. Everyone knowing and not seeming to mind. Maybe it was the peace and good will and all that shit, but whatever it was, he'd take it.

Chapter Twenty

S NOW DRIFTED DOWN on Christmas morning.
    Still under the covers, Logan watched fat fluffy flakes fall past the window in Seth's bedroom. The sky was cloudy, but he could tell by how bright it looked that everything below was thick with white. The perfect day for PJs and TV and all the leftovers Jenna had pushed on them.

They'd fallen into Seth's plush bed after sharing a lazy shower, full of turkey and stuffing and chocolate cake. Even though they'd been too tired to do anything, they'd cuddled up, their naked bodies still new and exciting.

He was spooned up behind Seth now, his morning wood prodding Seth's ass. Logan circled Seth's hole, wondering what it felt like to take a cock inside. He'd told Seth that he'd never done it, and that was true. He'd also told him he didn't want to, but that was...less true.

Becoming less damn true every minute.

"Mmm," Seth murmured, yawning.

"Merry Christmas." Logan kissed his shoulder.

Seth tensed. "Right. Christmas." He laughed unsteadily. "You'll think I'm nuts, but it feels naughty to let myself celebrate. This is the first year since I left home that I've done anything at all for Christmas. Let alone so many things. A proper turkey dinner, even."

Fuck Seth's family and him "leaving" home. Fuck their obituary. Fuck them all in their pious, hypocritical ass-faces. "You deserve every single bit of Christmas," he said fiercely.

Seth relaxed back against him, turning his head to kiss Logan softly. "Thank you. I wish I'd bought you more than a new tie."

Logan laughed, letting go of the fury toward the Marstons. They weren't worth hanging onto. Not when he had Seth naked in bed and the door locked. "Um, I might have gotten you socks that Jenna originally bought for Jun. In my defense, it's been really busy."

Grinning, Seth rolled onto his back. "We'll definitely up our gift game next year."

He knew they shouldn't be banking on a year from now, but what the hell. "Deal. At least there's some stuff for Connor."

"Yes, Jenna assured me she chose well and that we could take all the credit."

"She's always been the best at gifts, like our mom. I'll pay her back when—well, if I get that job. If not—"

"Nope. You're getting it. End of story. I have complete confidence in Angela Barker."

Logan laughed. "Fair enough." He dragged his fingers through Seth's chest hair and kissed his throat. "Now what was that about you being naughty? Because I've got a few ideas."

"Mmm. I bet you do." He ran his foot over Logan's calf. "I'm all ears."

"How about you fuck me?"

Seth's eyes went wide. "Oh! I… Are you sure? You don't need to. I mean, not to prove anything to me. Or because you think you have to."

"I want to," Logan insisted. "Maybe I've been curious for a long time, but I squashed it." He fidgeted, his face going hot. "Never even considered doing it for real. It's different with you." He shrugged. "I trust you."

Seth smiled and laughed and almost cried at the exact same

time, and Logan had to kiss him until they were panting. Then he got on his hands and knees on the soft bed. This had always been out of bounds, and now he shook with curiosity and lust. Even if he didn't like it, he wanted to *know*.

He wriggled his ass. "Come on. Plow me."

But Seth was apparently in no rush, and he smoothed his long fingers over Logan's thighs, kissing down his spine, murmuring to him and turning him over onto his back.

Logan froze up. He was all *exposed* like this, and he closed his eyes before realizing what he was doing.

"Logan. Look at me. Do you really want to do this? Because you don't have to. I love being…penetrated." Seth scratched the back of his neck, and he was so damn pretty kneeling between Logan's legs. "I'm not good at the words."

"You don't need to be. Just fuck me already."

They both laughed, and Logan breathed easier. Seth pushed at his knees, pressing them back and opening him up, palms against the bottom of his thighs. Logan squirmed, but let Seth look his fill. They were both hard, but Logan knew he was going to droop if he didn't relax.

"Tell me what you want," Seth whispered. "The way you would if you were me."

Logan caught the drift. Seth loved dirty talk but was too shy to say it himself. Now here was Logan being the shy one. He cleared his throat. "Want you to shove your big cock inside me."

Gasping, Seth shuddered. Oh yeah, he clearly liked that.

"You do have a big cock, you know that? You should be proud of it." Logan reached down to run his fingers over the shaft and head. "You're already dripping for me. Gonna feel so good inside. You're so big, you're gonna split me open, and I'll love every second of it. Want you so bad, want you to—*mmph*."

Logan couldn't talk anymore with Seth's tongue jammed down his throat. They kissed hard and wet, grunting, Seth rutting against him. Logan's legs were still bent back, Seth heavy on him, fingers clutched at Logan's head, tugging his short hair.

He loved unraveling Seth like this, and the earlier nerves faded. They broke apart to breath, spit strung between them. Logan asked, "You want to eat my ass?"

Seth jolted, his face going even more red. Oh yeah, he sure as hell wanted to eat Logan's ass. Logan tried not to grin.

"You want to lick my hole? Stick your tongue in me? Bet you do. Wanna lick me like a dog with a bone. Bury your face in my ass and—" It was Logan's turn to jolt as Seth did exactly that, spreading Logan even wider with his hands and pressing his face into Logan's crack.

His tongue lapped at the sensitive skin, and Logan bit his tongue, his hands grabbing at Seth's shoulders. "Oh fuck, baby. That's so good. I could come just like this. With your tongue inside me."

Seth moaned against his hole, hot and damp and fucking perfect as he opened Logan with his tongue. Logan had done some ass play with women in the past, but this was next level because Seth was so into it.

The words tripped out of Logan's mouth. "Never even thought about letting anyone fuck me, but I want you to pound my ass with your big cock. Want you to fuck me 'til I can't walk."

Moaning, Seth lifted his head. His eyes were dark, his wet lips parted as he breathed hard. He reached blindly for the condom and lube.

"Wish you could come right inside me. Nothing between us." Logan wasn't even thinking about what he was saying now, truths rocketing out of his mouth. "We can after we get tested. You want that? Wanna fuck raw, baby?"

"Yes," Seth groaned hoarsely, kissing Logan again messily. "Oh, *God,* yes."

Logan could taste his own ass, and instead of grossing him

out, it just made him even harder. "Come on. Do it." He lifted his hips as Seth pushed lube into him clumsily. "I'm good. Fuck me. Give me your dick."

With jerky motions, Seth lined up and pushed, and Logan bore down. They both gritted their teeth. Seth cried out as he pushed past the rim and rammed all the way inside.

Logan ignored the burning pain, reaching up to slap his hand over Seth's mouth. "Walls. Not that. Thick," he grunted. He kept his hand planted over Seth's mouth as he arched his back, his chest tight. Seth felt way too big to fit, but he was all the way inside, his pubes tickling Logan's ass. Sweat trickled down Seth's face, and Logan felt hot all over, his own skin slick.

"Does it feel good splitting me open?"

Against Logan's hand, Seth nodded hard, his nostrils flaring.

"Move. I can take it. I can take every inch of you." He slid his hand away from Seth's mouth, holding the side of his face.

Panting, his eyes locked on Logan's, Seth eased out and then slammed back in. *Hard.*

"Oh, fuck yeah. Like that. Drill me." Logan had to open his mouth to breathe, trying to keep his moans quiet. "You feel amazing."

Thrusting steadily, Seth flattened his hand on Logan's chest, his fingers moving. At first, Logan thought it was just for leverage, but through the fog of building pleasure, his dick throbbing now between them, Logan realized he was tracing the scars.

His breath stuttered, and for a moment, that old panic exploded. Logan wanted to shove Seth off him and run. He was naked in a way he'd never let anyone see—not even Veronica at their best.

He had Seth's cock deep inside him, and he loved it. He wasn't straight, and he'd never been straight, and fuck, he was going to start bawling if he wasn't careful.

He gripped Seth's head, fingers tangling in his hair, their

sweaty bodies rocking. Seth brushed against just the right spot, sending sparks to Logan's tight balls. He was bent almost in half, his hips getting sore.

"Please make me come," he begged. It wasn't dirty talk now. Logan needed it in a way he couldn't explain.

"You're beautiful," Seth whispered as he took Logan in hand, swiping at the fluid leaking from his dick and mixing it with the remnants of lube as he stroked. Leaning on his other hand beside Logan's shoulder, he thrust and stroked. "I love you."

Logan arched, shaking as he came all over himself, his mouth open and gasping. Waves of pleasure crashed through him until he relaxed back, totally empty. Except he wasn't empty. Well, his nuts were, but he was so full of love he didn't know what to do with it.

"Come on," he muttered, squeezing his sore ass around Seth's thick cock. "Let go. I can feel how hard you are. Imagine we're doing it raw, and you can come inside me until your jizz is dripping out."

Seth seized up, and Logan clapped a hand over his open mouth again, muffling his cry as he came, his head back and eyes shut. Logan loved seeing Seth let go—sharing the release with him as if he was coming again.

When Seth collapsed on top of him, Logan grunted. His ass was stinging and his legs were going numb, and Seth was heavy and sweaty.

"Best Christmas ever," Logan muttered.

Seth laughed weakly against his neck. "Ho-ho-ho." He lifted his head, sudden sharpness in his eyes, his hair standing up. "Does it hurt?"

"Yeah, but not in a bad way. Provided you get the fuck off sooner rather than later."

Of course Seth was almost unbearably gentle as he pulled out and lowered Logan's legs to the mattress, pressing kisses to Logan's knees. He got rid of the condom and cleaned them up with a wet cloth, and Logan took his face in his hands. Seth's stubble scratched his palms.

"I love you too."

Adam's apple bobbing, Seth's eyes practically glowed. "You don't have to say it just because I did. I know it's too soon."

"I'm saying it because it's true. I love you."

"Well…heck. I guess we're in love."

"*Heck*, I guess we are."

Seth laughed. "That doesn't sound right coming from you."

"Fuck-a-doodle-do, I guess we're in love. That better?"

"Much." Seth pulled the covers over them.

Logan figured they could stay there all damn day, and he wouldn't complain a bit.

SETH FOUND CONNOR in his PJs by the tree in the great room, looking out at the falling snow. The colored lights glowed, the shiny angel on top beaming down, the world white beyond. "Hey," Seth whispered, because it felt like he should. "Merry Christmas."

Connor turned. "Merry Christmas." His eyes were red, but he'd apparently stopped crying a while before.

Seth wanted so much to hug him, but he wasn't sure about overstepping. "You're up early."

"You guys are kinda noisy."

Oh, merciful lord. "I—I'm so sorry, we—it's—oh my."

Connor laughed. "Don't, like, pass out or anything. It's gross, but whatever." He quickly added, "Not because you're guys! Because you're so…old and stuff."

"We'll keep that in mind." He cast about for any change of topic. "Santa brought some gifts for you."

"Me?" Connor looked at the small pile of wrapped presents under the tree. "Really?"

"Really." Seth had removed the empty boxes Logan had wrapped for Angela's benefit.

Yawning in his boxer briefs and a tee, Logan shuffled in, passing Seth a mug of fresh coffee. "Merry Christmas. We having turkey for breakfast?"

Seth said, "I was thinking bacon and eggs and home fries cooked in the bacon grease. Save the turkey and stuff for dinner."

"Mmm. Sounds good." Logan flicked the collar of Seth's pajama top and winked. To Connor he said, "Yeah?"

Connor was watching them with an unreadable expression. "Yeah. Cool." He looked back at the presents.

Seth knelt by the tree. "Here you are. Come on. Don't be shy."

Hesitantly, Connor knelt by him, and then Logan did too. Seth passed out the presents, seven of the boxes for Connor. He ripped into the paper of one, pulling out some kind of speaker. "Sweet! It's the waterproof Bose. This is awesome!"

"Santa knows his stuff," Seth said. Jenna would definitely be getting a spa day for her help.

Connor was already ripping open another package. "The new *Call of Duty*!" He shrewdly eyed the remaining boxes, picking up a bigger one and tearing it open. "And the latest Xbox!" His face positively *glowed*, and Seth and Logan shared a grin.

"Glad you like it," Logan said.

"I love it! Can we hook it up?"

"Absolutely," Seth said.

Connor tore into his other gifts, a few more games and a pair of Adidas shoes that he declared "sick," which Seth took to be a good thing. Connor was readying the Xbox when he said, "Oh, wait. You guys have to open your stuff."

With wry smiles, Logan and Seth unwrapped their blue tie

and black socks, respectively. Connor scowled. "Seriously? That's it."

"We're gonna do better next year," Logan said.

"Shit, I hope so." Connor went back to the cables behind the TV. "But thanks. This stuff is awesome. I... I didn't get you guys anything."

"That's okay," Seth assured him.

Logan said, "How about you not be a little dickhead for the rest of the holidays? We'll take that."

After a pause, Connor burst out laughing. "I'll try my best. Can we make breakfast soon? I'm starving."

Seth chose the Christmas station on the stereo, and jazzy holiday music filled the main floor. He hummed as he got out the eggs and bacon, Logan insisting he and Connor would do the potatoes.

"I think you're supposed to cut them the long way," Logan said.

"Says who?" Connor grumbled.

"I dunno. It looks better like that."

Connor rolled his eyes. "Since when are you an expert in cooking?"

"Since never. Let's Google it."

"Fine. What Google says goes. Deal?"

Logan chuckled. "Deal."

Seth said, "We have a pretty good track record with deals." He grinned at Logan, who gave him a wink while Connor tapped his phone.

As Seth peeled off the strips of bacon, he sipped his coffee and hummed along to Sinatra singing about happy golden days, and all their troubles being miles and miles away.

Epilogue

Five Years Later

"HEY!" LOGAN TURNED from the pantry and tried to swat away Seth's hand, but he was too late. "You know you're not supposed to eat raw batter. It can kill you or some shit."

Seth sucked the chocolate cake batter off his index finger with a wet *pop*, making Logan's dick perk up and giving him all sorts of ideas they didn't have time for.

Seth said, "The risk of consuming raw eggs has been greatly overstated. They'll take my cookie dough and cake batter from my cold, dead hands." With a wink, he scooped up more with his finger. "It'll be worth it."

"Okay, but there has to be enough for the cake. And I haven't had any yet."

"Ah, the truth comes out! You're not worried about salmonella—you just want enough left for you to lick the bowl." He sucked his finger clean.

Logan shrugged, trying not to laugh. "Guilty as charged."

Sliding an arm around Logan's waist, warm hand stealing beneath his ratty tee, Seth leaned in. They kissed slowly and deeply, batter still on Seth's tongue. Logan relaxed into him, chasing the sugar.

When they parted, Seth lowered his voice in the cute way he did sometimes when he jokily faked a come-on. "Let me know when you're ready to lick the bowl."

"You know, everyone thinks you're so innocent, but you're really…" Logan tried to find the right word.

"A vixen?" Seth waggled his thick eyebrows. There was a bit of gray coming into the hair at his temples, and it was sexy as fuck.

"Sure. We'll go with that. Because only you would suggest that word. Right, Hercules?" Logan glanced down at their portly tabby cat, who rubbed against their legs, meowing for his snack. Seth had wanted to name him *Hercule* after some detective, and they'd compromised on Hercules.

Logan's phone buzzed where it sat on top of the island. "Might be work," he said as he reached for it. He'd recently been promoted to senior craftsman at Ricci and Sons and was in charge of his own renovation crew. He had to deal with more problems, but it was worth it.

"Oh, it's Connor." He tapped the screen with Connor's picture, a shot from his first day at Harvard several months earlier, exasperation showing in his smile and a few zits still dotting his face. He'd insisted it was no big deal to go to college and there was no reason to take a picture when Logan and Seth dropped him off.

"Hey, Con," Logan said, putting him on speaker. "Where are you?"

"Just past Auburn, but it's snowing." Connor's voice sounded deeper every time Logan heard it. He was taller than Logan and Seth now, but still a beanpole. "People are driving like they've never seen this foreign substance falling from the sky before." Logan could hear him rolling his eyes, and it made him smile.

Seth snorted. "Sounds about right. Take your time. Be safe. Tell Asher to drive carefully."

"*Yes*," Connor said with a sigh and probably another eye-roll. "He will."

Seth asked, "You're sure it's not out of his way to drop you off?"

"Huh? Yeah, I'm sure." Then Connor's voice faded as he

talked to someone else—probably his buddy Asher. "I'm coming! Just had to call my dads while I have a good signal. Order me a large fries and a root beer, okay?"

Logan's chest had gone tight, his breathing shallow as he and Seth stared at each other and then back down at the phone on the island.

"Sorry," Connor said, talking directly into the phone again. He paused. "You guys still there?"

"Yes!" Logan answered too loudly. He cleared his throat. "Thanks for calling. Drive safe. Doesn't matter if you're late, okay?"

"Yeah, but it'll suck ass to miss Aunt Jenna's turkey."

"We'll wait for you," Seth said, his voice a little hoarse. "Even if it's midnight."

"'K. But it really shouldn't be past seven. Later!"

Logan jabbed the disconnect button and leaned on the shiny counter, flattening his palms. Seth covered one of Logan's hands with his own and threaded their fingers together.

Logan met his gaze and muttered, "Fuck. Wow."

His *dads*.

"Yeah." Seth blinked rapidly, tears catching on his lashes. "Wow."

With a creak, the front door opened. "Ho, ho, ho!" Jun called from beyond the sitting room. Boots stamped the mat, voices and activity filling the air, a cold blast already finding its way toward the kitchen.

They hadn't even noticed the vehicle pulling up. Logan swallowed the lump in his throat and swiped his thumbs under Seth's eyes before kissing him soundly.

Seth nodded and gave him a shaky smile before going to greet their family with a hearty, "Merry Christmas!"

Logan scooped up his phone and looked at the home screen picture he'd seen a million times—him and Seth in fancy suits in front of the local Unitarian church, friends and the Derwoods surrounding them, Angela Barker and her family too, Connor giving a genuine smile.

The invites to the Marstons had been returned to sender, and Seth had made peace with not trying to contact them again.

Putting the phone in his pocket, Logan said hello as Pop grumbled by, leaning on his walker and making his way toward the great room and the reclining armchair they'd bought specially for him. Seth followed and sat next to Pop, and Logan listened to the rumble of their voices as Seth asked all the right questions to get him talking.

"Coming through!" Jenna carried the big, shiny silver disposable roast pan, foil covering the mound of the turkey. "Trivets!"

Logan quickly slapped down a couple of the big coaster things on the island. "Yes, ma'am."

She plonked the turkey on top. "You and Seth have the potatoes and squash done?"

"Shit, were we supposed to do that?"

She paled. "Tell me you're joking."

"I'm joking, I'm joking."

She kissed Logan's cheek. "You little shit. You'd better go put on some decent clothes." Then she spotted the cake batter. "Are you just baking the cake *now*? It has to cool before you ice it!"

"It'll be fine! It took a little longer than we expected to get the rest of the stuff ready. Chill. Have some wine."

Noah was racing after his older brother, shouting something. Jun told them to cut it out and sighed heavily. "Maybe Ian can drive home later. I need a drink too."

"Six more years until he can be our designated driver," Jenna said, pouring herself a glass of sweet white. "It'll fly by."

Seth came back and shooed Jenna and Jun into the great room to relax. The fresh smell of the pine tree wafted with him, and Logan inhaled deeply as he pulled Seth into a hug.

"Mmm." Seth relaxed against him. "We have got to get that cake in the oven."

"I know. In a minute."

Seth leaned their heads together. "I'm officially going with polka dots, by the way."

"But what colors?"

"Red and green."

Logan chuckled. "You think I got you holiday polka-dot socks?"

Each year, he bought Seth socks, and Seth got him a tie like the shitty gifts of their first Christmas. Betting on the colors and designs had become a tradition too. He'd actually gone with gray and navy stripes, because as much as Seth liked to joke about bright socks, he'd never wear them. At least not to work.

"Maybe you were feeling wild." Seth trailed his fingers down Logan's spine.

"Mmm. We'll get wild later."

After a laughing kiss, they went back to work, and a few hours later, their son's too-deep, grown-up voice called, "I'm home!"

Logan and Seth shared a smile before they went to greet him. They were all home.

THE END

Afterword

Thank you so much for reading *The Christmas Deal*! I hope Logan and Seth's story helps you get into a festive mood! I'd be grateful if you could take a few minutes to leave a review on Amazon, Goodreads, Bookbub, social media, or wherever you like. Just a couple of sentences can really help other readers discover the book. Thank you again.

Wishing you happy holidays and many happily ever afters!

Keira
<3

p.s. Keep reading to check out more sexy and sweet Christmas romances!

Read more holiday romance from Keira Andrews!

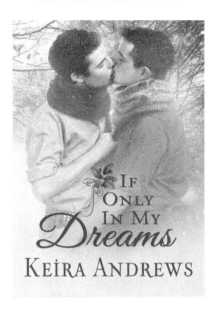

To be home for Christmas, they must bridge the distance between them.

Charlie Yates is desperate. It's almost Christmas and his flight home from college has been delayed. For days. Charlie promised his little sister Ava he'd be home for her first holiday season since going into remission from leukemia. Now he's stuck on the opposite coast and someone else grabbed the last rental car. Someone he hasn't even spoken to in four years. Someone who broke his heart.

Gavin Bloomberg's childhood friendship with Charlie ended overnight after a day of stolen kisses. With years of resentment between them, they don't want to be in the same room together, let alone a car. But for Ava's sake, Gavin agrees to share the rental and drive across the country together.

As they face unexpected bumps along the road, can Charlie and Gavin pave the way to a future together?

This gay holiday romance from Keira Andrews features new adult angst, enemies to lovers, steamy first times, and of course a happy ending.

Read now!

Four steamy and sweet MM holiday romances in one sizzling box set!

This gay romance collection from Keira Andrews includes four of her best-selling holiday novellas:

Eight Nights in December—A geek. A virgin. One sexy holiday.

Orphaned Lucas figures spending Hanukkah with his obnoxious roommate's family in New York City is better than staying alone on campus upstate. He ends up sharing a room again, this time with his roommate's brother. Geeky photographer Nate isn't at all what Lucas expects. In fact, he's incredibly sexy—especially when he invites Lucas into his darkroom…

Features secret trysts, new adult angst, spinning the dreidel, and of course a happy ending.

In Case of Emergency—Former stepbrothers find Christmas romance under the tree.

After years alone, Daniel Diaz is finally ready to shake up his orderly, solitary life. He's about to leave for a cozy Christmas getaway when he gets the call from the ER that his former stepbrother has been admitted with a concussion and a broken hand—and Cole put him down as his emergency contact. Why the hell would he do that? Daniel barely knows the guy. But Cole has no one else to look after him and strict doctor's orders not to be left alone. So, *fine*, Daniel will bring him along on vacation…

Features former stepbrothers reconnecting as adults, sexy hot-tub shenanigans, Christmas feels, and of course a happy ending.

Santa Daddy—Mall Santas aren't supposed to be hot!

Hunter Adams is still a virgin, can't find a real job, and has no clue what to do with his life. In desperation, he returns to his humiliating old job as an elf at the Santa's Village. The Santa on the job is an unexpectedly sexy lumberjack, twice Hunter's size and age. He's grumpy and intimidating, but he makes Hunter feel *very naughty.* When a surprise blizzard traps them alone on Nick's isolated tree farm, Nick's daddy instincts kick in…

Features an age gap, steamy mm first times, daddy role-playing and light spanking, and of course a happy ending.

Where the Lovelight Gleams—Will co-stars take their romance offscreen this Christmas?

Actor Ryan Drake is pining. He may get to kiss gorgeous Cary Holloway on the set of their hit sci-fi TV show, but he knows it'll never happen in real life. Charming Cary has a starlet girlfriend, and despite their sizzling onscreen chemistry, he and Ryan are just friends. Right? Then Cary accepts Ryan's invite to spend the holiday with his family in Canada. Little does Ryan know, Cary's coming to terms with his bisexuality and deep attraction to his co-star…

Features delicious pining, sexual awakening, snowball fights, cozy holiday cheer, and of course a happy ending.

Grab these sexy holiday romances now—available together in digital and print for the first

Read now!

Join the free gay romance newsletter!

My (mostly) monthly newsletter will keep you up to date on my latest releases and news from the world of LGBTQ romance. You'll also get access to exclusive giveaways, free reads, and much more. Join the mailing list today and you're automatically entered into my monthly giveaway. **Go here to sign up!** subscribepage.com/KAnewsletter

Here's where you can find me online:
Website
www.keiraandrews.com
Facebook
facebook.com/keira.andrews.author
Facebook Reader Group
bit.ly/2gpTQpc
Instagram
instagram.com/keiraandrewsauthor
Goodreads
bit.ly/2k7kMj0
Amazon Author Page
amzn.to/2jWUfCL
Twitter
twitter.com/keiraandrews
BookBub
bookbub.com/authors/keira-andrews

About the Author

After writing for years yet never really finding the right inspiration, Keira discovered her voice in gay romance, which has become a passion. She writes contemporary, historical, paranormal, and fantasy fiction, and—although she loves delicious angst along the way—Keira firmly believes in happy endings. For as Oscar Wilde once said, "The good ended happily, and the bad unhappily. That is what fiction means."

Made in United States
North Haven, CT
19 February 2024

48921995R00150